"Do you wan

Ashley's heart skipped around in her chest.

His eyebrow rose. "Be honest."

She bit her lip. "I do want to dance. But my dance partner is missing."

Micah nodded. "You don't need a partner, you know."

"So I've heard," she said on a huff. People who had never lost a spouse never quite understood that grief wasn't a monolith. It affected each person in a unique way. And right now it made the prospect of dancing alone more than she could bear. "But really, I'm not sure I remember how. And I might look stupid."

"Ah. A shy dancer. If you want, you can dance next to me."

"You dance?" The idea of Micah St. Pierre dancing to Jamal Robinson's band seemed odd and surprising.

He shrugged. "I shuffle my feet. I'm not exactly a twinkle toes."

Something about the way he said the word "twinkle" made her smile through the tears.

"Dance beside me, Ashley," he said. "It might help you remember Adam and smile instead of cry."

PRAISE FOR HOPE RAMSAY

The Moonlight Bay series

"Ramsay paints a quaint portrait of Magnolia Harbor and its earnest, salt-of-the-earth denizens, but she doesn't shy from drama and drops in a few deliciously hateable villains to liven up the tale. This cozy small-town romance will please Ramsay's fans and should attract new ones."

—Publishers Weekly

"I pick up a Hope Ramsay book anytime I see it . . . Ramsay is great at writing for 'real' people. The characters are just like us and I love that about her writing. Worth every page. Can't wait for the next in the series!"

—Books-n-Kisses.com on *A Wedding on Lilac Lane*

"*An Officer and a Gentleman* meets Nicholas Sparks's *Dear John* in the second captivating installment of the Moonlight Bay series."

—*Woman's World* on *Summer on Moonlight Bay*

"Ramsay mixes a tasty cocktail of sweet and sexy in this heartfelt launch of the Moonlight Bay series. Ramsay's expert characterization (particularly with the multi-layered hero and heroine), entertaining cast of secondary characters, and well-tuned plot will make readers long for a return trip to Magnolia Harbor."

—*Publishers Weekly* on *The Cottage on Rose Lane*

The Chapel of Love series

"[A] laugh-out-loud, play-on-words dramathon... It won't take long for fans to be sucked in while Ramsay weaves her latest tale of falling in love."

—RTBookReviews.com on *The Bride Next Door*

"Getting hitched was never funnier"

—FreshFiction.com on *Here Comes the Bride*

"Ramsay charms in her second Chapel of Love contemporary... [and] wins readers' hearts with likable characters, an engaging plot (and a hilarious subplot), and a well-deserved happy ending."

—*Publishers Weekly* on *A Small-Town Bride*

"Happiness is a new Hope Ramsay series."

–FreshFiction.com on *A Christmas Bride*

The Last Chance series

"I love visiting Last Chance and getting to revisit old friends, funny situations, the magic and the mystery that always seems to find their way into these wonderful stories."

—HarlequinJunkie.com on *Last Chance Hero*

"4 stars! Ramsay uses a light-toned plot and sweet characters to illustrate some important truths in this entry in the series."

—*RT Book Reviews* on *Last Chance Family*

"5 stars! I really enjoyed this book. I love a little mystery with my romance, and that is exactly what I got with *Inn at Last Chance*."

—HarlequinJunkie.com on *Inn at Last Chance*

"Ramsay writes with heart and humor. Truly a book to be treasured and a heartwarming foray into a great series."

—NightOwlReviews.com on *Last Chance Knit and Stitch*

"Last Chance is a place we've come to know as well as we know our own hometowns. It's become real, filled with people who could be our aunts, uncles, cousins, friends, or the crazy cat lady down the street. It's familiar, comfortable, welcoming."

—RubySlipperedSisterhood.com on *Last Chance Book Club*

"Amazing... This story spoke to me on so many levels about faith, strength, courage, and choices. If you're looking for a good Christmas story with a few angels, then *Last Chance Christmas* is a must-read."

—TheSeasonforRomance.com on *Last Chance Christmas*

"A little Bridget Jones meets *Sweet Home Alabama*."

—GrafWV.com on *Last Chance Beauty Queen*

"Full of small-town charm and Southern hospitality... You will want to grab a copy."

—TopRomanceNovels.com on *Home at Last Chance*

"Ramsay's delicious contemporary debut introduces the town of Last Chance, SC, and its warmhearted inhabitants...[she] strikes an excellent balance between tension and humor as she spins a fine yarn."

—*Publishers Weekly* (starred review)
on *Welcome to Last Chance*

BEACHSIDE BED AND BREAKFAST

Also by Hope Ramsay

The Last Chance series

Welcome to Last Chance

Home at Last Chance

Small Town Christmas (anthology)

Last Chance Beauty Queen

"Last Chance Bride" (short story)

Last Chance Christmas

Last Chance Book Club

"Last Chance Summer" (short story)

Last Chance Knit & Stitch

Inn at Last Chance

A Christmas to Remember (anthology)

Last Chance Family

Last Chance Hero

"A Midnight Clear" (short story)

The Chapel of Love series

"A Fairytale Bride" (short story)

A Christmas Bride

A Small-Town Bride

Here Comes the Bride

The Bride Next Door

The Moonlight Bay series

The Cottage on Rose Lane

Summer on Moonlight Bay

Return to Magnolia Harbor

A Wedding on Lilac Lane

BEACHSIDE BED AND BREAKFAST

HOPE RAMSAY

FOREVER
New York Boston

Forever
Hachette Book Group
1290 Avenue of the Americas, New York, NY 10104
read-forever.com
twitter.com/readforeverpub

First Edition: August 2022

Forever is an imprint of Grand Central Publishing. The Forever name and logo are trademarks of Hachette Book Group, Inc.

ISBNs: 978-1-5387-1019-7 (mass market); 978-1-5387-1020-3 (ebook)

Printed in the United States of America

OPM

10 9 8 7 6 5 4 3 2 1

To Bryan, I think of you every morning when I wake up and every night right before I go to sleep.

Acknowledgments

My good friend and critique partner J. Keely Thrall went above and beyond the call of duty for this book. I asked her a couple of questions about Episcopalian priests, and she took them all the way to the bishop of the Episcopal Archdiocese of the District of Columbia, who became instantly concerned about Micah and Ashley. Until that moment I had not fully realized how much trouble Micah faced in getting to a happy ending. I hope I portrayed the life of an Episcopalian priest accurately. Any errors are entirely my own.

I'd like to thank Mary Washington Hospital's Spousal Bereavement Group for helping me swim the currents of my own grief, which has informed the character of Ashley Scott for many years now.

As always, the writers in the Ruby Slippered Sisterhood's morning chat room were instrumental in keeping me on track. I want to especially thank Jan Whitson for providing a detailed list of what someone might find in the back of a minister's car, especially her suggestion of the preschooler's comfort blanket.

Finally, I would like to thank my readers. You have sustained me over the years, and my gratitude knows no bounds. Thank you so much for taking the time to read my words.

BEACHSIDE BED AND BREAKFAST

Chapter One

Rev. Micah St. Pierre stood on the sidewalk in front of Bread, Butter, and Beans, staring up at the sign above the coffeehouse, fighting the bright February glare from a cloudless sky. He closed his eyes, the winter sunlight warming his eyelids, promising spring.

But today it would only reach forty-five degrees, according to the weatherman. He took a deep breath, pulling in the crisp air and huffing it out in a cloud of steam. The expansion of his chest brought the tiny box inside his breast pocket tight against his rib cage.

He straightened his shoulders and hesitated, a vague sense of dread squeezing his gut. No, maybe not dread.

Fear.

But of what? He couldn't decide whether he feared failure or success. He gulped air. He could do this. It would be fine. Besides, it was Valentine's Day.

He squared his shoulders and strode through the door. The aroma inside the shop—a rich amalgam of coffee, fresh bread, and cinnamon—set his stomach growling. Brooklyn Huddleston's pastries were the best.

He crossed the small dining area to his regular table near the take-out counter. He'd been coming to breakfast for almost nine months now. It was time.

Brooklyn was waiting for him, although today her dark ponytail seemed tighter than usual, pulling her face taut and almost gaunt. She had the sinewy build of a ballet dancer, with blade-like cheekbones.

"Hi," she said, hurrying to his table with a cup of coffee and his favorite almond croissant. She placed the cup and plate in front of him, her ponytail swinging.

"Uh, wait," he said, reaching for her hand and missing.

"I...uh...I've got a million customers this morning. It's Valentine's Day, and I need to get back to the counter."

Only then did Micah notice the long line of people ordering coffee and sweets. Brooklyn's helpers were running around like squirrels on a wheel. Back and forth from coffee machine to counter. Rinse. Repeat.

"Uh, yeah, sorry. I didn't think about that."

"That's an odd thing to say. You didn't think about it or failed to notice?" she asked.

"Both," he said, and then regretted his honesty. He needed to move fast before she escaped. If he let her go back behind the counter, he'd have to wait until the morning rush ended. That might be an hour or more, and he had a meeting with the church's senior warden this morning to discuss the budget for a number of needed church repairs. He hated that part of his job. All the financial planning and begging for donations and dealing with paperwork. All that stuff kept him away from his calling.

"Uh, Brooklyn, there's something I need to ask you," he said, standing up, his chair moving back with a loud scrape. He dropped to one knee, the linoleum hard against his kneecap. He fumbled the ring box as he drew it from his pocket. It skittered across the floor and came to rest at Patsy Bauman's feet.

Oh boy. What a disaster. Patsy was the chairwoman of his altar guild, and was evidently at the coffee shop enjoying a Valentine's breakfast with her husband, Harry. Harry, a member of the town council and his church's vestry, bent down and retrieved the red leather box. He handed it back with a wink. "Carry on, Micah."

But Patsy made a funny noise in the back of her throat that didn't sound at all encouraging.

"Uh, sorry. Um, Brooklyn," he said, opening the box to display the antique rose gold diamond ring. "Will you marry me?"

He stared at Brooklyn, searching for joy. Instead her face widened into an expression of...horror? Surprise? Embarrassment?

Wait. This wasn't right. A smile might have been nice. Maybe a few tears of happy surprise.

But the water forming in her eyes didn't appear very happy. Maybe it had been a big mistake to surprise her.

She bit her lip and shook her head. "I can't," she said in a strangled voice and then hightailed it into the kitchen.

Micah got up off his knee. Numbness crept through him. At the next table, Patsy might have said, "Thank the lord," under her breath.

He turned toward Patsy and Harry, not seeing them.

"I'm so sorry, Micah." Harry stepped forward and patted him on the shoulder. "Better luck next time."

A lot of people were staring now. Boy, he sure had chosen a busy day to humiliate himself.

What the... she'd said no? How was that possible?

He stumbled from the coffee shop out onto the street and headed mindlessly up the hill toward the rectory, where he'd left his car. He crossed Palmetto Street and was halfway down the block when he spied Deputy Ethan Cuthbert checking the newly installed parking meters.

Without thinking, he dug into his pocket for some change—he'd been carrying quarters around for the last three months, ever since the new meters went in—and started pushing coins into each meter as he passed.

It seemed like a good thing to do. A normal thing to do. Something he'd done yesterday.

"Hey," Ethan called from up ahead. "What are you doing?"

"A kind deed," he said under his breath.

"Well, stop it. It's against the rules."

Micah stopped in his tracks. "What kind of stupid rule is that?"

"It's the law. You can't randomly put coins in parking meters."

"Why not?"

"Because I could arrest you for it."

"That's dumb."

"Yeah, well, the town put the meters in for a reason. It costs good money to maintain Harbor Drive."

"Okay. So I'm paying for that."

"But you don't own these cars."

Micah bit his lip as a toxic flare of anger burned up the column of his throat. He reflexively swallowed the emotion down. "Well, tough," he said. "If the town has such a big problem with Good Samaritans, it can come and arrest me anytime."

He stalked past Ethan, his gut growling with familiar shame and a deep, deep hunger that Brooklyn's croissants had never truly satisfied.

* * *

The aroma of bacon and freshly brewed coffee greeted Ashley Scott the moment she entered the gleaming kitchen at Howland House, her five-star bed and breakfast.

Dad was cooking again.

He'd taken charge of Ashley's kitchen like the colonel he'd been in the army. But today he wasn't wearing camo or wielding an M16. No, he'd come dressed for action in a white chef's apron and carried a pair of tongs. Dad was one of the most competent human beings on the face of the planet. Not only was he cool and collected under fire during breakfast service, he'd momentarily tamed Ashley's recalcitrant coffee machine.

He was amazing. And now he was burying himself in this job so he wouldn't have to think about losing Mom. Ashley's mother had died suddenly last December from pancreatic cancer. She'd suffered a DVT clot in her leg on Thanksgiving Day, and while in the hospital, she'd been diagnosed. She'd died right before Christmas.

Mom and Dad had been living in Kansas at the time. They had settled there after Dad had retired from the army in order to take care of Granny Horning, Ashley's maternal grandmother. But Granny had passed a year ago at the ripe age of ninety-six. Mom and Dad had been planning to do some traveling and had purchased tickets for a much-put-off a trip to Paris. Mom's death had ended all those dreams and plans.

Dad had lost interest in traveling. Instead, he'd put the Kansas house up for sale and returned to Magnolia Harbor, his hometown. He'd moved into the cottage behind Howland House in mid-January.

In the few weeks since, he'd invaded Ashley's kitchen, taken over the inn's webpage, and generally meddled in her business decisions. It was annoying as hell, but she let him get away with it because it was his way of coping with a catastrophic loss. Mom and Dad would have celebrated their forty-fifth wedding anniversary this June.

She resented his meddling sometimes, but she also appreciated his help. It freed up time for her to spend on other interests and eliminated the need to hire extra help during the weekdays.

"So you've got it all covered, I see," she said, taking her apron down from a peg. It was covered with daffodils and a quote from a poet. She tried to make her voice as sunny and bright as the flowers. She longed for the spring to get here already.

"Well, I didn't start biscuits," Dad said, turning with a gleam in his big, dark eyes. Dad had recently turned seventy-three but a lifelong commitment to fitness gave him a much younger vibe. He still ran five miles every day, and he'd never lost that tall, square-shouldered stance of a military man. "I am not about to try to re-create Mother's recipe." He winked and continued. "And just so you know, my heart fills with pleasure at the very sight of you this morning." His mouth curled at the corner.

He was paraphrasing the Wordsworth quote on her apron. "Thanks, Dad." It was kind of nice the way he always greeted her with love every morning. She'd been living alone, except for the guests, ever since Grandmother died. Adam, her husband, had been killed in Afghanistan almost six years ago.

She crossed to the industrial-sized fridge. "Speaking of daffodils, you think they're ever going to bloom this spring? It's only a few weeks until people will start booking rooms for the daffodil festival. They better be up and dancing the first week of March, or people will post unhappy reviews on Yelp."

"I see you're in a full-out February funk," he said.

She refrained from pointing out that today was Valentine's Day, and she was alone, because the same could be said of Dad. Maybe Dad hadn't checked the calendar this morning, and Ashley didn't want to be the one to remind him of their shared loneliness.

She got busy making biscuits the way her grandmother had. She had just started to combine the dry ingredients with flakes of butter she kept on hand in the freezer when her eleven-year-old son, Jackie, came rushing down the stairs.

Jackie had started to shoot up in the last few months, and he'd gotten that rail-thin look of a boy growing too fast. This morning, his school uniform was more disheveled than usual. How did the boy manage to wrinkle his polyester, no-iron pants? He took the last three steps in a single bound, raced around the kitchen island, and helped himself to several pieces of bacon while simultaneously dodging his grandfather's attempt at a hug.

"Mom, Reverend St. Pierre is coming up the walk. I saw him from my bedroom window. You think he's coming to breakfast?"

"The preacher is coming to breakfast?" she asked, suddenly worried that she might appear as disheveled as her son. She stomped on that thought. It had been months—almost a year—since The Rev had come to breakfast. He'd been courting Brooklyn Huddleston.

Jackie chomped down on a second piece of bacon and headed toward the dining room door. "Don't worry, Mom, I'll greet the preacher and find out what he wants for breakfast. My guess is oatmeal, same as me," he said. He flew through the door, leaving it flapping behind him.

"I wonder how he manages to get creases in the back of his pants that way?" Dad asked.

"It's a mystery," Ashley said, trying to quell the urgent beat of her heart. Why had The Rev come to breakfast? She stifled the urge to follow Jackie and pepper the minister with questions. Everyone in town knew he was courting Brooklyn. It didn't make sense for him to show up here, especially on Valentine's Day.

Dad glanced at the clock. "The minister knows that breakfast doesn't start for another twenty minutes, right?"

"Reverend St. Pierre used to come to breakfast all the time. And usually showed up earlier than most." Ashley plopped the biscuit dough onto the counter and began rolling it, adding layers of butter.

"Oh?" Dad drew out the word until it became a question, and his eyebrow arched.

"Dad, it's like a tradition around here that we feed the ministers. You know how Grandmother was."

"Yes, I do." He gave her a full-on daddy look. "And you are not your grandmother. I loved Mother, but she was insufferably stubborn and blind about some things." He aimed his bacon tongs in her direction. "Just saying."

Dad had joined the army against Grandmother's wishes,

and during Ashley's childhood they visited Magnolia Harbor only sporadically, usually when Dad was off on some deployment. Dad and Grandmother had issues.

After Adam died, Dad had been coolly furious with Ashley for accepting Grandmother's invitation to come stay for a while. But at the time, it only seemed fair, since Granny Horning had Mom and Dad, and Grandmother lived alone.

Although in reality, Grandmother wasn't lonely. She had friends, her quilting circle, all kinds of civic activities, and Heavenly Rest Church, which the Howland family had helped to establish hundreds of years ago.

Grandmother hadn't desperately needed Ashley, but she'd given her a place to stay and heal. When Grandmother died unexpectedly two years later, she left everything to Ashley, not Dad. The legacy had come with its own problems. Howland House had been in desperate need of repair, and Ashley didn't have the funds to fix it. But thanks to an angel investor, she'd been able to get a small business loan and had turned the old family compound into a bed and breakfast.

Grandmother had given her so much more than a place to stay. She'd given her a future.

Jackie slammed through the dining room door again, popping his head into the kitchen. "The Rev wants biscuits and gravy. And a cup of coffee," he announced.

"What?" Ashley finished cutting out the first batch of biscuits for the day and started placing them on a baking sheet. "Not oatmeal?"

"He says he's especially hungry today," Jackie said.

* * *

Micah sat at Ashley's group dining table, studying his hands and wondering if he should have driven down to the new Starbucks across the street from City Hall. Coming here was a mistake.

But somehow his feet had carried him up the hill and right to Ashley's door, where the scent of bacon hung in the air. It was safe here.

He could eat his emotions, even if he couldn't quite describe what they were. Humiliation and shame, surely. Anger at Ethan Cuthbert's stupidity and the idiocy of the town council for putting in the parking meters? Relief? Wow. Maybe he was relieved.

The swinging door to the kitchen whooshed, and Ashley appeared. His emotions teetered on yet another precipice. Anger melted away, leaving him with a deep longing to cross the distance between them and smooth the frown that rode Ashley's forehead. Maybe he could make her smile, and it would reach all the way to her dark eyes.

But today the perpetual sadness hovered there.

The rumors about Howland House were right. It *was* haunted...by the ghost of Ashley's late husband.

Ashley paused by the door, coffee carafe poised while she studied him. Thank the Lord she didn't have X-ray vision, because she might be surprised by the direction of his thoughts.

Most likely, the Magnolia Harbor grapevine had already alerted her to the disaster at Bread, Butter, and Beans, and that explained her hesitation.

"Good morning," he said, trying to sound normal.

"Good morning, Reverend St. Pierre," she said, using his formal title. "Jackie told me that you wanted biscuits and gravy. It'll take a minute. The biscuits just went into the oven."

She crossed the room with a hip-swinging walk he was professionally required to ignore. Her familiar scent—a rich floral amalgam that rivaled her famous rose garden—captured him the moment she leaned close to fill his coffee cup.

He inhaled that scent and held it in his lungs for a long moment. This was torture. He needed to stop. Tomorrow he would make his own darn breakfast.

He braced for some remark indicating that she'd heard all about what had happened at Bread, Butter, and Beans. Instead she cocked her head, the frown deepening a fraction. "Are you okay?"

Maybe she didn't know yet. And maybe he hid his emotions too well. He put on a smile that rivaled hers for its lack of depth. "I'm fine. I just had a hankering for a real breakfast."

A tiny moat of light shone in her eyes, the lower lids bending upward, deepening a few laugh lines. At the same time, her grin melted into something more sincere. "You're always welcome here, Rev."

Chapter Two

Jackie hung back, leaning against the school's brick wall. The other boys were playing kickball, but not him. He hated kickball. He was no good at it.

He would much rather be inside, instead of leaning against this rough wall with his hands freezing because he'd lost his mittens. If Mr. Helme found him here hiding behind the big magnolia at the edge of the playground, he'd be in trouble. Recess was supposed to be for kids to run around and play outside.

He preferred reading.

Which he was managing to do, even if he was tucked away in this corner in the shade by the tree. He'd sneaked the library book out of his cubby because it was really good. *Ghostology* had a wealth of cool information about ghosts, hauntings through history, and the stuff a ghostologist needed to study unusual phenomena.

And Captain William Teal, a pirate who had once sailed Moonlight Bay, had been haunting the old live oak behind Mom's bed and breakfast for centuries, probably ever since he drowned in the big hurricane of 1713. Jackie had encountered the ghost when he first moved to the house, back when Great-Grandmother was still alive.

Mom didn't believe the captain was real. Most grown-ups didn't. They all said the ghost was a figment of his imagination. And also that he'd invented the ghost because Dad had died when he was little. He didn't believe any of that.

But he was worried because the captain didn't come to talk with him as often as he'd used to. Jackie hated to think that he was "growing out" of his ghost, as Mom would say. The ghost was real. How could he grow out of it?

Jackie had come to believe that the ghost only showed himself to kids. And since he was growing up—almost twelve now—the ghost was having a harder time appearing. Jackie worried about that. Not the growing-up part, but the ghost being stuck alone.

He wanted to find a way to send the ghost into the light, or over to the other side, or whatever. The ghost hunters had lots of descriptions for where ghosts go when they finally retire from haunting.

Ghostology also had a lot of information about contacting ghosts through séances and other stuff like that. So he was deep into studying it when someone found his hiding spot.

"Hey, Jackie, whatcha doing back here?" The voice was deep.

Jayden Walsh had found him. Crap. Jayden stood a foot taller than Jackie and outweighed him by a lot. The kid should have been in seventh grade, but everyone knew Jayden had been held back a year when he'd been little. If he'd ever been little. Now Jayden was a freaking giant like his daddy was. And Jayden's daddy had played football for Clemson, which made him a hero. Everyone said he was going to grow up and become a linebacker like his daddy was.

"Reading again?" Jayden asked in a singsong voice that grated up and down Jackie's spine. "Whatcha got, asswipe?" He lunged and ripped the library book from Jackie's hands.

"Give that back," Jackie said.

Jayden roughly thumbed through the pages. "You still on that ghost thing? You're such a jerk, Scott."

Just then, several of the boys who hung with Jayden came through the magnolia. Now Jackie was outnumbered, not that it mattered much since Jayden was a beast.

"Please give me back the book. It's from the library."

"Oh, it's from the library," Jayden said in a high, mocking tone. "And look here, Liam, it's got stories about haunted ships." He turned to show one of the boys the page with the pictures of the haunted pirate ship.

"Hey, Scott, I heard they sent you to see a shrink because of crap like this. Does your momma know you took this book out from the library?"

As a matter of fact, he had not mentioned the book to anyone, mostly because Granddad would give him a lecture about the ghost and telling stories that weren't true. In some ways, Granddad was worse than Jayden and his pack of bullies.

But Jackie figured it was okay to have this book because Mrs. Wilson, the librarian, had specifically pulled it from the shelves when he'd told her he needed to do research on ghosts. Mrs. Wilson was helping him figure out what he needed to know in order to help the ghost.

"Please. Give it back," Jackie said. His voice shook a little.

"No." Jayden gave him a wicked grin and then started ripping pages from the library book.

That did it. Something deep inside Jackie snapped. Maybe Granddad wouldn't approve of him reading this book. Maybe he hadn't told Mom about it. Maybe he was a jerk for believing the inn was haunted. But Mrs. Wilson would have his ass if he returned that beautiful book all torn up.

Ripping up a book—any book—was the most horrible thing he could think of, so he had to stop Jayden. No matter what.

"Stop it," he yelled. Then he charged at the bigger boy, aiming low for his legs because Cousin Topher, who had also played football in college, had once told him the legs were the weakest place.

And sure enough, he toppled Jayden back. The bigger boy fell hard against the magnolia, knocking his head against the trunk and then hitting it again when he landed on the ground. Jayden didn't get up. He just lay there groaning like he was really hurt. Good.

Jackie felt almost no remorse for tackling him. And he didn't wait around for Jayden's friends to retaliate. He grabbed the book and tried to pick up the pages that Jayden had tossed on the ground. But a wind came along and scattered then, and then Mr. Helme discovered them. Before Jackie could say one word about Jayden, Liam accused Jackie of ripping up the book. He even told Mr. Helme that Jayden had tried to stop Jackie but Jackie had attacked him. Mr. Helme believed Liam because all of Jayden's friends ganged up and lied.

So Jackie ended up spending the next forty-five

minutes in the principal's office. Which was bad. But it was even worse when Granddad showed up to "deal with this situation." Granddad gave him the expected lecture about the book, not only its destruction but its subject matter.

And worse yet, Granddad believed Liam's lie, too. Even though Jackie had tried to tell him the truth. It was as if Granddad truly thought he was the kind of kid who would rip up a book. Mom would never have believed that. But she hadn't come. She'd sent Granddad instead.

* * *

Valentine's Day was a bust for Ashley. She was alone, missing Adam, and Jackie had been suspended from school. And Dad, in a spectacular overreach, had taken it upon himself to impose punishments on Jackie without first consulting with her.

This is what she got for leaving him in charge while she ran off to the grocery store.

He should have called her. She should have been the one facing off with Mrs. Thacker, the principal who had first suggested that Jackie needed counseling because of his obsession with the ghost of Captain Teal. Ashley and Edith Thacker had had more than one run-in over the years.

But no, she'd been cut right out of the discussion. And now her mood verged on incendiary as she strolled down Harbor Drive to Patsy Bauman's house for the weekly meeting of the Piece Makers, the quilting group originally founded by her grandmother.

She should have canceled tonight, but if she'd stayed

at the inn for one minute longer she might have picked a screaming fight with Dad. And that would not have solved anything.

It was easier to breathe out here in the cold. She stopped a block from Patsy's house and gazed out at the bay, dark this time of evening, the soft lap of the water against the shore deep and lonely. She could have used Mom's help today, talking Dad down from his outrage at Jackie's behavior. She missed Mom so much. And Adam and Grandmother. But most of all, she missed her old self. Where had that Ashley gone?

Of course if Adam had been here, he would probably have done the same thing Dad had done. And really Jackie deserved to be punished. The other boy had suffered a head injury. There needed to be consequences.

Tears filled her eyes and dripped cold down her cheeks, and for a moment the world was too small to contain her sorrow. She was screwing this up, and Adam wasn't here to help. And she couldn't shake the feeling that her love for her dead husband was killing her in some way. But how was she supposed to fall out of love with him? He'd been her soul mate. Her rock. Her world had revolved around him.

But this perpetual sadness wasn't good for her either, even though the grief was the last connection with him. The one she would never be able to give up.

She stood staring at the bay until the tears passed, as they always did. Once, the grief had dragged her down like the undertow along the inlet. Now she'd learned how to swim the currents and tides of it. But she couldn't figure out how the hell to get out of the water.

She checked her watch. She was going to be late for the quilting group. She straightened her shoulders and continued to Patsy's house. She didn't bother ringing the bell. The door was open, and the girls were gathered around Patsy's kitchen table, helping themselves to some cake.

It was Karen's week for refreshments, so the cake would be store-bought, which was a good thing because Karen was no baker. Ashley doffed her winter coat and rubbed her hands together to generate a little heat.

"Well," Patsy said on a huff, "now that we're all finally here, we need to talk about Reverend St. Pierre."

Ashley stared at Patsy. "What about him?" she asked.

"He asked Brooklyn to marry him."

"Oh." Her heart twisted in her chest. And then she knew that Brooklyn had refused him, even before Patsy said the words. If Brooklyn hadn't rejected his proposal, Micah would never have darkened her door this morning.

"The poor man went to the coffee shop on Valentine's Day morning, got down on bended knee, and Brooklyn rejected him right there in front of everyone," Patsy said. "I was there with Harry for Valentine's Day breakfast. I saw the whole thing."

"The hussy," Nancy said. Her quiet voice underscoring the venom in her delivery.

"Now, Nancy, that's not nice," Patsy said. "And besides, ladies, we were all uncomfortable with Micah's courtship of Brooklyn."

"Only because she's a Methodist," Barbara said with a sniff. "We Methodists would have been happy to see Micah convert."

Karen rolled her eyes. "It wasn't ever going to work out that way, I'm sure."

"Ladies," Patsy said like a schoolteacher quieting an unruly class, "we don't need to argue that point anymore.

We all now know that it wasn't going to work out. I think we need to put our heads together and find him a suitable wife."

"What?" The word exploded from Ashley's mouth. "Why on earth would we do that? Leave the man alone."

"He clearly needs help." Patsy said this with the conviction of the converted.

"What makes you say that?" Ashley asked.

"Because he's almost forty years old, and he's now ready to take a wife. Some men are like that. And now that he's ready, we can be of enormous help. After all, some of us are members of his altar guild. And the rest of us are good church women."

"Oh good lord," Ashley muttered under her breath, earning her a glare from Patsy.

Patsy remained undeterred. "So, ladies," she said with that authoritative voice of hers, "we need to make a list of eligible women in the congregation."

"No, we don't," Ashley said, anxiety racing through her. Technically, she was one of the eligible women in the congregation. But she never checked the "single" box on forms. She always checked the box labeled "widow." And if the idiots who had made the form didn't have a "widow" box, she wrote it in.

She was not an unmarried woman.

"We should stay out of Micah's life," she said.

"No. I think we could be of help. And I think he might welcome our assistance."

"I doubt it."

"Maybe we should ask," Nancy suggested in a low voice.

"Good idea," Patsy said, turning on Ashley with an ominous gleam in her eye. "You could ask him, Ashley, and maybe you could find out how he's feeling. You know, if he's sad or depressed. We need to support him, and I think of all the members of the altar guild, you probably know him best. Maybe you could invite him to have breakfast at the inn again, like he used to. We're all concerned about him."

Ashley ground her back teeth but did not divulge the fact that Micah had already returned to her dining room on his own, seeking out a breakfast he'd never once ordered before. What did that mean? Nothing good, she suspected. Poor man.

The last thing he needed was a bunch of meddling church women. She ought to warn him about this. So she met Patsy's stare. "I'll talk to him," she said. Of course she had no intention of doing any matchmaking for him. She would just let him know he was sailing into shark-infested waters.

"Thank you," Patsy said. "Now, in the meantime, I think we should make a list."

"I agree," Sandra said. "And we should put Emily Wilson at the top of it."

"What about Sarah Wilcox?" Nancy asked. "Her pralines are to die for."

Karen got out a notepad and started jotting down names while Ashley poured herself a second cup of coffee. It was going to be a long night.

* * *

Micah's brothers showed up at the rectory at six thirty on Valentine's evening, catching him in the act of scooping out some ice cream for dinner. What the heck? Jude was married and should be with his wife on Valentine's Day, and Colton had never had any problems finding dates. Why were they here?

One look at the ice cream scoop in his hand, and Jude asked, "How often exactly do you eat ice cream for dinner?"

Micah pressed his lips together. There were laws that protected him from self-incrimination.

"Good thing we're here to make an intervention," Colton said. "We're taking you to Rafferty's for a steak." Micah's younger brother snatched the scoop and returned the ice cream to the freezer. Of course he noticed the lineup of Marie Callender's frozen dinners stashed there.

"Don't you guys have dinner plans tonight?" Micah asked, his irritation and maybe a little bit of embarrassment bleeding through his tone.

"Yes, we do. With you," they said in unison as Jude helped him into his coat and dragged him out to Colton's pickup.

"Well, you ought to be dining with your wife and girlfriend," he muttered.

"Valentine's Day is a stupid holiday," Colton said. "It's designed to make people without dates feel bad."

"Jenna's under the weather," Jude said. "She insisted I get out of the house."

"I'm fine, really," Micah insisted. "I was just fixing to watch the Clemson game."

"I'm sure they'll have it on the TV at Rafferty's. We're not leaving you alone tonight," Jude said. "And I'm thinking maybe Jenna should start sending over care packages. Ice cream for dinner. Dude, really?"

Micah found himself wedged between his younger brothers, his stomach rumbling. The ice cream had been a rash decision. One of Rafferty's twelve-ounce New York strip steaks might actually fill his troublesome belly better.

Rafferty's Raw Bar occupied a spot right in the center of town, along the boardwalk and adjacent to the public pier. Tonight's crowd consisted mostly of couples out to celebrate Valentine's Day. There were, however, an odd assortment of what could only be called lonely hearts.

Colton and Jude snagged a table in the back corner of the main dining room where they could see the basketball game on the large screen. The game had just started.

Micah settled in, and his brothers ordered a pitcher of beer. Not much was said until the waitress had brought their drinks. Colton did the pouring, and when he pressed the glass into Micah's hands, he said, "Drink up, brother. You escaped today."

"Escaped?" Jude asked. "He didn't escape. She broke his heart."

Micah took a deep draft of beer and put down his glass. Clemson had turned over the ball. "Come on, y'all, can we watch the basketball game, please?"

"No. You need to talk about this," Jude said.

"Maybe he doesn't want to," Colton replied, rolling his eyes in Micah's direction. "I want to make it clear that I'm here in a show of solidarity. If you don't want to talk, I'm down with that."

Jude scowled at Colton, and Colton returned the look. Micah took another gulp of beer. "Am I going to have to break up a fight?" Micah asked.

"No," his brothers said in unison.

"But you should talk about your feelings," Jude said.

"Right."

"You know this is true. You're a preacher."

Technically, he was an Episcopalian priest, but folk around here called anyone who stood in the pulpit a preacher. And if he started talking about his emotions, Micah feared he might confess stuff that neither of his brothers wanted to hear.

Stuff about his guilt for leaving them years ago.

Stuff about his interest in Ashley Scott.

Stuff about his anger with Mom and Daddy.

Stuff about how he had decided to settle for Brooklyn instead of love her.

Better not to talk about this stuff. He took another gulp of beer.

"So . . ." Jude leaned in.

"I don't want to talk about my feelings," Micah snapped.

"See." Colton grinned at Jude and picked up his menu. "I suggest you get the biggest steak on the menu."

"Seems reasonable to me," Micah said.

"Come on, Micah. It's okay to feel sad. After all, you loved her, and she said no." Jude stared at him out of worried eyes. Micah appreciated his brother's concern, but he was not ready to talk. Not about his most important thoughts. Sadly, losing Brooklyn might not be the biggest disaster in his life.

"Jeez, Jude, leave him alone."

Micah hid behind his menu until the waitress came by and they ordered their steaks. By then, Micah was working on his second beer, and his grumpiness was fading into a little buzz. Also, Clemson was ahead by five points.

"For what it's worth, I've decided never to order muffins at Bread, Butter, and Beans again," Colton said.

Micah huffed out a breath. "Don't penalize Brooklyn. It's all my fault."

"And why do you say that?" Jude asked, pouncing on this confession like a cat on a mouse.

Oh great. That had been a mistake. Maybe he should give them a tiny sliver of truth that Jude could take home to his wife. And then they could congratulate themselves for helping him. He had no doubt this brotherly dinner was all Jenna's idea.

He gulped down some more beer. UVA was staging a comeback.

"You know, Micah, you're always taking the blame for stuff that you're not responsible for," Jude said.

"What?" He tightened his grip on his beer.

"The part about it being your fault. It's not. Just sayin'."

He shrugged, unable to counter this obvious truth. But there were other truths beneath the surface. Otherwise, how could he explain that he was more humiliated than heartbroken? He studied the big screen for a moment and decided to speak the unvarnished truth. "I was settling."

"What?" Jude sounded horrified.

"Oh boy," Colton said, squirming in his chair.

"You proposed to a woman you didn't love? Were you hoping to fail?" Jude asked, leaning in.

"Maybe."

Colton scrubbed his face with his hands. "Y'all, do we really want talk about this?"

"Grow up," Jude said, shooting Colton a sharp glance. It was a funny thing for Jude to say since he was younger than Colton. But maybe more mature than any of them. "Why did you want to fail?" he asked Micah.

Micah drained his beer, and Colton refilled it. "Look, you guys, it's not that easy when you're a priest." He turned toward Colton. "There are rules I have to follow."

"What rules?" Jude pressed. The ref blew the halftime. Clemson was down by five.

"I can't date just anyone."

"Oh? What does that mean?"

He huffed out a breath. "It's against the rules for me to date anyone with whom I have a pastoral relationship."

"What does that mean?" Colton asked.

"It means he can't date members of his congregation," Jude said, then frowned. "Holy crap, Micah, is there someone in the congregation that you'd *like* to date?"

He stared at Jude without the fig leaf of being able to tell him to watch the game since it was halftime. "No," he said as firmly as he could. "It makes the pool of potential dates smaller, is all."

It was the truth. But it wasn't the whole truth. He wasn't being entirely honest with them or himself.

* * *

"And then," Shawna Braddock said, waving her glass of Chardonnay with a flourish, "after he dropped the ring, Brooklyn said no."

"She didn't," Marcie Harvey said, looking up from the somewhat lopsided scarf she was kitting.

Shawna nodded, and Kerri Eaton, who was trying, unsuccessfully, to shape the crown of a beanie hat, let go of her knitting in frustration. She'd started this "easy" project right before Christmas and had ripped it out five times. Now her yarn was kinky and split in places, making the decreases along the crown an unholy mess.

Her girlfriends had formed this knitting circle, unofficially named the Stitch and Bitch Club, a few months ago. They usually met on Wednesday, but Marcie had called an emergency Valentine's Day meeting because they were all over thirty-five and dateless.

"Why on earth would a woman Brooklyn Huddleston's age say no to Micah St. Pierre? I mean, it's not as if there are that many marriageable men floating around this island during the off season," Shawna said.

"Amen to that, girlfriend," Marcie said, stuffing her project into her knitting bag and pouring herself another glass of Chardonnay. "In fact, y'all, I've been thinking about moving back to the mainland. I could get a job at a bank anywhere. Preferably somewhere there are available men. I'm tired of living like a nun."

"Maybe you should make a play for Micah St. Pierre," Shawna said, taking a sip of wine.

Marcie wrinkled her nose. "I don't want a minister. I suspect that's why Brooklyn said no. On the other hand, the preacher's brother... Well, that's a whole different story. Only problem with Colton St. Pierre is that he's married to his business, near as I can tell."

"And not likely to commit anytime soon," Kerri muttered, putting her sad hat aside and picking up her wine. Summer before last, she'd had a whirlwind and completely secret affair with Colton St. Pierre. The man had commitment issues. He was not the Prince Charming Kerri was looking for. But then again, there was no such thing as Prince Charming. If only her stupid heart would believe that.

Marcie heaved a big sigh. "I know he's a player, but one day he might get a notion. I live in hope of being the first woman he sets eyes on when that happens."

"Right, and you might be too old to notice when he gets around to it," Shawna said, cocking her head and staring at Kerri in a peculiar way.

Had Kerri said too much? Had her friend connected the dots? She didn't want to expose her own foolishness over Colton. She'd known right from the start that her fling with him wasn't going to be permanent. At the time, Colton had been carrying a gigantic torch for Jessica Blackwood. He probably still did, although Jessica had married Topher Martin.

"You know," Shawna said, aiming her gaze at Kerri, "you'd be perfect for Micah St. Pierre since you're such a good church woman."

"What?" Kerri almost spilled her wine.

"You heard me. Why don't you give him comfort in his hour of need?"

Kerri shook her head, searching for something that would end this conversation. "Shawna, we go to different churches."

"So. You're both Christians." Marcie drained her glass and reached for the bottle.

"Well, yes, but I don't know the man that well."

"I'm sure you could wrangle an introduction."

"No."

"Why not?"

Shawna wasn't getting the hint. She wasn't going to drop this subject, which was a problem. Kerri could not date Rev. St. Pierre when she'd slept with his younger brother.

It was icky.

And probably immoral.

Or something.

"No. Just... no," Kerri said, reaching for the bottle and draining the last bit of wine into her glass.

"Well, if not you, then who? I mean, there are plenty of single women here in town. Maybe we can help him out and get him hooked up with someone we know."

"Shut up, Shawna. I'm sure he doesn't need a matchmaker. The man is tall, dark, handsome, and reliable. I bet he has to beat the ladies off with a stick," Marcie said.

"Well, if that's true, why hasn't he gotten married before this?" Kerri asked. She suspected that Micah suffered from the same commitment phobia as Colton. They'd both come from a dysfunctional family where addiction had been present. It made for screwed-up adults.

"Girl, are you suggesting that he doesn't like women?" Marcie asked.

"No," Kerri said with a firm headshake. "But he might be terrified of commitment. He comes from a broken home, you know. And besides, it's got to be complicated for a minister. I mean, what if his congregation doesn't like his choice?"

"Good point," Shawna said, an unholy, wine-fed glow in her eye. "Clearly, you have given this some thought, haven't you?"

"What makes you say that?"

"That bit about him coming from a broken home, girl," Marcie said with a little giggle.

"Well, he did."

"Right. And you know this because...?"

"Everyone knows Colton came from a broken home. Don't they?"

"I didn't," Shawna said.

"Oh. Well, I'm surprised because it seems to be general knowledge. And the minister has to be approaching forty years old. What's been keeping him from getting married all these years, if not some deep-seated problem with commitment?"

"Right. Like I said, you seem to know a lot about it."

"No, it's not that at all." Kerri took a breath and stopped speaking before she dug herself a great big hole she could not get out of.

"Well," Shawna said, standing up, "I'm going to get more wine. I think we need to discuss this further, girl-friend. Because I think you have a little crush on the minister. And really, if you're looking for a reliable man who probably wants a family, Micah St. Pierre is the one for you."

Chapter Three

Micah strolled into one of the meeting rooms at the new City Hall building for the monthly meeting of the Jonquil Island Museum Board of Directors. This would be the first time the group had met in the new building, which would also house their new museum. He took a moment to appreciate the light-filled room with its ultramodern, modular furniture—a far cry from the dingy basement room they'd been meeting in for the last three years.

Tonight's meeting marked a transition for the board. Most of the work on exhibits had been done, a museum director had been hired, and the museum would officially open in mid-March. Instead of hashing out history, tonight they'd be planning the museum's unveiling ceremony and reception.

Micah had already announced his intention to step down as chair right after the museum opened. He had too many things on his agenda these days, chief among them the renovation of Heavenly Rest Church, which was two hundred years old and had weathered a lot of history itself.

Pride might be a sin, but he was especially proud of the way the board had come together in the face of a lot of political pull and tug. When they opened their doors, the museum would present a fair and balanced picture of the island's history.

A lot of the space would be devoted to presenting the story of the formerly enslaved people who had settled this island in the nineteenth century. Those people, known as the Gullah, had left the rice plantations, migrated to this island, which was remote at the time, and purchased their own land, making them distinct from the sharecroppers of the post–Civil War era in most parts of the South.

These first settlers preserved some of the culture they'd brought with them from the west coast of Africa. To this day, a visitor to the island could still hear people speaking the Gullah language, derived from hundreds of African dialects. The new museum would present the history of the Gullah culture and have special events including storytellers and sweetgrass basketmaking demonstrations. A foundation had also been created to study the language and try to preserve it in written form for future generations.

And a special gallery would be reserved for the story of Rose Howland, who, with Henri St. Pierre, planted the daffodils that had given Jonquil Island its name.

Micah took a seat at one of the tables. He was early. His meeting with one of the architectural consultants hired to provide advice on church repairs had ended early. So he had a moment alone before Harry Bauman and Dylan Killough came through the door talking about the Frigid Digit regatta coming up this Saturday.

"Ah, Micah, I'm glad you're here early," Harry said. The older man took the seat to Micah's left. "I need a word with you."

"Oh? What's up?"

Harry swiveled on the fancy new chairs and leaned in close. He spoke in a near whisper. "On the QT, you should know that my wife is lining up potential prospects for you like some dowager in one of those Masterpiece Theater shows."

"What?"

"You know. Those period pieces set in England where the women are obsessed with getting their sons and daughters married off."

"Oh." Micah's stomach clutched.

"She's decided that you can't manage on your own."

Great. Just what he needed. He wanted to tell Harry to ask his wife to back off, but before he could open his mouth, Ashley Scott sailed into the room, her cheeks rosy from the cold outside. She pulled off a knit hat, and a few strands of dark hair, charged with electricity, lifted from her scalp.

A different kind of electricity jolted Micah at the sight of her. She'd lost her perfect-ponytail, buttoned-up, do-not-ever-approach vibe. But he wasn't supposed to notice that. Sometimes Adam Scott's ghost had been a welcome barrier between Micah and his straying thoughts.

"Anyway," Harry continued, oblivious to Micah's wandering eye, "forewarned is forearmed."

"Thanks for the advice, Harry," he said, pretending to study his meeting notes.

"What advice?" Ashley asked as she found the chair to his right.

Micah braced himself, his mind going blank.

Harry muttered, "Nothing," under his breath. "Just church stuff. You know the endless talk about the roof and the ancient plumbing."

Ashley squinted her eyes at Harry as if she wasn't buying that line, although lord only knew the church's roof needed to be replaced and the plumbing was a mess. "What are you two up to?" she asked.

"Nothing," Micah said, echoing Harry. "Truly. We just got another architectural report this afternoon. Filled with gigantic cost estimates."

Ashley's gaze moved between them a couple of times, but she bought the little white lie.

A few minutes remained before seven, when the meeting was scheduled to start. He prayed for time to get a move on, but this was one of those prayers God was never going to answer. Instead, time seemed to slow down while Ashley shuffled papers. Harry turned to talk to Annie Robinson on his other side. Cousin Charlotte came over just to whisper a few unwanted condolences in Micah's ear.

He breathed in and out and looked down at his agenda. That way he wouldn't have to notice any pitying looks. He was sure he'd gotten a few. His breakup with Brooklyn was topic number one on the gossip hit parade.

And then the worst happened. Ashley leaned a little closer, her left arm touching his right.

The world seemed to narrow down to that tiny bit of pressure.

"Do you have some time after the meeting?" The space between them filled with her flowery scent.

"Time?" he asked, momentarily confused.

"I need to talk to you about something."

"About what?" For a moment, he worried that she

might be about to change her mind about Rose Howland's diary. It had taken some convincing for Ashley to agree to donate the diary. Some white folk didn't want history to be fully and accurately told. Ashley wasn't one of those people, but she was worried about potential backlash. Micah wished he could assure her that her worries were unfounded. But he couldn't. There would be some people who didn't want to know the truth.

He studied her for a moment. The groove in her forehead seemed unusually deep tonight. "Is something troubling you?" he asked in a quiet voice when she didn't answer his earlier question.

She shook her head, biting her lip. "No. Yes. Maybe. I don't know. I need a minute, okay?"

Oh. Maybe this was not about the museum or the diary or the church's roof. Maybe she needed a minutc with her minister. How easy it was these days, with all the distractions, to forget his true calling.

"Of course. After the meeting." He glanced at the clock on the wall.

She cocked her head like an adorable, sad-eyed puppy. "That would be good. I'll buy you a coffee at the new Starbucks across the street."

He nodded and then checked the wall clock again. Finally, it was time to start the meeting.

* * *

A tiny pang of remorse nudged Ashley. She'd misled The Rev when he'd asked if something was troubling her. Patsy's matchmaking plans for him *were* troubling her, but she doubted that's what he'd meant. Micah had a way of focusing on a person when they needed his help. He was an exceptionally good listener, and he probably thought she was in need of guidance or some such thing.

They walked in silence, a mounting sense of dread swelling within her. How the hell was she supposed to raise this issue with him without embarrassing him? Or herself. But how could she not warn him?

By the time they crossed the street, her anxiety got the best of her, and she opened her mouth and said, "I'm sorry things didn't work out for you and Brooklyn." She regretted the words the moment she said them.

"I'm okay." His tone conveyed the opposite. The poor man.

She zipped her lip, and they lapsed into quiet. When they arrived at the coffee shop, he opened the door for her. She hesitated a moment before going through it. She'd been opening doors for herself for most of her life, so this courtesy struck her as odd and old-fashioned. But maybe nice.

The coffee shop wasn't as busy as it would be in a few weeks when college kids descended for spring break. They didn't have to wait in line and found a small table with two easy chairs by the front window, which provided a stellar view of the new City Hall with the harbor lights beyond.

"The new building is really amazing," she said, mostly to fill up the silence. This time she'd chosen a safer topic.

"Colton says they're still putting the finishing touches on the council chamber, but the office staff moved into their new digs last Friday," Micah said, folding his large frame into the chair beside her.

"I imagine Colton's happy the job's finished," she said.

"The contract was bigger than anything Colton ever

took on before. And now he's so busy he's had to hire a few more employees. He's moving his office to a bigger building with more parking and warehouse space, way out on Elm Street east of town."

Ashley took a sip of her chai latte, the sweet spiciness of it lingering on her tongue. The small talk seemed forced, and she expected The Rev to change the subject at any moment.

So she took the proverbial bull by the horns. She only hoped she didn't get gored in the process. She put her paper coffee cup down on the small table between them and leaned in, bracing her elbows on her knees. "I may have gotten you here under false pretenses," she said. "I am troubled but not with a personal matter. The truth is, well, I need to give you a warning."

His mouth twitched. "Is this the same warning Harry gave me earlier?"

"He gave you a warning?"

"Yes. He told me the altar guild is behaving like a bunch of matchmaking matrons."

"He knows about their plans?" She leaned back, snagging her cup from the table and taking a healthy gulp. Jeez, she could have saved herself the angst.

"Patsy isn't very good at keeping secrets. I'm sure she told Harry everything about her plans," The Rev said in a dry tone.

"And you're not offended?"

"Well..." His voice faded off. He stared out at the new building across the way.

Damn. This wasn't going well. "I'm sorry. I've offended you. And you know what? You should be offended. I'm offended on your behalf. And for the record, I'm just the messenger."

He pierced her with an intense gaze. "And why are you the messenger? Did they ask you to talk to me?"

Heat suffused her cheeks. The Rev had asked her this question many times. He didn't like the way Patsy bossed people around.

But Patsy had not bullied her this time.

"Look," she said, "I let them think I was doing their bidding."

"And what exactly is that?"

"To quiz you on what sort of wife you might be looking for, so they can flesh out their list of good Episcopalians."

He collapsed back in the chair, his head hitting the leather with an audible slap. He closed his eyes.

Remorse tugged at her insides. "I'm sorry."

"So am I." His voice had the ring of defeat in it.

"I'll tell Patsy to back off, okay?"

He snorted a laugh and opened his eyes. "And you think she'll listen?"

He had a point.

He straightened in his chair and took another gulp of coffee. "Let me ask you, do you think Patsy would listen to the bishop about this?"

"The bishop? Why would you bring the bishop into this?"

"Because I have to ask the bishop's permission to date anyone in the congregation. Just to be clear, I'm certain the bishop would say no."

"Really?"

His stare connected with her, deep brown to deep brown. "Think about it, Ashley. The church has rules about this sort of thing."

Of course they did. She didn't know whether to be

relieved or disappointed. Wait. Disappointed? What was up with that?

Her emotions tumbled with various implications, and he continued. "To date anyone in the congregation would be to abuse my position."

"Of course," she said in a tiny voice. "That's why you were dating Brooklyn. Because she's a Methodist."

"Well, yes. I was free to date her. But I also liked her."

Liked her? Whoa. That was wrong. And then she blurted, "Wait, are you saying you didn't love her?"

He closed his eyes again, the picture of misery.

"Oh, uh, I'm sorry. I should have—"

"No. It's a fair question. Maybe I didn't love her enough. And clearly she didn't want to settle for me. It's not easy being a priest's wife."

No, she imagined not. It would be . . . kind of like being an army wife. A priest's wife would have to pull up stakes and move on if her husband's calling demanded it. It would require sacrifice.

You'd have to love someone a lot for that.

His naked look hit her in the midsection, knocking her off kilter. A man as handsome, thoughtful, and kind as Micah St. Pierre shouldn't be having such a hard time finding someone to love him.

Chapter Four

Micah's aunt Daisy was turning eighty-six, and the family planned a huge birthday party for Saturday afternoon, which was supposed to be Micah's day off. But Ken Nyberg, the church's volunteer youth minister, ended up shorthanded for the skateboard derby he'd organized for the church's teen group. Since it was scheduled for Saturday morning, Micah filled in. He didn't mind. Getting to spend time with the kids in his congregation was a joy—so much more fulfilling than the mountain of paperwork he had to deal with on a daily basis.

It was a glorious day, that hinted at the summer heat that would soon be upon them. The temperatures spiked to almost seventy, and the kids had a great time. Everyone needed the February thaw.

But the program ran long. And then Ken pulled Micah aside for a personal conversation about a boy named Danny Beckett. Up until recently, Danny had been attending the local high school, where Ken was a science teacher and the coach of the basketball team. Danny had been one of his students but had dropped out of school right before Christmas.

Ken was concerned. The boy's parents had died a little over a year ago in a freak boating accident, and that's how Danny had ended up in Magnolia Harbor, living with his grandmother, who had health issues. Mary Beckett was not a member of Micah's congregation. She didn't go to any church, evidently. Ken thought she needed help, not only in managing Danny but maybe in more ways than that.

Micah's ability to help was limited, but he promised to see if Mary Beckett would talk to him. And he also agreed to contact the local senior center to make sure they were aware of her needs. He also gave Ken a few telephone numbers for grief counselors for the teen. Most of the counselors were located on the mainland, which was a problem because Mary was going blind, and Danny did not have a driver's license. Ken was trying to remedy that issue, but finding the boy a car was also a problem.

Ken was truly worried about this boy. He'd been trying to get him involved in Heavenly Rest's youth programs for the last three months, with no luck. He'd hoped the boy would come to the skateboard event, because Danny liked to board. But he hadn't come today.

Assuring Ken that he'd do all that he could for Danny took some time, so Micah was running extremely late for Aunt Daisy's party, and when he got to her house there were no more parking spots in the drive.

He had to back down the gravel road and park behind Colton's pickup. He killed the engine just as winter made another assault on the island. The skies opened up in a downpour, sending rivulets snaking across the windshield of his twelve-year-old Forester.

He unbuckled his seat belt and searched the car's back seat, looking for an umbrella. Unfortunately, the clutter in the back of his SUV had grown to ridiculous proportions. He always carried a couple of copies of the Bible and the *Book of Common Prayer*, as well as a traveling communion kit. But today, his back seat also had a stack of catalogs from Christian booksellers and a plastic bag of baptism napkins, hand-embroidered by members of the congregation, as well as a box of books the Bible study group had ordered that had been wrongly sent to the rectory. The napkins should have been taken into the church a week ago, and the box of books had overturned, spilling all over the floor.

And high atop the mess, folded carefully, sat Isabelle Gerst's beloved and slightly grubby comfort blanket. Izzy had left it at the church-sponsored preschool on Friday. Last night, when Diane Gerst had called frantic for the blankie, he'd promised to search the schoolroom for it and return it as soon as possible. He'd found it this morning, hiding under one of the preschool tables.

He stared at the blanket for a long moment. He should take it back to the child now. But he was expected at the party too.

A heavy sense of exhaustion pulled at him. He didn't mind helping out at the teen event today or taking care of Isabelle Gerst's blanket. But all the paperwork he had to deal with made time precious. And today he had to show up for his family.

With a twinge of guilt because Izzy had gone without her blankie for a day and a half, he decided to go wish

Daisy a happy birthday. Then he'd leave early and drop the blanket at the Gersts on his way home.

He gave up trying to find his umbrella and resigned himself to getting wet, which was exactly what happened during his sprint up the road to the porch. Rain soaked through his suit jacket and got under his Roman collar. It trickled down his back. When he reached the wraparound porch, he shook himself like a dog and followed the music to the backyard.

Aunt Daisy's house had been originally built in the late 1800s. The family had added onto the small cabin several times over the years, and his brothers had footed the bill for a major renovation last year.

The original, hand-hewn clapboard siding now wore a new coat of pale-yellow paint, set off by green windowsills and shutters. His brothers had replaced the old rusty roof, jacked up the sagging porch, and added a fancy patio out back that provided killer views of Moonlight Bay. They'd also redone the interior. Daisy's house could have been featured in *Southern Living*'s travel section.

Micah didn't have the means to help pay for the project, although he'd escaped the paperwork on his desk a few weekends to help sand drywall and paint a few walls. When he'd left the navy to become a pastor, he'd had no real understanding of the demands a church community would make on his time. The navy had been a piece of cake in comparison.

Someone had erected a big tent over the new patio, where Cousin Jamal's band had set up. They were covering the Ranky Tanky song "Good Time," and the party guests were enjoying themselves. The patio was chockablock with dancers clapping and stomping their feet, and a buffet-style feast catered by Jamal's mother had been laid out on the back porch.

Aunt Daisy sat up under the eaves in a wicker rocking chair, wearing a kitenge-cloth head wrap and dress in shades of blue, yellow, and orange. The dress seemed a little too big for her, the voluminous skirt almost swallowing her thin form whole.

Despite her frail health, she beamed at the crowd like some reigning monarch. He loved that woman. Daisy had kept the family together when it had started unraveling. She had been his rock as a boy.

And he'd needed a rock because his parents had never been fully present. Micah had tried to bridge the gap for his younger siblings, but he'd been inadequate. And then he'd gone to college. For as long as Micah lived, he'd be paying a penance for leaving his brothers behind. He had vowed never to leave them again. Although they didn't need him these days.

He scanned the crowd. No sign of Daddy, which was not much of a surprise. Daddy had never gotten along with Aunt Daisy, who was his mother's sister and Micah's great-aunt.

He headed in Daisy's direction, but before he could take two steps, Cousin Archie, Daisy's son, stopped to greet him and press a beer into his hand. Archie could talk a mile a minute, and he always had a lot to say, usually about the state of politics in America.

Micah managed to escape after five minutes only to be accosted by Cousin Annie, the owner of Annie's Kitchen, who had catered the event.

"We're s'posed to be having a good time, Micah. Why are you wearing that collar?"

"Uh, well, I just came from a church thing and..."

"Honey, you spend too much time at the church. And the Desmond Tutu vibe is not cutting it here today." She swept her hand over the crowd, which sported colorful Hawaiian shirts, dashikis, and a lot of sweatshirts since the day's warmth was fading fast.

"I'm sorry. I had a shirt hanging on the back of the bedroom door, and I forgot it this morning. I was in a rush for this—"

"Church thing. I get it. Take off the collar, Micah."

He unbuttoned the shank button at the back of his neck, which held the collar in place. He removed the two studs from the back and the front of his shirt.

"Better," Annie said. "But you're still wearing black in a sea of colors." She gave him a slap on the back and a kiss on the cheek. "Honey, you need to loosen up and live a little. The Lord commanded that we rest at least one day a week. And since you have to work on Sunday..."

"I'll keep that in mind." He turned away, finally making it all the way up to where Aunt Daisy was sitting. He bent over to touch her shoulder and give her a kiss.

"Oh, Micah, there you be," she said, taking his hand in a fierce grip, her gaze over-bright. He'd spent enough hours at bedsides to know that Aunt Daisy was ill. Cousin Charlotte said it was heart failure.

This would probably be her last birthday, which explained why the family had pulled out all the stops for her. He gently squeezed her hand, riddled with arthritis from years of making sweetgrass baskets. "How you doing, Miz Daisy?"

"I be fine," she said with a wave. She turned toward Cousin Benton's son, who was standing beside her. "Honey, you go get one of those folding chairs so Reverend Micah can set here with me."

"Yes ma'am," the boy said and scurried away, returning a moment later with a chair.

Micah sat, and Daisy pulled her hand away. "Now, son, I need to talk with you."

"Yes ma'am." He held his breath.

"I heard all about that woman saying no to you. And let me just say, she ain't worth nothing if she don't see the worth in you."

He took a pull on his beer. "Well, Aunt Daisy, I think maybe she didn't love me."

Daisy's skin seemed to be stretched tight over her bones these days. She'd lost a lot of weight. "She's stupid then."

He managed a laugh. "Thank you."

"Don't be thanking me. Now listen here." She waved him closer, and he leaned in, catching the faint scent of jasmine.

"Charlotte's been saying that maybe you don't really want a wife."

"What?"

Daisy's eyes shone with love and age. "I am so very proud of you, Micah, being a man of God. If you've been carrying around a secret, maybe you need to lay it down, you know? Charlotte was just telling me that you Episcopalians don't have any objections to, you know…folk who are different."

Micah had to button his lip to keep from laughing out loud. His eighty-six-year-old great-aunt, who didn't have the most open of minds when it came to the LGBTQ+ community, seemed to be giving him permission to come out of the closet.

"Aunt Daisy," he said, patting her hand where it lay on the chair's arm, "I don't have any secrets I need to lay down."

Daisy's gaze firmed up. "So you say Brooklyn didn't love you. Did you love her?"

This time he chose to tell the truth. "To be honest, I thought I did."

Daisy expelled a short breath between her lips. "You *thought* you did. You didn't *know*?"

She had a point.

"I reckon you're one of those men who hasn't yet met the right gal." She waved again at the crowd. "Bet there's someone out there for you."

He smiled and nodded. No sense in trying to stop her from matchmaking when everyone else in town was at it. In the last few days, he'd gotten half a dozen phone calls from people who knew a nice Christian single woman.

It was beyond humiliating.

Especially since there was one woman who had already caught his eye. But she was so far beyond his reach, it was absurd to think about it. He could count all the reasons: She was a white member of his own congregation who still loved her dead husband.

He didn't think race was much of an issue since he was biracial himself and his younger brother was in a happy interracial marriage. He also hoped that one day Ashley would learn to love again.

But the prohibition against dating within his congregation couldn't be bypassed that easily. It could cost him his career. So it was best not to dwell on his friendship with Ashley. It wasn't healthy.

Just then, Jude got up on stage and captured the microphone. He toasted Daisy and then told a few stories about how Daisy had taught him how to speak Gullah and make sweetgrass baskets. He thanked her for helping him pay for his education at Howard University and for accepting Jenna into the family. "And, Daisy, we got a birthday present for you," he said, a bright smile on his face.

"And what's that?" Daisy asked.

"Jenna is going to have a baby, and—"

The guests hooted and clapped, and Jude had to hush them. "If it's a girl, we're going to name her after you."

"Oh Lord, I am blessed," Daisy said, tears in her eyes. Micah handed her his handkerchief. He forced a smile, although deep inside a wave of envy seized him. He pushed back on it. His own loneliness was no excuse for not sharing Jude and Jenna's joy. He was going to be little Daisy's uncle. That was enough to be joyful about.

And thinking about little Daisy reminded him of little Isabelle Gerst. He leaned forward. "I have something I have to do, Aunt Daisy. I'm sorry I can't stay."

She turned and frowned at him. "More church paperwork?"

He shook his head. "No, I need to return a little girl's comfort blanket."

Daisy's eyes glittered with amusement. "All right, that's a good excuse. You eat before you go, you hear. Jude told me he saw nothing but TV dinners in your freezer." She stared up at him through her bifocals with a no-nonsense look.

He didn't really need too much convincing since his cousin Annie was catering the party. "Yes ma'am," he said, and went off to find some supper.

* * *

Kerri Eaton stood at the edge of Ms. Daisy's patio, under a tent that provided protection against the rain. Daisy's family had invited the world to her party: family, friends, and business associates like Kerri, who had been selling Daisy's sweetgrass baskets at Daffy Down Dilly for the last several years.

The baskets were a big seller, so of course she'd left the store in the care of one of her part-time employees so she could wish one of her most important suppliers a happy day. But getting up to the porch where the guest of honor was sitting would be difficult. She'd have to sharpen her elbows in order to work her way through the crowd of Joneses, Robinsons, and St. Pierres. Daisy's family was huge.

She stepped into the crowd, preparing to do battle, but before she made much progress, someone gave her dress a tug from behind.

"Hey." A voice cut through the music and the noise of the party guests.

She turned...and faced her worst nightmare...or maybe her best fantasy. It was hard to tell which.

"Hello," Colton St. Pierre said above the music. He met her gaze with eyes the color of Spanish moss.

"Um, hi," she said, the spit drying in her mouth. Colton was the sexiest man alive. Tall, muscled, with skin the color of a cypress knee.

He was a magnet. For her fantasies. And every chick in town. Which, no doubt, explained his talent between the sheets. But sex wasn't everything, was it?

No, it was not. Her brain knew this lesson. Unfortunately, her heart just couldn't manage to figure that out. Kerri had tried casual and knew she couldn't do it.

And she wouldn't do it again with Colton St. Pierre

because, like all her exes, he was a man who could break a woman's heart without trying. And her heart had been broken so many times it was Scotch-taped together.

"So, um, I was wondering if..." His voice faded out, and she had to read his lips above the blare of Jamal Robinson's band.

What kind of game was he playing? Whatever it was, she didn't want to participate. "What do you want, Colton?" she snapped.

His eyes widened. "I, uh, well, I'd like to apologize."

She blinked a few times. Had she heard that right? "For what?"

His brows lowered. "Um, well, I don't really know why. I mean, I know you're mad at me about something, but—"

"Oh for god's sake. Grow up, okay?" She walked away from him and abandoned her plan to say hey to Ms. Daisy. In this mood, she was likely to say something grumpy. She needed an attitude adjustment, so she swerved toward the buffet and loaded her plate with fried chicken, okra and tomatoes, mac and cheese, and a bunch of other comfort food. She ducked inside the house searching for a place where she could sit down to eat. Eventually, she found an empty barstool at the kitchen counter, but her solitude was soon interrupted when Rev. St. Pierre strolled into the kitchen, a beer in one hand and a plate in the other, and dropped to the stool beside her.

Something about his body language gave off warning signals. He seemed...*stressed.* Like he had a lot on his mind or needed to eat fast because he had a long to-do list. That made him a whole lot different from Colton, who had this cool, calm thing going for him.

But Micah was easy on the eye too, with darker eyes than his brother's. He also didn't have that I-work-in-construction ripped body of his brother. Micah seemed softer around the edges, and maybe squeezably soft in the middle.

"Hi," she said, deciding to be sociable.

"Hello." His voice rumbled from deep in his chest. He was a baritone to his brother's tenor.

"Great news about Jude and Jenna," she said.

"Yeah, it is." He started shoveling food like a man who hadn't had a good meal in days.

Awkwardness descended, and the silence rose between them like a barrier. She focused on her food, her mind bouncing as she compared and contrasted Micah and Colton. And then she paused, fork midway to her mouth, as she realized how stupid it would be to rule out Micah St. Pierre as possible husband material.

He was, by all accounts, a good man in need of a long-term relationship. That was rare in her experience. All her exes had run from commitment. Micah wouldn't do that. And then she figured that, as a minister, he would probably insist on no sex before marriage.

Boy, that would be different. Liberating even. Because Kerri had mistaken lust for love more times than she could count.

She leaned in a bit. "I don't mean to be forward or anything. But you seem a little stressed out. Is something bothering you?"

He barked a laugh and swiveled on the barstool. "You have to ask?"

She blinked a moment and then realized her mistake. "Oh, I'm sorry. I guess that was a stupid question. I had forgotten all about Valentine's Day."

"Well, that makes you unique."

"I'm sorry. Can we start over?"

The minister's mouth curled ever so slightly. "You think? People are watching us."

"What?"

"Well, not you particularly. But they're watching me. And if you're caught having a conversation with me, the tongues are going to wag."

Was he paranoid? No. But he was Magnolia Harbor's most eligible bachelor. Every church woman in town would be trying to find him a mate. Hadn't she been doing that herself last Tuesday with Marcie and Shawna?

"So I guess the matchmakers are on the move," she said.

"I'm afraid they are. You're in peril."

Kerri laughed and weighed the possibilities. "And what about you? Sadder but wiser, or determined to forge ahead in your search?"

He chuckled and shook his head. He looked away, staring out through the kitchen window above the sink. Out on the front porch, away from the blare of the music, a group of older white women had gathered. Kerri suspected that a number of them were members of his church. "Well," he said finally, "I don't know. But my altar guild is formidable. I have it on good authority that they are making a list for me. Careful, now, your name might end up on that list."

She refrained from saying that she might even like being on that list, except for one not-so-minor problem: his younger brother.

Chapter Five

Ashley didn't usually attend parties up here in the north part of town. She rarely attended parties at all. But today she'd escaped the inn for a few hours, leaving Dad in charge.

Which might be a huge mistake. On the other hand, hanging around the inn while Jackie sulked and Dad mansplained would have been too depressing for words.

But now, hesitating at the edge of the dance floor like a wallflower, she had second thoughts. She hadn't realized this was going to be a dance party. Once upon a time, she'd loved dancing—with Adam. Now, without a partner, the loss burned a hole in her chest.

Someone had pressed a glass of champagne into her hand to toast Daisy. She'd gulped the wine and then hadn't had quite enough to toast Jenna and Jude's wonderful news. Jenna was her angel investor. She'd swooped in with a loan and a lot of business acumen when Howland House had been teetering on the brink.

Without Jenna's help, Ashley wouldn't have a business or life here in Magnolia Harbor. Jenna was a newcomer too, but clearly she'd made a place for herself here.

Someone refilled her cup, and she drank again, watching the dancers for a long time before deciding that staying here was more depressing than going home. She headed up the stairs to the wraparound porch and followed it to the front of the house. She didn't get far, though, before Jenna came up behind her.

"Ashley," she said, "I've been looking all over for you. Where have you been hiding?" Jenna gave her a big hug, despite the fact that she was carrying around a magnum of champagne.

"I hope you're not planning to drink that," Ashley said.

Jenna laughed. "Of course not. But I'm in a bubbly mood, filling everyone else's glasses." She topped off Ashley's drink. "Isn't it a wonderful day for a party?" Jenna continued, her dark eyes alive with joy.

Ashley cast her gaze beyond the porch rail, where the rain came down in sheets. "I miss this morning's sunshine. I spent some time in my greenhouse today, planting a bunch of annual seeds. Maybe spring will come sometime, and I can plant them in the garden."

"Well, as Buddha says, it might be stormy now, but it can't rain forever. Also, Buddha says, winter always turns into spring." Jenna was prone to random Buddhisms.

"I hope he's right." Ashley raised her glass. "Congratulations on the baby. I am so happy for you and Jude."

"I'm pretty excited about it, although less excited about naming her Daisy. Jude didn't consult me when he made that announcement."

"Maybe it will be a boy."

"Maybe. So, how's your dad settling in?"

"I guess he's doing all right." This was not even close to the truth. Then again, Ashley had learned how to sidestep questions like this. It was a skill widows learned quickly.

"You guess?" Unfortunately, Jenna had the uncanny ability to see through her lies.

Ashley took a gulp of her wine. "Maybe I've lived alone for so long that I'm not used to a man around who thinks he's in charge. He's second-guessed my parenting. He feels the need to explain things to me all the time. And he's redesigned the inn's webpage and reservation portal to make them more complicated. He's pretty good as a short-order cook, and I do appreciate his offers of help. But he's driving me crazy."

"Poor thing. Maybe you should get him sailing lessons so he can join the yacht club. Or encourage him to play golf."

"Yeah, it would be nice if he had some hobbies. But until Mom died, his main hobby was taking care of her and planning their grand world tour. The poor man doesn't know what to do with himself. I'd love to send him off to Europe, but he doesn't want to travel alone, and I can't blame him."

Jenna splashed more champagne into Ashley's glass, replacing the wine she'd gulped. "Are you okay? You weren't about to leave, were you? I mean, the party's just getting started."

"Well..."

Jenna put the now-empty bottle down on the porch floor and draped an arm around Ashley. "I can see you're feeling sad. Come on, cough it up."

Ashley took a deep breath. What was it about Jenna?

She had this uncanny way of worming out secrets. "I don't know. I was watching the dancers, and it made me miss Adam."

"You know, you could have walked onto the dance floor and started dancing. You don't need a partner to dance."

"I know. But I was missing him."

"As you should. But you should dance too. You can't have joy without sorrow, you know."

Ashley ground her teeth. People who had never lost a spouse never quite understood that grief wasn't a monolith. It affected each person in a unique way. And right now it made the prospect of dancing alone more than she could bear.

"Come on. You can dance with me." Jenna grabbed her by the arm and started hauling her back to the patio.

Ashley pulled away. "No. I'm not in the mood, okay?" And dammitall, her eyes started to fill with tears. A familiar loneliness began to burn a hole in the middle of her chest.

Just then, Rev. St. Pierre came through the front door, almost knocking Ashley down. He grabbed her by the shoulders and steadied her, his big hands warming her shoulders, his dark eyes full of kindness and concern.

"What's the matter?" he asked. He'd seen the tears, dammit.

"It's nothing."

He dropped his hands. "It's not nothing. What?"

"She was feeling sad," Jenna said. "You know, about the dancing."

Micah blinked. "Do you want to dance?" he asked.

Her heart skipped around in her chest. "Not really."

His eyebrow rose. "Be honest."

She bit her lip. "I do want to dance. But my dance partner is missing."

Micah nodded. "You don't need a partner, you know."

"So I've heard," she said on a huff. "But really, I'm not sure I remember how. And I might look stupid."

"Ah. A shy dancer. If you want, you can dance next to me."

"You dance?" The idea of Micah St. Pierre dancing to Jamal Robinson's band seemed odd and surprising.

He shrugged. "I shuffle my feet. I'm not exactly a twinkle toes."

Something about the way he said the word "twinkle" made her smile through the tears.

"Dance beside me, Ashley," he said. "It might help you remember Adam and smile instead of cry."

And for some stupid reason, she nodded her head.

* * *

Micah swallowed hard. What had he done?

He was supposed to be taking Isabelle Gerst's blanket back to her. But instead he'd let Ashley's tears trap him.

Then again, Isabelle had been surviving without her blanket for a day, and Ashley needed a dance right now. He wasn't offering this dance for himself. This was all about her grief.

He led the way back to the patio, where Jamal's band was covering 50 Cent's "In da Club." This would be easy. He didn't have to do much more than stomp his feet to the beat. Dancing had never been his thing.

He opted not to elbow his way into the crowd. He gave

her a somewhat frantic smile. He was about to expose himself as a klutz.

She started to move, more a sway than a stomp, the skirt of her dress swishing around her legs. He'd seen that navy-blue dress before—at church, where it blended into the background. Here it was about as appropriate as his dark jacket, slacks, and black collarless shirt.

At least she hadn't worn her grandmother's pearls, which often made an appearance on Sundays. Instead, a pair of sexy, oversized hoops decorated her ears and brought attention to her utterly naked neck.

He found himself focused on her collarbones. She might be standing three feet away, and they might be moving to entirely different beats, but his mind had chugged its way onto an extremely dangerous track.

The song ended almost as soon as they had started dancing. He breathed a sigh of relief, but then Jamal stepped to the mic and invited his momma up to sing. Annie Robinson was one hell of a great cook. No one could make a chop like she could. But she was also the main soloist at Bethel Church and usually sang at least one solo with the Christmas Chorale during the annual holiday fundraising gala for the free clinic.

"Oh, I'd like to stay and hear this," Ashley said.

Micah didn't object. He loved to hear Annie sing, and since she was his cousin, he couldn't leave the dance floor now.

Jamal struck up a rhythm line on his bass that was as old as time, with a syncopated African drumbeat blending in. Darius Williams hit a chord on his guitar, and Annie started to sing "Turtle Dove Done Drooped His Wings," a spiritual as old as the folk who'd settled the sea islands in the middle 1800s. Jamal had rocked out this version a good deal more than the lullaby Aunt Daisy had sung to all of the young'uns at one time or another.

The party guests crowded the patio and started to clap and raise their arms and sway to the beat. Micah let the music carry him away.

Songs like this were the soundtrack of his early years on the island.

So he started clapping and then raised his arms as the swell of people pressed him closer to Ashley, until they were practically on top of each other. She stood in front of and slightly to the left of him, surrounded by partygoers, her high ponytail brushing against the skin of his chin and neck.

And then, as the swaying and clapping swelled, disaster struck. Somehow, Micah managed to snag onc of her large hoop earrings on his pinkie finger as he clapped. Her head yanked sideways, and the earring's clasp let go.

The motion of his hand half spun her around to face him, grabbing her earlobe. "Ow, ow, ow."

"I'm sorry. Are you okay?"

"Ow," Ashley repeated, grabbing her ear.

"Let me see." He gently moved her hand away, the brief touch electric. He took the earring from her ear. "You're not bleeding, at least. I'm sorry," he said again.

"It's okay. You didn't do it on purpose."

Annie finished the song and left the makeshift stage, but by now a much bigger crowd surrounded Ashley and Micah. The band struck up another upbeat song, and Ashley stumbled. He grabbed her shoulders to steady her, another jolt rocking his body. "Whoa, there."

"I'm okay." She removed her second earring. "Not a good choice of jewelry in such tight quarters, I guess."

He tried to give the earring in his hand to her. The metal seemed suddenly hot enough to brand his palm.

"No, um, you hang on to it. And this one too. I don't have any pockets, and my purse is in the house." She handed him the second one, and he jammed both earrings into the same pocket as his collar and studs.

"Let's dance," she said, with a grin that turned up the corners of her eyes. She seemed utterly unaware that her proximity was beating down his self-restraint.

He needed to escape. But there was no way out.

So he danced, which entailed shuffling his feet while she gyrated in a completely sensuous way that made him hot under his not-so-tight collar. He enjoyed every moment, especially when the crowd thinned a bit and he caught glimpses of her dress drifting around her legs.

Ashley loved to dance.

This new information warmed him until the trap sprang closed. Jamal's band shifted gears and played a slow John Legend song.

Now would have been the time to exit the patio and get on with returning Isabelle Gerst's blankie. But Ashley grabbed him by the hand and swung him into the dance, evidently not caring if he led or not. Instead she stepped around him as he moved his feet. She seemed to have gotten lost in some other time or place when she'd danced with Adam.

Meanwhile, people were watching. And putting two and two together. He couldn't let this go on much longer.

When the song ended, he let go of her hand and made a show of inspecting his watch. "Uh, it's getting late, and I have things I need to do," he said.

"Oh?"

"Yeah, Isabelle Gerst left her blankie at the preschool, and I should have returned it before I came to the party, but I forgot. I have to get it back to her, so I need to run."

And then he did.

Chapter Six

Dad liked to sit in the front pew at church because it allowed him to hear better. In Ashley's view, it was high time the man got some hearing aids. But lord help the woman who suggested that he was going deaf.

Luckily Ashley was responsible for organizing fellowship hour this week, which gave her the perfect excuse to leave Dad up there in front while she sat way in the back and ducked out early.

Most Sundays, Ashley didn't mind sitting in the front pew with Dad, but after yesterday's dance with The Rev, hiding in the back seemed appropriate.

What was wrong with her? Once Micah and Jenna had cajoled her onto the dance floor, she'd lost herself. And yes, she'd had fun. She hadn't missed Adam. But every time she recalled the moment right after her earring had become ensnared in Micah St. Pierre's fingers, electricity flitted through her middle. She had become obsessed with the memory of his fingers brushing against her ear. His touch had thrilled and appalled her. Even now, thinking about it raised gooseflesh on her arms.

So hiding and then escaping to the fellowship hall and making coffee seemed like a perfect antidote for her inappropriate reaction. And yet, her memory of Saturday still tripped her up. She found herself scooping coffee and losing track of the count. Heaven help her if the coffee was too strong or too weak. Someone—Patsy Bauman—would say something.

This was ridiculous. She couldn't have a crush on her parish priest. It was... adolescent or something.

"So, what did he say?" Patsy asked from behind, once again disrupting her scoop counting. She gave up trying to estimate the coffee. She closed the lid and started the cycle before facing the chair of the altar guild.

"What did who say?" she asked, pretending innocence.

"Oh for goodness' sake. I was at Daisy's birthday party and I saw you dancing with Reverend St. Pierre. You must have talked to him about our plans."

Ashley crossed her arms over her chest. "Patsy, we need to stay out of his life."

"Why?"

She huffed a breath. "For starters, he can't date anyone from the congregation."

"Why not?"

"Because it would be wrong. You know. He's our rector and..." She let her voice trail off and gave a small hand gesture.

Patsy frowned, clearly not understanding. The woman was eighty years old and from a different generation.

"He's got to worry about sexual harassment issues."

"What?"

"He told me quite clearly that a priest cannot date a

woman with whom he has a pastoral relationship. It's not allowed. It could cost him his career."

"Well, that's—" Patsy bit off the rest of her words as congregants began to file into the fellowship hall. She leaned a little closer and whispered, "After everyone's gone, we need to talk about this."

"There's nothing to talk about."

Patsy crossed her arms and tapped her upper lip with one of her French-manicured fingernails. "Well, I guess that explains why he was dating Brooklyn."

"I guess," Ashley said, her tone a bit sharp.

"You know," Patsy said, continuing to tap her upper lip, "I saw him at the party with Kerri Eaton. They were eating dinner together in the kitchen, and they seemed... Hmmm."

Oh boy, Ashley could see the wheels spinning in Patsy's brain. A hot thread of irritation crawled up her neck. "You need to stop," she said, putting her hands on her hips.

The older woman blinked at Ashley's tone. "Boy, you're snippy this morning."

"I'm sorry. But I think we should let the minister have his privacy, okay? Count me out of your matchmaking plans."

Ashley turned away and marched into the kitchen, where she spent the next five minutes telling herself she was hiding from Patsy and her misguided matchmaking attempts. She almost believed it. But the truth was a harder pill to swallow.

She was hiding from the priest and her own schoolgirl reaction to what had happened yesterday.

This was bad. She needed to stop or she'd lose the careful equilibrium she'd worked so hard to find after Adam died. She was too old for romance. And certainly too mature to be in here hiding from a man who wasn't allowed to be interested in her that way, and who wasn't in any case. Interested in her.

He was recovering from Brooklyn, right?

Exactly.

So these emotions were lunacy. She would give them up for Lent, which started on Wednesday.

She emerged from the kitchen, newly determined to push this madness aside. And then she caught sight of Micah, hunkered down so he could speak with Isabelle Gerst, age three, and lightning crackled through her, bringing heat she hadn't felt in years.

* * *

Ashley overslept on Monday morning, waking to the aroma of frying bacon wafting up from the kitchen two floors below. She hauled herself out of bed and took a quick shower.

Not that she had to hurry. If she didn't make it down in time for breakfast service this morning, Dad would handle it, including the biscuit making. He might pretend not to know how to make them, but Grandmother had taught him all her secrets.

Ashley still remembered the German chocolate cake he'd baked for her tenth birthday, when they'd been living in Holland. Ashley suspected Dad knew all the secret ingredients in Grandmother's hummingbird cake recipe too. He just hated to admit that he had a knack for baking because it wasn't exactly macho. And also, he rejected any notion that he took after his mother. In fact, they were much the same. Both of them were stubborn, organized, and annoyingly competent.

Since it was Presidents' Day, she tiptoed past Jackie's bedroom door, which was closed. This indicated that Dad hadn't awakened him at oh-dark-thirty for push-ups or KP duty or some other penance. Thank goodness. He was just a little boy, and it was a holiday.

She found her way downstairs. "Morning," she muttered.

"Top of the morning to you too, sweetie," Dad said brightly.

Oh yeah, she recognized that gratingly jovial tone. She'd employed it on numerous occasions. He was burying his grief by working and organizing and taking control and pretending everything was just hunky and dory. Yeah. She knew this phase.

She refrained from calling him on his fake joviality and got to work, rolling out biscuits, folding in the layers of butter that would make them light and flaky.

Rolling out biscuits was Zen. But this morning her thoughts drifted to Micah St. Pierre and her earring malfunction. The Zen disappeared in a full-body flush.

Thankfully, Dad didn't notice, because at that moment a middle-aged woman sailed into the kitchen like a battleship with all its flags flying. She was presumably a guest, although Ashley had not met her. That was unusual, but several people had checked in last evening when she'd made a quick run to the fabric store. And, of course, Dad had been handling reservations so Ashley had no idea who had reserved rooms this week.

"There you are, Andre," the woman said with an Eastern European lilt to her words.

Andre? Dad's name was Andrew, not Andre. Her father turned away from the griddle with one of his brilliant smiles. For a seventy-three-year-old, Dad had beautiful teeth. “Morning, Nadia. Did you sleep well?”

Nadia? They seemed awfully chummy.

“I did not. House energy is—oh.” She turned, cocking her head as she stared at the Bunn coffee machine behaving semi-normally in the corner. “Is causing trouble, yes?” she asked.

“Uh, well, it can be cantankerous,” Dad said, “if you don’t talk to it before you use it. It isn’t really a morning person and needs to wake up slowly.” He winked.

Winked!

Who the hell was this platinum blonde with the Betty Ford bouffant? Amber teardrop earrings dripped from her lobes, and the heavy silver chain around her neck held a four-inch-wide crystal of some sort that rested on the shelf of her bosom. Half a dozen silver bangle bracelets and a caftan-like blouse in shades of turquoise and purple completed the ensemble. “Ah, talking is good,” she said, nodding sagaciously.

“I’m sorry, Ms.—?” Ashley interrupted.

“Oh, am sorry. Nadia Kovic.”

Ashley forced a smile. “I’m Ashley, the innkeeper. And, Ms. Kovic, we prefer guests to avoid the kitchen at breakfast. We get very busy in here. The rest of the day you’re welcome. If you like, I can bring you a cup of coffee in the dining room. Breakfast starts in ten minutes.”

“Please, no coffee. Machine not right.” Nadia squinted at the coffeemaker.

Ashley stomped on the urge to defend her coffee machine, which was ancient, sometimes refused to turn on, and frequently misbehaved. But she cleaned it regularly.

"How 'bout some tea?" Dad asked, smooth as silk.

"That will be delightful. But no hurry." Nadia withdrew, leaving the door to the dining room swinging.

Ashley slapped the dough for the second batch of biscuits on the marble counter. "So, Nadia?" She forced herself to roll the dough gently. "What's the deal, Dad? Is she here doing some kind of review or something?"

He shook his head. "No, why?" Something in his tone seemed off.

"I don't know. She seems... different."

"Different? What do you mean by that exactly?"

"Dad, that crack about the coffee. Honestly. I'm hoping she isn't the kind of person who will turn us in to the health department or complain on Yelp about the cleanliness of our kitchen and coffee machine. It's more than merely unsettling to have people staying here that I haven't met." She bit her tongue before she said anything else.

Dad chortled in response. *Chortled.*

"What? It's not funny."

"She isn't worried about our cleanliness, Ash."

"Oh? Then what? You seem awfully chummy with her."

"Well, we chatted for a bit before..."

He was evading her question. "Before what? And what did you chat about exactly?" Ashley started cutting biscuits.

"Captain Teal."

Ashley's hand paused above the dough, the well-used biscuit cutter gleaming in the bright kitchen lights as a confused mélange of emotions roiled in her gut.

Captain Teal, the infamous pirate of the golden age, and his lover Rose Howland were Ashley's ancestors. Captain Teal had died in a shipwreck while rushing to return to his lover, creating a sad, romantic tragedy that had become something of a local myth. To this day, folks on the island swore that Captain Teal still haunted Howland House's grounds looking for his lost Rose. In fact, Jackie insisted that he'd seen and conversed with the ghost on many occasions.

Ashley did not believe in ghosts. She had sent Jackie off to several psychologists who had assured her that her son would eventually grow out of his fascination with the story.

She was still waiting. The very last thing she wanted was a guest who was caught up in the same mythology, which, as it turned out, had nothing to do with the real history of Captain Teal and Rose Howland.

"Dad," she said carefully. "Are you saying she's a historian?" Ashley put the biscuit cutter down on the counter and stared at her father.

"Uh, no."

"Oh my god. Please tell me she isn't a ghost hunter?"

"I think the proper description of her profession is paranormal investigator."

"Why on earth did you let her make a reservation? I thought we both agreed that—"

"Captain Teal is a real ghost," Jackie said from the doorway to the hall. Evidently he hadn't been in his room. He looked as if he'd just come in from the cold. What the hell? Had he gone up to that tree house of his last night?

She turned toward her son, who was wearing his stubborn frown along with his slightly too-short jeans, an Atlanta Braves sweatshirt, and the knit hat that Mom had made last Christmas.

"I didn't know she was a paranormal investigator until

she checked in," Dad said. "I couldn't send her packing. That would have been rude." He put his hands on his hips and stared at Jackie.

What? Had Jackie hired a ghost hunter? And if so, just exactly how had the eleven-year-old paid for it? She was about to demand answers when Micah St. Pierre's unmistakable voice came from the front foyer. "Hello! Ashley, are you there?"

What the hell? Did the man think he now needed an engraved invitation to eat breakfast at the inn? Usually, The Rev strolled into the dining room or kitchen and made himself at home.

On the other hand, she didn't exactly want him to make himself at home. If he started doing that, she'd lose her mind. Or something else. Clearly some ground rules were in order. It disquieted her to think that The Rev realized this too. Otherwise he wouldn't have called from the foyer.

"Don't let the biscuits burn," she commanded as she picked up a dish towel, wiping the flour and butter from her hands. "I'll go see what the preacher wants. And afterward, young man, we're going to have a talk." She threw the towel on the counter and stalked across the kitchen and down the front hall.

The Rev stood by the front door, hands jammed into the pockets of his dark overcoat. A wave of cold rippled across her skin. She tried to tell herself that it came from outside, where the winter sky wore heavy gray clouds promising more rain. But she knew better.

Micah had clearly realized something had changed.

"Good morning," he said in an oddly formal tone. "I came to bring you these." He extended his hand. Her oversized hoop earrings rested in his palm.

"I meant to return them yesterday," he continued, "but you escaped the fellowship hall early."

She met his deep-brown gaze. The word "escape" had been well chosen. And maybe it was exactly the same thing he'd done on Saturday when they'd both danced a little too close to the flame.

She picked up the earrings, careful not to touch him, and yet his hand had heated the metal. She curled her fingers around them and let the warmth seep through her, like the April sun waking up the garden. She yearned to divest him of his coat, invite him into her dining room, and feed him. It had been such a long time since he'd come to breakfast on a regular basis. She missed him.

But things couldn't return to the way they'd been. She'd grown too aware of him.

He gestured, pointing awkwardly over his shoulder with his thumb. "I need to go. I—"

"Hey, Rev," Jackie said in a booming voice as he came charging down the center hall. "I need your help with the ghost hunter."

"What?" Micah said.

The boy took the preacher by the hand. "Come on, she needs to know all the details about the captain's life. And there's no one as good at telling that story as you." Jackie yanked the priest toward the dining room.

Micah resisted. "You let a ghost hunter into your house?" he asked.

Her face heated. "I didn't hire her. I think she's a guest. Although..." She eyed Jackie, and he gave her a far-too-innocent look.

"Did you promise to pay that woman?" she asked.

He shook his head. "I just called her to ask a few questions. I got her name on the internet."

Oh good lord. Her son was out of control.

"Come on, Rev. I really need your help." The boy tugged on Micah's hand, and he followed, his expression mirroring her concern.

Well, dammitall to hell and back. The whole world would be judging her parenting before this was over. She stalked back into the kitchen, where Dad was taking the biscuits out of the oven. "Daddy, this is all your fault."

He turned with a who-me expression on his face. "What's my fault?"

"That ghost hunter or whatever she is."

"I had nothing to do with her. She made a reservation like anyone else, but when she checked in, she asked a lot of questions. I couldn't exactly tell her to leave after she'd paid for the room, could I?"

"Of course not. But she wouldn't be here at all if you'd handled Jackie better. He's the one who invited her."

"What?"

"He obviously found a way to surf the web. He found that woman, called her, and now she's here. I don't think he would have done any of that if you'd listened to him."

"Listen to him about a make-believe ghost? You've been doing that for almost six years now, and near as I can tell it hasn't fixed the problem."

"Well, your approach didn't work either. He's out there talking to a ghost hunter right now. Even worse, he's enlisted the preacher to help."

"Well, we'll just have to put a stop to—"

"*We're* not doing anything, Dad. He's my son. Leave this to me."

Chapter Seven

Micah hadn't intended to have breakfast at the inn, but once Jackie took his hand, it was game over. He had a soft spot for Jackie Scott. Besides, the conversation in the foyer about ghost hunters had surprised and concerned him. So he allowed the boy to drag him into the dining room.

He took a seat at the communal table and introduced himself to a woman named Nadia, whose Eastern European accent seemed a skosh phony to him. That increased his concern. He didn't trust anyone who labeled themselves a ghost hunter.

"Reverend St. Pierre knows all about Captain Teal," the boy explained to the older woman before turning toward Micah. "He can tell you everything about the history. He and Mom are part of a museum that's going to tell the truth about that stuff."

Just then, Ashley came out of the kitchen with a tray containing a carafe of coffee and one of her flowery china teapots. She was frowning, and the set of her shoulders told him she was upset. He could understand why.

She placed the pot in front of Nadia along with a small wooden chest filled with a variety of teas. Then she turned toward him, and for an instant their gazes collided and held. Her agitation became a palpable thing, resonating deep within him. She needed his help.

"Coffee?" she asked.

He nodded, despite his best intentions to make this visit brief. She leaned over his left shoulder, bringing her flowery scent as she poured.

"Come on, Rev. Tell the story," Jackie nagged.

Ashley hovered over Micah's shoulder, close enough for him to hear the hitch in her breathing right before she asked, "Did you want biscuits again?" She might have been whispering in his ear.

He shook his head. "No. I better stick to oatmeal. I'm trying to lose some weight."

"Are biscuits good?" Nadia asked.

"Very good," Micah replied. Something about that accent activated his BS detector. At the same time Ashley's presence at his back unsettled him in entirely different ways. He willed Ashley to move away. But when she did, it left his skin cool and clammy, and his pulse elevated.

"I will have biscuit," Nadia said.

Ashley gave him an eye roll before she scurried back into the kitchen. Her departure left the dining room cool and cloudy as the day outside. Clearly, Ashley wanted this woman out of her house, but Nadia was a paying guest.

"So. About ghost?" Nadia asked, pulling Micah's gaze away from the swinging door into the kitchen.

"Tell her, Rev," Jackie said again. The boy's urgency also worried him. Jackie hadn't talked much about his ghost recently. Micah had assumed he was merely growing up. But maybe not. Even more worrisome was the fact that this investigator had shown up directly after Jackie's fight at school. Something wasn't quite right at Howland House. Ashley seemed overly tense. Jackie was getting into trouble. And the main change had been the arrival of Andrew Howland, Ashley's father.

"History is important part of investigation," Nadia said, pulling Micah from his concerns. "Spirits come to places with much energy. This ghost was pirate, yes?"

"He was a famous pirate," Jackie said. "Tell her!"

Micah almost jumped at the boy's tone. Jackie was as agitated as his mother. He seemed to be having trouble sitting still.

"All right," he said, turning toward the woman. "I'll tell the true story of William Teal, Rose Howland, and Henri St. Pierre. If you come back to Magnolia Harbor in mid-March, you'll be able to visit a museum of the island's history, where this will be prominently displayed, with artifacts and interpretive exhibits. The true story is a great deal different from the myth."

"How interesting," Nadia said as she selected a foil packet of oolong tea from the chest. The musty scent of the tea filled the space between them.

"The larceny of Captain Teal has been well documented," Micah began. "He was a famous pirate. One of the most famous."

"Famous pirate is problem," Nadia said.

"A problem why?" Jackie asked.

"People always want famous ghosts."

"What does that mean?" Jackie asked, his voice rising.

Nadia turned toward him with a tiny smile. "You speak with ghost of famous pirate."

The boy nodded.

The ghost hunter shook her head. "Is uncommon. Ghosts do not speak usually. And famous means ghost is probably fraud. You know, for marketing. Haunted inns are popular."

Jackie gave Nadia a furious frown. At the same time, Micah relaxed a little. Maybe Nadia with her crystal jewelry and phony accent was not here to take advantage. Maybe she was here to expose a fraud. In which case, everyone could relax. There was no fraud. Just a boy with an imaginary ghost.

"I don't think Ashley is interested in marketing a ghost," Micah said quietly.

"No?" Nadia slurped her tea.

"Would you like to hear the rest of the story?" he asked.

Nadia nodded.

"Captain Teal was returning to this island in order to make Rose his bride when he ran right into the hurricane of 1713 and lost his life. All of his crew died in the shipwreck except his first mate, Henri St. Pierre."

Nadia looked up from her tea. "Same name as yours?"

Micah nodded. "He was my ancestor."

"Ah. Interesting. Spirits can come to a place where many lives were lost."

"Maybe. But the inlet is miles away. People loved to tell the story of Rose grieving the loss of her captain, but the truth is she rescued Henri, nursed him back to life, then fell in love with him. Together they planted the daffodils that have given this island its name. And documents show they did it not to honor Captain Teal, but simply because they loved daffodils.

"Unfortunately, their love story also ended in tragedy when Rose's father forced her to return to his plantation up the river. Henri and their child were both enslaved." Micah's voice hardened just a little bit. Rose and Henri's ending was more tragic than any shipwreck, and yet that story had been repressed and almost lost to history.

Just then, Ashley came through the door bringing a bowl of oatmeal and a helping of biscuits and gravy. Once again, she hesitated a moment too long as she placed the bowl in front of him. He closed his eyes and breathed her in. And for a moment, he connected through the span of time with his own ancestor.

"She's on your side," Jackie said, jolting Micah's eyes open.

"What?" Ashley sounded bewildered.

"She doesn't believe in famous ghosts," Jackie said, while Micah added brown sugar to his oatmeal and wondered how on earth he'd ended up having breakfast here when he'd promised himself not to.

"Really?" Ashley sat down beside Micah. None of the other guests had arrived, otherwise she would never have done that. Now her unique scent threatened to make him dizzy.

"Am always skeptic," Nadia said. "People lie."

"I'm not lying," Jackie said.

"No one said you were," Micah said gently. He stared down at his oatmeal, his appetite suddenly gone. He should leave. Now.

"I have questions," Nadia said. "Do you think—"

"Just wait one second," Ashley said. "I know you're a paying guest, but no one hired you to go hunting for ghosts. Is that clear?"

"Might not be a ghost," Nadia said. "When there is

trouble, energy is left behind, and you just said that this man, Henri, was a slave, no?"

"Yes," Micah said.

Jackie scowled. "Henri St. Pierre isn't haunting the tree. It's Captain Teal. And he's not jealous. Well, I don't think so. I mean, he never said anything about being jealous."

"Like I said before. Ghosts do not speak with living people," Nadia said.

Jackie gave the ghost hunter a classic preteen look that said, *I think you're an idiot.*

Micah decided it was best for him to depart, even though he sensed that Ashley and Jackie needed someone in this moment. It wasn't his place. He had not been asked to help. So he made a show of examining his watch. "I need to go. It's Monday, and that's always a busy day for me."

"You aren't going to eat your oatmeal?" Ashley said.

"Uh, well, I'm not hungry." In truth, he was starved. But he needed to go.

He pushed back from the table and headed toward the door. He got as far as the front foyer before Jackie caught up with him, giving his suit jacket a swift tug.

"Don't go, Rev. I need your help. No one believes me. Not even the ghost hunter."

The pain in the boy's voice arrowed straight into Micah's chest. He turned and met the boy's bright-blue eyes. Just a year ago, he had to hunker down to get eye-to-eye with Jackie. But the kid had recently sprouted up. If he kept growing, he was going to make a pretty good basketball player. Assuming he could get his nose out of the books he loved to read.

"What can I do?" he asked gently.

"You believe in the ghost, don't you?"

Oh boy, this was going to be hard.

"I believe that our memories of those who have passed do come back to haunt us. But that's not like the ghosts you see on TV, Jackie."

"You sound like that BS ghost hunter. I'm sorry I called her." Jackie crossed his arms over his chest. "So you don't think I'm telling the truth either. Just like Granddad didn't believe me when I told him Jayden Walsh started the fight."

Ah. So. Micah put his hand on Jackie's shoulder. "I believe you're telling the truth about that."

"I would never destroy a library book."

No, Jackie Scott would never do a thing like that. Micah nodded. "I know. I believe you."

"I'm telling the truth. About everything."

Micah let go of a long breath. Behind him in the dining room, Ashley's voice carried. She was telling Nadia, in her nice way, that no one here wanted any ghosts investigated.

"Jackie, I believe that you're telling the truth as you know it. But sometimes the truth is a slippery thing. Sometimes one person believes one thing and the next person believes something else. And in the absence of facts, the truth can be hard to prove."

The kid frowned. "I've spoken with Captain Teal. He's real. It's the same as God. You talk to Him all the time, but you can't prove He's real."

Jackie was smart as a whip. He'd certainly drawn an apt analogy. "No. But I *believe* He's real. And I accept that you *believe* the captain is real. But not everyone shares that belief. Especially not your mother or grandfather."

"But I thought preachers believed in ghosts. I thought preachers could, you know, pray or something and send them into the light or whatever."

Oh great. Micah did not want to discuss the church's views on exorcism with an eleven-year-old boy.

"I'm sorry, Jackie. I believe that when someone passes away, their spirit leaves their body and goes to God. Spirits of the once living don't hang around."

He refrained from going into the church's thinking about paranormal activity, which was generally regarded as the work of something evil. He didn't think Jackie was possessed. The child simply had a vivid imagination.

"So you won't help me. You're just like all the rest of the grown-ups." Jackie's voice had developed a sharp, angry edge. Stiff-shouldered and almost hugging himself, Jackie was the picture of someone fighting alone.

Micah wanted to help him, but there were so many rules regarding exorcisms. And besides, an exorcism was not necessary. What Jackie needed was a big hug and a little understanding. Micah could listen and try to understand, but the hug was not allowed either.

"I'm really sorry, Jackie. But I don't think I'm qualified to help Captain Teal into the light," he said.

"Well, neither is Nadia." Jackie almost spat the words before he turned on his heel and raced up the stairs.

* * *

Micah hated Mondays. And this particular Monday had started out badly. Jackie's dilemma was breaking his heart. And Ashley was...

Well, forbidden.

Better to think about all the work that faced him today.

Mondays were filled with all the tasks he liked least about being a parish rector: administrative work, answering emails, and firming up his schedule for the week. Mondays frequently meant church governance meetings as well. The second Monday was reserved for dinner with the church's senior warden, Len Huxley, where they talked about ministries and missions as well as the many problems with the aging church building. Tonight, the third Monday of the month, the vestry, the church's board of directors, met to make decisions.

Vestry meetings were always interminable. Micah never ceased to be amazed by the way good Christian people could argue about everything. There was something to be said for the navy's command structure. Less democratic, of course, but so much more efficient.

Mondays also brought distractions. Unscheduled visitors would drop by in greater numbers on Mondays than any other day of the week. A lot of these visitors were moved by his sermon to come chat; others came to talk about problems or needs. He welcomed these distractions. Helping people, listening to their needs, was always the best part of his day. And he never resented those visitors.

But a great many people also came by to gossip about what was said at fellowship hour. He often worried that the parish needed more fellowship and less gossip.

When he arrived at the church, the preschool was in full swing. It occupied the Sunday school rooms, which were tucked behind the sanctuary in a small building. His office, not much more than a tiny cubbyhole, sat at the end of the hallway. The sound of loud and happy children usually made him smile, but Jackie Scott's problem still weighed heavy on his mind as he headed toward his office.

His first Monday visitor was already waiting for him.

"Colton?" he said in a surprised tone when he found his brother sitting with slumped shoulders in the side chair.

"Hey," Colton said, glancing up for a moment before returning his gaze to his slightly muddy work boots.

"What's the matter?" Micah closed the door behind him before he came to sit in the facing chair. Something bad must have happened because Colton never set foot inside a church if he could possibly help it. "Is it Aunt Daisy?"

Colton shook his head.

"Dad?"

"Isn't it always Dad?" Colton said on a long breath. "I'm pissed that he didn't bother to show up at Daisy's party. I went by the house to give him a piece of my mind, but he's not there, and none of the neighbors have any idea where he's gone off to. Jude's worried that he's back on the bottle."

Micah rolled his neck, where the tension of this early morning had come to rest, creating an incipient headache. Dad would do whatever he wanted to do. That had always been his MO. He'd been sober for a while, but that meant nothing.

Dad often went on benders. The only good thing anyone could say about him was that he'd stuck around after Mom had left. Micah and his brothers had been raised by Aunt Daisy and her momma, Old Granny, his great-grandmother.

But all this was water under the bridge. The family had been dealing with Dad's disappearances for years. Never once had it brought Colton to his church office before.

So the whole Dad-is-missing thing was a ruse. Something else was up. "Dad's not why you're here, is it?"

"How did you figure that out?"

He shrugged. "Comes with the occupation."

Colton nodded but said nothing.

"Then what's on your mind?" Dragging stuff out of Colton often took a lot of patience and energy. He wasn't good at talking about his emotions.

Colton didn't say anything for the longest time, and Micah let the pressure of the silence build until his brother finally said, "At Daisy's party..."

But his voice trailed off, leaving Micah to worry that someone had noticed that he'd danced a little too close to the flame named Ashley Scott.

"What about the party?" Micah finally asked into Colton's silence.

Colton raised his head and stared. "Well, it's just that I noticed you talking to Kerri Eaton."

Whoa. Wait. What? "We talked."

"So, uh, well..."

"What, Colton? Just spit it out, please."

"I wanted to know if your church ladies have her on their list."

"What?"

"I'm sorry. I didn't want to...I don't know...freak you out or anything. But it's all over town that Patsy Bauman and her crew are helping you find a woman. I won't comment on that. I want to know if Kerri is on their list?"

Micah laughed. Hard. And not because he was amused.

"You think this is funny?" Colton asked.

"Yes. And no. My altar guild is a trial. But, um, I'm curious. Are you here because you think it's unmanly for me to allow my altar guild to behave this way or because you don't like the idea of me dating Kerri Eaton?" He leaned forward a little when he got to the woman's name.

"Well..."

"So this is about Kerri?" It was a wild leap of faith, but Micah took it.

His brother brought the heels of his palms up to his eyes. "I guess. Maybe."

"You don't know?"

Colton didn't answer the question. Instead of pushing him, Micah decided to let him twist in the wind for a moment.

A long time passed—a minute maybe—before Colton vocalized a long sigh. "Well..." Another pause, and then he started again. "The thing is...I wish you wouldn't."

"You wish I wouldn't what? Date her?"

"Yes."

"Do you mind my asking why? Because it had occurred to me that she might be a nice person to date."

"You can't."

"Why?" He leaned forward.

Colton's gaze shifted around the room. "Because you can't. And I can't talk about it."

Oh. Now Micah got it. Colton had a history of playing the field. At least he hadn't blurted out information best kept private. It meant he'd learned an important lesson these last few years. As a teen, Colton had told all sorts of untrue stories about a girl—a turn of events that landed him on the wrong side of the law and right into juvenile detention on an overblown drug charge.

That unfortunate episode had happened after Micah had left home to attend college. Colton's brush with the law might never have happened if Micah had been there to keep his brother in line. But he'd chosen to accept the scholarship to Clemson. Taking the scholarship might not have been selfish because Micah had worked hard for it. But choosing not to come home for years had been selfish. He'd run away from his dysfunctional family. And now he deeply regretted that choice.

He'd dedicated himself to making amends. To Colton and Jude especially. They had relied on him, and he had let them down.

"So," Micah said, drawing out the word, "is this a situation where you'd feel embarrassed if I dated her? Or is there something else?"

Colton's flighty gaze finally settled. "What do you mean?"

"Oh for goodness' sake, do you have feelings for Kerri?"

"Uh, well..." Colton shifted in his seat like a teenager who couldn't quite sit still. "The truth is she dumped me."

"She dumped you?" Micah leaned back, utterly surprised.

"I didn't tell you that to make you want to, you know, date her or anything."

Micah swallowed back a laugh. Instead he asked, "Why, exactly, did she dump you?"

"I don't know." His words were almost a whine. "She had some stupid idea that I was using her to make someone else jealous. And she wouldn't listen to me when I tried to explain."

"I see. Did you try to apologize?"

"Uh, for what? She was wrong."

"Did you examine your actions leading up to this

dumping to see if perhaps you'd given her reason to think this way?"

"Um..."

"Colton, you can't expect to be forgiven if you refuse to talk about what happened. And if you refuse to accept that you may have given her a reason to doubt you. And an apology is more than words spoken. There needs to be a sincere effort at atonement or restitution or, at the very least, a commitment to try to be a better person."

Colton braced his elbows on his knees again and studied his boots some more. "Okay. I get that. But honestly, I got the feeling that she didn't give me a chance. Like she was expecting me to screw up, you know? And then *bam*..." His sentence ended in a sigh.

"Maybe you have a reputation."

"Yeah." He paused a moment. "I wish I didn't."

"You can repair your reputation."

"Really?"

Micah nodded. "It's possible. But it requires thinking about other people."

"Okay. I didn't come here for a sermon. I just came to tell you not to date Kerri Eaton."

"I get it. I understand," he said. "But if you want to figure out how to win Kerri back, you have to start thinking about her and not yourself."

"Thanks," Colton said, twisting the word. He stood up. "Just stay away from her, okay?"

Chapter Eight

Kerri liked the cold, and Monday morning dawned brisk enough to make her breath fog as she hurried down Harbor Drive to Daffy Down Dilly, the boutique she owned.

It might be cool for mid-February in the Carolinas, but it was also Presidents' Day—the unofficial demarcation point for the turning of the seasons. The winter doldrums were behind her. Business would be picking up from now until Christmas.

She was in a happy frame of mind. Her new spring merchandise had just arrived, and she planned to spend a portion of the day creating a sunshiny new display for the front windows.

Kerri opened the shop, started a pot of coffee, and was just about to open one of the boxes of new sundresses when the little bell above the shop's door jingled. A customer. And early in the morning.

She left the back room, but when she entered the sales

floor, she discovered that skateboard kid. He'd been in the store a couple of times, and she didn't like the look of him in his baggy cargo pants and oversized black sweatshirt. He had an unkempt crown of sand-colored hair that bushed out from under a mustard-colored knit hat. His face was painfully pale, with a few pimples around his long, narrow nose. Several pale hairs sprouted on his chin, but he couldn't have been more than seventeen, maybe younger.

A kid his age ought to be in school.

She checked herself. Today was a holiday, so maybe he had a reason to be hanging out downtown. But she'd seen him plenty of times during school hours riding his skateboard up and down the boardwalk or creating a nuisance of himself down at the public dock. Ethan Cuthbert, a deputy on the Magnolia Harbor police force, had told her he was trouble.

And he sure looked like trouble, right down to the logo across his narrow chest, which read ANTI HERO. Evidently, a brand of skateboard. Even so, if that boy was her kid, she would never have allowed him to wear something like that around town.

But then a Black kid wearing a hoodie like that might find himself in a whole heap of trouble that a white boy would not. But still.

Today he'd come into the store, carrying his beat-up board under his arm. She winced, imagining him knocking stuff off shelves with that thing. She was about to tell him to get out. But she hesitated.

She knew better than to judge anyone by the way they dressed. Other people did that. She didn't have to. The boy had as much right as anyone to come into her store, as long as he behaved.

By the same token, she intended to stay right there at the point-of-sale counter to keep an eye on him.

And so she saw it—the moment the kid picked the daffodil mug off the sale table and tucked it into one of the pockets in his baggy cargo pants. He didn't head straight for the door. Instead, he coolly continued to pretend-shop, moving in a loose-limbed shuffle.

She weighed her choices in the moments before he moved toward the door. She could hang back and call Ethan Cuthbert later, probably putting the kid in a heap of trouble. Or she could call him out right now and find out whether he was redeemable.

"And where do you think you're going with that mug?" she asked when the kid was a good five paces from the door.

He stopped mid-stride, frozen. Good thing he didn't run. A boy who stopped might be salvageable.

"Son?" she asked, when he didn't move or speak.

"What do you mean?" he said, turning toward her with a who-me expression.

"The mug you took. Off the table back there. It's on sale. Only three dollars. Hardly worth calling the police. But I'm curious. Why do you even want that mug? You don't look like the kind of guy who drinks coffee at all, much less from a mug that has daffodils all over it. I mean, the mug is kind of girlie." She gave him the raised eyebrow she sometimes employed with the unruly teens at church. She was the coordinator for the youth ministry at Bethel AME.

"Ma'am?" the boy drawled as if he didn't quite understand her. But he'd given himself away by using the word "ma'am." Someone had taught him manners.

She cocked her head. "Put the mug on the counter. I'm not going to call the police."

His eyes widened a little right before he dug the mug out of his pocket. His shoulders slumped slightly. "Can I go now?"

"I don't think so. What's your name?"

"Danny Beckett," he muttered.

"And you live here year-round?"

One shoulder shrugged. "I came to live with my grandmother last year."

"Well, I can't let you go. You have to make amends. Stealing is a crime. Even if the mug is only worth three dollars."

He met her gaze, wide-eyed. She couldn't be sure, but he seemed surprised. Like maybe he'd been getting away with stuff for a while. "I'm sorry," he said. He almost sounded sincere.

"So, first of all, tell me why you wanted the mug?"

He looked down at the floor and studied his Converse shoes. Those shoes looked worn out. They had holes in them. He was poor, then. Or neglected. Or both.

"Son?" she asked, prodding him.

He let go of a long breath. "It was for my granny. It's her birthday, and she loves daffodils. She's been sick."

Deep within her chest, Kerri got the warm fuzzies. So he wasn't really a bad boy. Just a troubled one.

"You didn't have three dollars?"

He looked up, his eyes a little shiny. "I can't get a job."

"No?"

He shook his head. "I been trying but no one wants to hire me."

"What kind of work have you been looking for?"

"I'd like to be a carpenter. I like building things, you know, out of wood."

"You have a high school diploma."

Something changed in his demeanor. "I don't need to learn a bunch of English literature to be a carpenter. But I can't get a job anywhere." His tone had turned angry.

"Well, I don't have any carpentry jobs. But I do need someone to sweep out the back room and open a bunch of heavy boxes for me. It's about an hour's work, and I'll pay you twenty dollars and throw in the mug for free. I suggest you use the twenty to buy your granny some flowers to go with the coffee mug. The florist is right down the street."

He blinked, the angry look softening. "I don't want to be a janitor," he said.

"I know. But without a high school diploma, that's all anyone is going to hire you for. You can't be too choosy when you drop out of school. I have a job for you. It's only for an hour. But it pays better than minimum wage. You want it or not?"

He nodded. "Yeah, I guess." Oh, he was surly. But no surlier than some of the boys she'd had to deal with at church. With teens, all that surliness was mostly for show. And she knew how hard it sometimes could be for a grandmother who suddenly found herself raising up a teenager. Kerri had been raised by her grandmother. She had a feeling Danny's granny was at her wit's end with the kid.

"All right then," she said. "Welcome to Daffy Down Dilly. I'll show you the broom and the back room."

* * *

Patsy Bauman called after breakfast service, while Ashley was in her small office trying to figure out what Dad had done to her reservation system. He'd made "improvements" since the last time she'd used it.

"I know you don't want to meddle in the preacher's life," the altar guild chair said, "but I've been thinking about Kerri Eaton all last night and this morning. She'd be perfect for him."

Of course Kerri would be perfect. In fact, logically, Kerri would be the ideal woman for Micah St. Pierre.

She was stylish, beautiful, successful, and smart. Best of all, she was a church woman of the same race. The points in her favor added up to an overwhelming sum. Of course, Ashley hated the idea that Pasty was still in matchmaking mode. But she acknowledged the truth.

"Kerri would be good." It was, in every respect, an underwhelming endorsement of the woman.

"I'm going down to Daffy Down Dilly to talk to her," Patsy announced.

"What? No. Patsy, stay out of it."

"Why? I think we should be up-front."

"And scare her away?" The words came out of her mouth without thought.

But they stopped Patsy for a nanosecond before she said, "Why would she be scared away? This is Micah St. Pierre. In case you haven't noticed, he's handsome, kind, and thoughtful. Ashley, sometimes I think that, when Adam died, you stopped living too. I mean really, every woman in town has Micah on their list of eligible bachelors."

"Yes, but don't you think being a minister's wife might be a challenge?"

"Not for Kerri. From what I hear, she is very involved in the youth ministry at Bethel Church."

"Have you been checking her references?" Ashley asked.

"Of course I have. Although really, I know her. Everyone does. She's lovely. And there are so many things to recommend her."

Yes, there were. And if Patsy waltzed into Daffy Down Dilly on a mission to force the issue, Kerri would probably run for the hills.

Ashley leaned back in the office chair and studied the ceiling. She ought to back away... now. Micah didn't want or need anyone to do any matchmaking for him. On the other hand, what if Kerri was the right woman for him? She couldn't let Patsy screw that up in her ham-handed fashion. Besides, maybe helping Micah find the perfect wife would be the best way to exorcise this sudden adolescent, and totally unacceptable, attraction she'd developed for him.

"Look, I need to go downtown this morning for some errands. Let me talk to her."

"I thought you weren't interested in helping," Patsy said.

Patsy had played her. Somehow. But it was all right, for Micah's sake.

"I heard they were quite chummy at Daisy's party." Her face heated. Had no one noticed how she and Micah had danced? Evidently not. Thank god.

"I'm glad you're finally with the program. And since that's the case, I was wondering if you could, you know, put a good word in the minister's ear."

"A good word?"

"About Kerri."

Ashley should have seen that one coming. But she hadn't. Still, she might as well hang for a sheep as a lamb.

"All right," she said, surrendering to this plan.

But when the call ended, she bowed her head over the neat stacks of paperwork Dad had left on her desk and spent several minutes doing deep yoga breathing. When she felt sufficiently calm, she got up from the desk, but not before purposefully messing up the neatly stacked papers. She hated Dad's military neatness. How interesting to discover that she thrived on a tiny bit of chaos.

She informed Dad that she was going out and asked him to keep an eye on Jackie, who had returned from his tree house and was sulking in his bedroom. She decided to walk down into Magnolia Harbor instead of drive, even though it was unseasonably cold. But it wasn't a long walk. Daffy Down Dilly stood in the heart of Magnolia Harbor's business district.

As she approached the shop, a young man wearing baggy cargo pants and a black hoodie slammed open the boutique's door, threw a skateboard down on the sidewalk, and scooted away. It was kind of odd. Kids like that, wearing ANTI HERO hoodies, weren't Kerri's usual clientele.

Ashley continued into the store. Kerri was in the back, a steamer in hand, unpacking new spring dresses.

"Oh, those are pretty," Ashley said. She couldn't wait for the arrival of warmer weather. She was ready to go shopping and buy something new. Which was odd because she hadn't upgraded her wardrobe in a long, long time.

"Aren't they? They just came in."

"So, I saw that boy with the skateboard. He looked like trouble."

"Oh, not really. I caught him trying to shoplift. A mug, if you can believe it. He wanted it for his grandmother. I found out that his parents died last fall. They were those people who got stuck in the storm out by the inlet. Remember? It was last October or November."

"Oh. Yeah. I do remember. Those poor people who drowned."

Kerri nodded. "Yeah. He's living here now, with his grandmother. And I think he's sad and lost."

"Poor kid." She empathized with him. His whole life had been destroyed by that storm.

"So I gave him a job sweeping up and helping me rack some of these dresses," Kerri said.

The unwanted tension within Ashley eased. Kerri *was* perfect for Micah. Not because she was active in her church or because of the color of her skin. But because of the quality of her character. Because of her kindness. She hated to admit it, but for once Patsy was right. This would be a good match.

"So," Ashley said on a long breath. "I have to be honest. I didn't exactly come to buy a new sundress in the middle of February."

Kerri gave her a knowing smile. "I figured. Something tells me you've been deputized by the Heavenly Rest Altar Guild."

Ashley laughed in spite of herself and this crazy mission. "Well, yes. But for the record I wasn't deputized. I volunteered when Patsy Bauman told me she was planning to talk to you herself."

"So you've come to talk with me about Micah St. Pierre," Kerri said. It wasn't a question.

"I guess we are utterly transparent."

Kerri shook her head as she moved the steamer across the fabric of a particularly pretty dress with embroidered roses along the hemline. "Well, not that transparent. Micah mentioned the altar guild on Saturday. I ran into him at Daisy Jones's birthday party. But I guess you already know that."

"I do. So, are you interested? It's okay if you're not. If I report that back, it would be the end of it."

"But I am interested," Kerri said.

"You are?" For some reason, this flabbergasted her. She'd been semi-certain Kerri would run in the opposite direction when directly queried on the issue.

"Yes, I am. He's really a very nice man."

"That's great," Ashley said, but she had to force her enthusiasm. Kerri was perfect. Why didn't she feel good about this?

"So what's the next move?" Kerri asked.

"I guess I need to convince Reverend St. Pierre to give you a call."

"He'll need my number then." Kerri turned off the steamer and moved to the point-of-sale counter, where she picked up a business card and a pen with a daffodil-flowered top. "Here's my cell phone number. Feel free to pass it along to Micah. Tell him I enjoyed our chat on Saturday."

* * *

At five thirty in the afternoon, Micah's final unscheduled visitor showed up.

Ashley Scott strode into his parish office like a woman on an important mission, and for the second time that day the door to his office was closed.

Her dark hair fell to her shoulders, and she wore the same navy-blue-striped sweater and jeans she'd had on this morning. The only difference was some lip balm that made her lips kind of shiny. And alluring.

He pushed that unwanted thought away.

"What's up?" he asked, trying for a casual tone.

She slipped into one of his side chairs, folding her winter jacket over her knees like a barrier. "Well, to be honest, I'm here as a messenger."

He leaned back, the springs in his office chair squealing. "I'm going to take a wild guess. Patsy sent you."

"And, you're wrong. Sort of. I'm here with a message from Kerri Eaton."

"What?" His gut clenched. Had she gone to Kerri first? Evidently so.

Ashley pulled Kerri's business card out of her pocket. "Kerri's cell phone number is on the back, and she told me to tell you that she enjoyed talking with you at Daisy's party." She slid the card across the small clean space at the front of his desk.

He picked up the card. Printed on the front were Daffy Down Dilly's location and hours of operation. On the flip side, someone had written Kerri's name and phone number in kelly-green ink. "Kerri knows about this?" he asked.

"Of course she does. That's her handwriting. And before you give me a lecture about meddling in people's lives, I want to make it clear that I volunteered to go speak with Kerri in order to keep Patsy from doing it."

"Huh?"

"There was no way to stop Patsy. So I handled this more discreetly. And if you don't want to call her, that's your business."

For a tiny instant, he was tempted to say, *Speak for yourself, Ashley*. But of course that was forbidden. "You didn't have to do that, you know."

She nodded. "I know. But you know what? Kerri

is terrific. She's beautiful and smart. And I think she'd make a great preacher's wife. When I visited her this morning, she was helping this kid who'd lost his parents. He looked like trouble. She even caught him shoplifting. But instead of calling the police, she gave him a job. She took the time to figure out that he was sad. His parents died in that boating accident last November. You remember that one?"

"She gave Danny Beckett a job?" he asked.

"You know the kid?"

He shook his head. "No, but I heard a lot about his problems from Ken Nyberg. Evidently Ken was his coach before he dropped out of school. Ken said he and his grandmother need help. But when I called his grandmother, she got all up in my face about not wanting any meddlesome preachers darkening her door. Ken thinks Danny is a problem waiting to happen if no one intercedes."

"Well, there you go. Kerri took the time to talk to him. And I've been thinking about that all day. About how sad he must feel. He lost both his parents, and then he had to move and his grandmother is sick. Ken's right. He needs help. Grief counseling at least."

Kerri wasn't the only empathetic woman in town. "Well, I'll see what I can do. I have it on my to-do list to give Sally Burns a call. She runs the senior programs at Grace Church. She might have some ideas for getting Danny's grandmother some help."

She nodded. "That's a good idea. But in any case, Kerri's kindness to that kid should tell you all you need to know. She's perfect for you. And the thing is, she told me she would like to go out with you. I mean, if you're interested."

He stared at her for a long time, letting his gaze linger. She was so earnest sitting there trying to match him up with someone else.

Someone he couldn't date either, unless he wanted to tick off his younger brother. He forced himself to look away, dropping his gaze to the card still clutched in his fingers.

He studied Kerri's handwriting for a long moment as a crazy idea formed in his head. He couldn't date Kerri, but he could talk to her about Colton. Maybe he could figure out how to get the two of them together.

"Thank you," he said, lifting his gaze to meet Ashley's. She was frowning again, that perpetual sorrow that hovered over her like a cloud.

Her eyebrows rose. "Thank you? Really? For meddling? I expected a lecture, to be honest."

He made a big show of shrugging. "Maybe I need meddlers," he said, the irony lost on Ashley. He forced a smile.

"Right. I'm not going to tell Patsy that."

He chuckled. "Good. Tell her I'll be giving Kerri a call. What do you think? Should I take her to dinner at Rafferty's, Annie's, or that new Italian place?"

"Not the Italian place. I've heard it's not that great."

"Annie's?"

"It's comfortable and quiet. And your cousin knows how to cook."

He nodded. "You're right. It would be the best place." And if he took her there, everyone in the family would know about it because Annie was a gossip.

Colton would be thoroughly ticked off. And that was the point.

Chapter Nine

Kerri stood outside Annie's Kitchen with Rev. Micah St. Pierre, wondering why she had said yes to this little escapade. Was it curiosity or desperation? Probably a little of both.

At least the date had started off well. Micah met her in the town parking lot, strolled with her down to Annie's place, and even held the door for her as they entered the restaurant. The whole door-holding thing was nice.

But then everything ran off the rails.

Since it was Fat Tuesday, the restaurant was crowded. Evidently a lot of folk wanted one last helping of pork chops and hush puppies before having to give up fried food for Lent.

Even so, an inordinate number of Micah's flock seemed to be dining at Annie's this evening, as if his altar guild had broadcast the time and place of the date. Ashley Scott and the rest of those women were a bunch of busybodies.

It took almost five minutes to cross the room. People had to stop and chat. Several asked questions about the upcoming museum unveiling, and then Marge Lewis stopped Micah to ask about the upcoming interfaith day of service.

"Do you know where and when the kids are supposed to arrive on Saturday?" she asked.

"Uh, well...um...I—"

"Nine thirty at the public pier," Kerri supplied, stepping in to save the floundering priest.

Marge gave Kerri a questioning gaze, as if she didn't quite believe the information because it hadn't come from the minister himself.

"I'm the interfaith service day coordinator for Bethel Church," Kerri said.

"Oh, okay. Great. Nine thirty then." Marge sat down, her face a little red.

Micah ushered Kerri the final few steps to the open booth. "Thanks," he said under his breath. "I should have known the answer to that question."

"Why? Ken Nyberg is handling the event for y'all."

"Yes, but I—"

"Micah, I hope you're not one of those ministers who thinks he has to be everywhere and know everything." She slid into the booth, and Micah did the same.

"I do feel that way sometimes," he said.

"Well, stop. You delegated to Ken, and he's doing a great job."

"That's good to know."

"There's nothing wrong with saying no to people."

Micah cocked his head and studied her with a little frown, as if he thought she was a puzzle that needed solving, instead of a woman he'd asked out for dinner.

Maybe lecturing him about his time management skills had been over the top.

Boy, she was out of practice. When was the last time she'd gone on a real date?

Damn. It had been that sunset cruise with Colton. She snapped the menu up, afraid that somehow this secret might shine through or something.

And then Annie came over and gave the preacher one of those I'm-so-glad-to-see-you-here-on-a-date looks. That didn't settle Kerri's suddenly queasy stomach. Good god, there were a crap-ton of St. Pierres living on this island, and evidently they had also gotten the broadcast announcement about Micah's date.

Never before had it occurred to her that going out with a minister would be like dating in a fishbowl. Everyone would be judging her all the time.

They ordered their dinners, and when Annie left the table she leaned forward and said, "I need to be honest here, I'm a little uncomfortable. Either your congregation has come here for one last fried meal before Lent, or someone tipped them off that we'd be here."

He chuckled. "Well, I didn't tell anyone, except Cousin Charlotte. So she's the one who blabbed. It's kind of nice to know that gossip that starts with the Black folk eventually finds its way to the white folk. It suggests that we are talking to each other more than we think we are."

He was a dewy-eyed idealist, obviously. And a biracial man who had not quite chosen sides. Colton identified as a Black. His brother Jude as well, even though Jude had married a white woman. Then again, Micah was presiding over the new museum project, which was designed to tell the truth about history, including all the painful parts that white folk sometimes wanted to gloss right over. So maybe she was wrong about him. Maybe she had judged him a little because he'd chosen to become an Episcopal priest, instead of an American Methodist Episcopal pastor. Either way, he was a man of God, with a lot of people interested in his personal character and life.

"It's always going to be like this, isn't it?" she said.

He nodded. "Afraid so, which begs the question, why did you say yes to this ridiculous matchmaking scheme?"

"Is it ridiculous?" she asked out loud, even though dating Micah would be utterly ridiculous. Not because he was the rector at the Episcopal church, but because she'd slept with his younger brother. Yeah. Ridiculous on steroids.

"I'm sorry," he said. "That didn't come out right. I'm not saying that you and me together is ridiculous. I'm just saying that my altar guild is often ridiculous."

She should tell him the truth. But she didn't. Instead she said, "I guess your congregation wants you to be happy."

The corners of his mouth twitched. "Thanks for reminding me of that. I should count my blessings."

"Well... that's not exactly what I meant. I mean, you dated Brooklyn for a while. It's not like you needed help to find a date."

"Right." He looked away from her.

"I'm sorry," Kerri said. "I shouldn't have raised your ex. We'll make a rule, no conversation about exes, okay?"

"Do you have an ex?" He fired the question at her.

Oh boy, she'd asked for that. Her exes—and there were quite a few—were not a topic she wished to discuss. Especially not Colton.

Crap. This was impossible. She would have to talk

about Colton. Eventually. It wasn't as if she could keep something like that secret. The wishful-thinking house of cards she'd built in her mind came tumbling down. Micah St. Pierre was a very nice man. She could even see herself dating him. But she could not lie to him.

* * *

Micah prided himself on his ability to read body language. Years of serving as a navy chaplain had honed this particular skill, and Kerri's posture had just closed tighter than a drum. She'd leaned back and crossed her arms, as if she was trying to hide something from him.

Of course he already knew this. But now he desperately wanted to know how she felt about Colton. So he waited patiently to see what she'd do next. Waiting was often a good strategy for getting people to talk about their feelings.

"I'm sorry. I—" she finally said, biting off the end of her sentence as she reached for her purse. "I really should go. I should never have agreed to—"

"Don't go. Our food is coming." He nodded toward Annie, who came bearing pork chops, okra, and coleslaw.

"Y'all eat up, now," Annie said, grinning. She gave Micah a wink before she left the table.

"There are some things you don't know," Kerri said, her distress showing in the lines that appeared on her forehead.

"Relax," he said gently. "If anyone should apologize, it's me. I asked you out under false pretenses."

"What?" The lines on her forehead got deeper.

"I know you and Colton dated for a short while."

Her mouth pinched, and her eyes widened. "Then why...? How? Did he blab his mouth about us?"

Micah shook his head. It wasn't exactly the truth, but sometimes a little lie was needed to protect the innocent. "He didn't do any blabbing at all. He just laid down the law and told me not to date you."

"What? He did not. The nerve of that man."

Micah leaned forward. "You misunderstand. It wasn't because he thought you were wrong for me. It was because, well, how to put this..." He paused for a moment, mostly for effect. "In my opinion, he is still interested in you, Kerri. He's jealous. Of me. Which is idiotic but revealing."

She flopped back into the booth, astonishment on her face. "He is not. He ghosted me."

"Hmm. Interesting. Because he seems to think you dumped him."

"What?"

Micah picked up his steak knife, cut a slice off his pork chop, and popped it into his mouth. Boy, Annie could cook. He savored the flavor while Kerri sat opposite him, staring as if he'd just dropped in from Mars.

He didn't speak again until he'd swallowed. "Eat your dinner, Kerri. We need to talk about how to bridge this gap between you and Colton, because honestly, I've never seen Colton so upset as he was yesterday. He stormed my office and told me to stay the heck away from you."

"Wait a sec. I thought you were opposed to matchmaking. This sounds a whole lot like you're trying to fix me up with your brother."

He smiled. "I'm not matchmaking. Y'all already matched yourself up. I'm just problem solving."

Her mouth finally fell open, and it took a while before she closed it again.

He hunched forward. "I like to solve problems. Or more accurately, I sometimes feel as if my calling is to help people find a way to fix their own problems. So, let's talk."

"And he's willing to fix this problem?" she asked, doubt lacing her words.

"I would say yes."

She shook her head. "No. He doesn't get a free pass."

"What, exactly, are you annoyed about?"

"To be frank, he took me out a few times and then suddenly stopped calling me. Which, according to the word on the street, is his usual MO when it comes to women. He's a player. And he played me. And I'm tired of being played."

Micah swallowed another delicious bite of pork chop and nodded. "I don't blame you."

"You agree and you're still here trying to talk me into dating him or something?"

"I'm not here to talk you into anything, Kerri. But if you are still interested in Colton, then you need to know that he's still interested in you."

Kerri stared at him for almost thirty seconds. He couldn't read her thoughts on her face, but she was sure doing a lot of thinking.

"He has to earn his way back into my trust," she said. Then she finally picked up her own knife and cut into her chop.

"And how would he do such a thing?" Micah asked.

She chewed for a moment, her eyes narrowing. When she'd swallowed, she said, "Well, there is this kid in town. He's got troubles. And I won't lie, I caught him trying to shoplift something. Anyway, he says he wants to become a carpenter. If Colton wants to get back into my good graces, he'll show me that he can think about someone other than himself and he'll give this boy a job."

"How old is this kid?"

"I don't know exactly. Maybe seventeen. He's dropped out of school, so he isn't eligible for most of the carpenter's apprenticeship programs. If he took this boy on, Colton would be doing a huge service. To me. And to the community."

"And if Colton does this, what would you give in return?"

She swallowed another bite of chop. "Well, I guess if he gives the boy a job, I'll agree to have dinner with him."

"And this boy wouldn't happen to be Danny Beckett, by any chance?"

"You know him?"

He shook his head. "I haven't met him, but one of my parishioners brought his situation to my attention. In fact, over the last several days, more than one person has darkened my door and spoken his name to me. When that happens, it's usually a sign that God is calling me to do something. How 'bout you?"

She grinned. "I could see how that would be the case."

"Well, then. I will put this proposition to my younger brother. I hope he sees the value in it. I personally think it's a wonderful idea. Colton had a hard time as a kid. We all did. But he overcame a lot of issues to become a success. He has a lot to give. Maybe if he gives something back, he might become a better person."

"Well, I don't know if this will work on him, Reverend, but if I can help Danny get an internship or some other job learning the basics of carpentry, then I will have done something good. And I guess it's worth a dinner with a total player to make it happen."

Just then, Annie came sailing across the dining room with a worried expression on her face. Uh-oh, something had happened. Maybe Ms. Taylor, who was ninety-nine years old, had finally met her maker. Or perhaps Paul Maguire, who was battling pancreatic cancer, had taken a turn. Micah visited the hospital every Wednesday afternoon, but people didn't get sick on a weekly schedule.

"What is it, Annie?" he asked.

Annie was breathing hard when she stopped at their table. "Micah, honey, I'm afraid I've got some bad news. Jude just called. Your daddy's in the hospital."

Chapter Ten

Micah dropped Kerri off at her house on the way out of town. It took twenty minutes to make it to the hospital on the mainland, during which time his cell phone blew up with dozens of messages.

He didn't own a late-model car with the latest electronic features. His twelve-year-old Forester had 120,000 miles on it, but it was still going strong. He'd been contemplating an upgrade, but he hated car payments. Right at this moment, though, he wished he had a hands-free option.

So he couldn't read any of the text messages until he parked the car in a slot reserved for clergy. The messages weren't comforting. Dad had experienced an episode of some kind and had been taken to the cardiac care unit. Micah donned his hospital ID, bypassed the visitor's desk, and took the elevator to the third floor.

He hit the double doors to the cardiac care unit at a

run, rounded the corner into room fourteen, and came to a dead stop, face-to-face with a ghost.

The hairs on the back of his neck stood up at attention, and in the space between one erratic heartbeat and the next, he relived all the pain of his childhood.

Mom.

She stood apart from the rest of the family like a specter with her graying blond hair hanging down to her shoulders and her pale, white skin. He studied her, a choking agitation flowing through him. Not a ghost. She appeared to be breathing.

"Hello, Micah," she said, her voice husky and broken, probably from too many cigarettes. She seemed to be fascinated with his collar.

Memory flowed through him like toxic sludge. Mom, too drunk or drugged to get up and make sure they had breakfast every morning. Mom, too out of control or lazy to get the laundry done so they had clean underwear. Mom, opening a single can of ravioli and thinking it was a sufficient dinner for three growing boys.

He almost gagged at the remembered taste of Chef Boyardee.

His white mother had abandoned them years before she'd actually left. And Dad, for all of his failings, had stayed and tried his best. Dad had a business to run, and Mom's leaving had devastated him. It had devastated them all.

Only forgiveness could purge this poison. But deep inside the hidden chambers of his heart, he couldn't forgive. He didn't even know how to pray for the willingness to consider forgiving her. He'd learned to live with the poison.

But what now?

He didn't know, so he did the only thing he could do. He pretended she wasn't in the room. Maybe she was still alive, but he would turn her into a ghost by never, ever acknowledging her.

"Daddy," he said, approaching the bed where his father lay connected to the beeping monitors tracking his pulse, blood pressure, and oxygen levels. Micah had visited many parishioners in this unit, some of them gravely ill. But this was different. Daddy's gray complexion raised a flock of butterflies in his gut.

"I'm fine," Daddy said, before Micah could speak further. "Don't go all nursemaid on me or start praying, okay?" Daddy gave him that grumpy look he'd perfected over the years. "I was a little out of breath, is all. And then they did an EKG, and the doctor didn't like the results."

"They've ordered a bunch of tests for tomorrow," Jude said. "They think he might need a cardiac catheterization—"

"Or a bypass," Colton said, his voice edgy. Colton rocked back and forth on the balls of his feet, glancing behind him every once in a while. So that made two of them who were painfully aware of the elephant in the room.

"Listen," Daddy said, "there's something I need to tell y'all." Daddy reached for Jenna's hand, and Micah's gut clenched. What was Jenna up to? He loved his sister-in-law because she tried to bridge gaps between people. But she'd stayed out of the family business. Except now, carrying the first grandchild, she *was* family business.

"You know, Daddy," Jude said, his voice edgy, "we should save big announcements until tomorrow. You need to rest."

Jude turned toward Micah with an odd, frantic expression. Obviously, Jude knew something about what Dad wanted to announce. Jude wanted Micah to head it off at the pass because that's what he'd once done. When things ran off the rails, Micah had frequently inserted himself between the boys and his parents.

But Micah didn't want to be the one everyone depended on. He'd been that once, and he'd failed. Just like Mom, he'd abandoned them. And right now he stood there, hands in his pockets, and said nothing.

"What I have to say needs to be said right now." Daddy's voice rang through the tiny room.

"We're listening, Charles," Jenna said.

"Rachel, honey, come on over here."

Mom crossed the floor slowly, and Jenna made a space for her at the bedside. Daddy dropped Jenna's hand and took hold of Mom's. "Now, I know y'all are surprised to see your mother here. But the thing is, we started corresponding a few years ago, about the time I went to the recovery center. I needed to apologize, you know, as part of my twelve steps. And—"

"I needed to do the same," Mom said.

"And anyway, we started talking on the phone and checking in on Facebook. And then after a couple of years, when we both had stayed sober, we met in Charleston, where—"

"I was living there. I had a job as a health care aide." Mom gave Daddy a quick smile. It wrinkled up her face. She wasn't the young mother he remembered.

A tiny inkling of pity tried to fight its way into his heart. He crushed it. How many addicted people had he counseled and prayed over in his life? Too many to count.

Addiction could happen to anyone. It was a *disease*, not a moral failing. And yet... He bit his lip to keep from speaking out his pain.

"Anyway," Dad said, "I know a bunch of you were pissed off at me for missing Daisy's party. I'm sorry. But I got pissed off at Daisy. I told her I was asking Rachel to come back and live with me. And she told me not to come."

"What?" Three voices said the word in unison.

Daddy nodded. "She told me not to bring your mother to the party so I didn't. We went off to Myrtle Beach for the weekend instead. Now y'all need to know that she's come back and we're together again."

"I'm done here," Colton said, turning and stalking out of the room. Jude watched his brother leave with a wild, almost frightened expression on his face. Jenna took him by the arm in a gentle caress that also restrained him.

Good for her, but she hadn't lived through the pain, so she had nothing to forgive.

"I'm glad you're happy," Micah said in a monotone. "It's late. I'm going."

He escaped, but his anger followed him down the corridor like a dark shadow.

* * *

This week, the women of the Piece Makers had spent their three hours around the quilting frame discussing Micah St. Pierre and Kerri Eaton—a natural turn of events since Donna, Karen, and Patsy had all received texts from various church members alerting them to the fact that Micah and Kerri had been spotted at Annie's

Kitchen. By the end of the meeting the altar guild had all but named Micah and Kerri's firstborn child.

Now Ashley huddled into her coat, hunching her shoulders to thwart the cold wind whipping from the bay. She tried to shake a vague sense of apprehension as she walked up the hill to Howland House.

She was jealous. And utterly pathetic.

Damn, it was cold. The mercury had dropped below freezing, and ice crystals had begun to form around the edges of the puddles left from the earlier rain. Would spring ever come? Maybe if spring arrived she could excise this untoward fascination with Micah from her brain. She suspected her sudden interest in the minister had more to do with the deep of winter. Once spring arrived, she could get back into the garden. She could distract herself, and this madness would pass.

But winter always seemed to raise gloomy thoughts. It crept into her heart and soul and reminded her daily that she was *not* happy.

Being *not* happy wasn't at all the same as being unhappy. A person could embrace sorrow. It penetrated deep. It brought tears. It made you crazy.

But this shadowy state was much, much worse. She wasn't happy...and not sad exactly either. More hollow and numb, like the tips of her un-gloved fingers. Micah had landed into this wasteland like a ray of sunshine. That was all. When spring came, she'd get over it.

She walked on, her breath coming in clouds of steam.

She had to get over it. There wasn't much choice.

She arrived at Howland House well after ten o'clock, but the front door was still opened. All the guests had front door keys, but she left the doors unlocked until about nine o'clock. Evenings when she had to be away from the inn, she hired someone to mind Jackie, take care of guest issues, and lock up. Dad had assumed this job since he'd moved in. And he'd forgotten. Again.

The nothingness within Ashley became a burning, sour anger. What the hell? Dad had spent the last few weeks telling her how to run her business, and raise her child, but when it came to the simplest of things, he screwed up.

She would talk to him in the morning. She would suggest that maybe he needed something else in *his* life besides meddling in *hers*.

She shucked her coat and headed toward the closet right off the kitchen, but the light in the private office drew her attention. The door should have been closed and the light off.

A hundred creepy thoughts suffused her mind as she crept forward until the sound of someone hammering on a computer keyboard eased her untoward fear. She peeked around the corner.

Dad sat hunched over the computer, the room dark except for the light from the flat-panel screen. For once, his posture wasn't military-straight.

"Dad?" she asked.

He straightened, flashing her that charming smile. But she wasn't buying it. He hadn't been sleeping, given the bloodshot eyes. He hadn't been taking care of himself. His hair had grown long, and today it stuck out as if he'd been trying to pull it out of his scalp. A little spot marred the pristine white of his T-shirt. Definitely ketchup, which probably came from the greasy bag of Burger Boys french fries sitting beside him on the desk.

"You ordered takeout? I left you pot roast."

"Jackie was in the mood for a burger." He scratched

the back of his head, making his too-long hair stand out a little more.

He wasn't telling the truth. "And you decided to get him some. Were you *spoiling* him?" she asked a little caustically. How many times had Dad accused her of doing the same? "Jackie loves pot roast, Dad."

"That's what you think. My mother thought the same thing about me." His chin came down in a defensive posture.

And that was it. Her fury rose like mercury on a hot July day. She pointed her finger at him. "Jackie loves pot roast, Dad. If you got him burgers, that's just your guilt talking. Also, I'm tired of being compared to Grandmother. I may have inherited her recipe box and this house but we are two different people. So stop doing that. It's annoying as hell."

He shook his head. "No, I won't. Because you're behaving just like your grandmother."

"And what does that mean?"

"You go off to your quilting group every week. You let those women run you ragged. You bake cakes because you've confused love with sugar. And you don't listen. Jackie hates your pot roast about as much as I do."

His words might have been stones. They rained down on her with such hateful, hurtful force that she found herself shrinking back, folding her arms over her middle, her stomach curling inward on itself.

She opened her mouth, intending to vent about his meddling in her life. About his hard-handed approach to Jackie, about the webpage and the unlocked front door. But the words would not come.

He'd hurt her, but it made no sense to hurt him back. He was already so clearly out of control. And besides, there were guests upstairs. They didn't need to be privy to the family drama playing down here. Especially since this was Dad lashing out because he'd reached the angry phase of grieving.

She also didn't need to take his abuse. So she denied him the fight he so desperately wanted and left the office.

She didn't go upstairs. Instead, she escaped through the front door intent on walking off her fury.

The brutal kiss of the frozen air didn't do one thing to slow her racing heart or untwist the knot in her stomach. But at least no one would hear her out here if she let out one long, agonizing scream, like the subject of Edvard Munch's iconic painting.

Of course she didn't scream. She muttered and spat a lot of profanity while she paced back and forth along the sidewalk waiting for calm to reassert itself. She walked Lilac Lane from the corner of Harbor Drive to the intersection with Rose, and then back again. On the second circuit, Rev. St. Pierre's ancient SUV came speeding up the hill so fast it almost left the ground when it hit the bump in the road right before the rectory.

He swung the car into the driveway, tires screeching in the night, headlights splitting the darkness like a lighthouse beacon. What the hell? He was in a hurry. But then she'd ridden with Micah once or twice. He was a wild man behind the wheel of a car.

She checked her watch. It was almost eleven. Boy, his date with Kerri must have been a good one for him to be getting home so late. Against her better judgment, she crossed the street and headed toward the rectory.

It occurred to her as she approached that she was exactly like the curious cat. She was probably going to pay a price for this.

The lamps on either side of the rectory's doors cast hard shadows across The Rev's face as he left his SUV. His stiff posture told her something was off. Maybe his date with Kerri had been a disaster. Or maybe something else.

"What's wrong?" she asked, but he asked very same question.

In unison.

* * *

Huddled in a puffy down coat that might have been two sizes too big, Ashley Scott appeared small and vulnerable.

His breath hitched. Why was she out here at almost eleven o'clock on the coldest night of the year? He stifled the urge to cross the distance and enfold her in a warm embrace.

"What—" They spoke at the same time.

"You first," she said. "What's wrong?"

"What are you doing out here so late?" Micah asked, ignoring her question. It was his job to comfort the needy and downtrodden. His own emotions were secondary. Besides, he didn't need or want to dump his unmovable anger onto one of his parishioners. His inability to forgive was something he needed to take up with God. And if God refused to answer, then there was always the bishop.

"I needed some air," she said, coming up the driveway. She stopped a couple of feet in front of him. "Something's happened. What?" she asked.

What the heck? Was his fury that transparent?

"Nothing."

She huffed out a breath that created a plume of steam. “Oh for goodness’ sake. What is it with you strong, silent types anyway?”

“What’s that supposed to mean?”

“It means I’m out here pacing the sidewalk because my father is in denial. He’s trying to avoid his grief by messing with my life. I’m pretty sure he’s trying to be strong because, you know, he’s a military man, and also my dad. So he thinks he needs to take charge of Jackie and take care of me. Or maybe he misses taking care of Mom. But anyway, right now I want to strangle him.”

“Maybe I should chat with him about grief counseling. We have a group that meets—”

“Oh no you don’t. I’m not letting you deflect by going all priestly on me. I saw the way you drove up the hill. You’re kind of crazy behind the wheel of a car, Micah, but that was reckless. What’s going on?” She flapped her arms like a goose trying to take off.

She was adorable. And also angry, which meant he was not allowed to smile at her adorableness. And besides, her being angry was probably a step in the right direction.

“It’s nothing,” he said. “Why don’t I stop by tomorrow morning and chat with your father.”

“Micah. Stop avoiding. You don’t usually stay out so late on Tuesdays. Is someone in the hospital? You know the altar guild will hear of it soon enough.”

His lips pressed together as if that could keep the truth from leaking out of him. She was right, of course. The altar guild would find out, and then she’d scold him about being stoic. And he hated it when Ashley scolded him.

She stepped closer, cocking her head. She had sweet,

sad puppy eyes. "Someone *is* in the hospital." It wasn't a question this time.

He inhaled, trying to find some balance, or maybe a modicum of calm. Both evaded him. He stepped back.

She stepped forward.

"It's complicated," he said, crossing his arms like a barrier.

"Uh-huh." She jutted one hip, telegraphing her skepticism and a whole bunch of attitude. Clearly she had a bone to pick with the male gender. Maybe he should give her something to gnaw on before she blamed him for the state of the world.

"My father had some kind of cardiac episode. But he's fine." He tossed off the words like it was no biggie.

Her gaze narrowed and invaded him like penetrating radar. "Cardiac episode?" She wrinkled her nose.

He fought the urge to grab her and hug her. Then it occurred to him that maybe the Lord had put her in his path tonight. "They're doing tests." He paused a moment. "He might need a bypass."

"Oh, Micah, I'm sorry. You must be—"

"That's not why I'm so angry," he blurted.

She stepped back. "Angry?" Her tone conveyed surprise. Maybe she didn't have radar after all.

"Yeah. I'm angry. My mom showed up. She and Dad are getting back together. I'm not okay with it. And I know I should be okay with it. But..." His voice trailed off as his throat tied itself into a knot. Talking about his fury didn't release the hurt or tension. His voice shook, and she noticed.

She stepped closer, until she stood mere inches from him, her dark eyes filled with an empathy he'd never noticed before. "You want to talk about it?" she asked.

He swallowed against the knot in his throat. He did not want to talk about it. He shook his head. But tears filled his eyes.

And right then, before he could escape, Ashley Scott took him by the arm and pulled him into an embrace. He wrapped his arms around her, her jacket's fabric cooling his hands. But the breath against his neck sent heat flowing through him despite the freezing temperatures.

He should pull away. He should run. But instead, he settled down into her hug, resting his forehead against her narrow shoulder. She stood half a head shorter than him, and yet she held him up. Like all the great women he'd known, she had a steel rod for a backbone. It made her stubborn as heck, but stronger than anyone could ever give her credit for.

She'd come in answer to his prayer. The Lord was supposed to carry burdens, and in that moment, Ashley was His angel. The dam of emotion broke. Tears came hard and choking, but she was his rock in the flood.

* * *

Ashley had been wrong about Micah. He wasn't at all like her dad...or Adam. Neither one of them had ever cried in her presence. That was the sort of thing a big, strong man would never do.

A few tears during "God Bless America" were acceptable, but a full-out crying jag was frowned upon. She drew the minister closer and ran her hands over the worsted of his suit jacket. The hard muscles under the fabric thrilled her in forbidden ways.

But when he leaned against her, she held him up, reveling in her own strength. She rested her cheek against his chest, and his strong, steady heartbeat connected her to the world of the living, and him too. A tiny, disquieting vibration of lust hummed low in her core.

No. Not now. The man needed someone to share his burdens, not a stupid woman who'd spent the last five years sleeping alone. *Get your mind out of the gutter, Ashley.*

Micah must have read her mind or something because he stepped away, breaking the embrace with a quick movement akin to pulling a Band-Aid off a wound.

Ouch. Painful. But quick.

To her relief, the familiar pastor reemerged, brushing tears from his cheeks, and the universe righted itself.

"Uh, thanks, I..." he started.

"Don't worry, I won't go blabbing all over town about your mom," she said softly.

He barked out a mirthless laugh. "Thanks. I have a feeling the news will make its way onto the grapevine anyway."

"Well, it won't come from me. And..." She ran out of words as she captured his gaze. Tiny flames flickered there, created by the front door lanterns.

"Thanks," he repeated, but he didn't move away.

"I, um..." she started, but she didn't know where to go with her words.

He nodded but said nothing.

"Look, it's—"

"I meant what I said earlier. If you want me to come by tomorrow morning and talk to your dad, I'll—"

"No," she said a little too quickly, because the idea of facing Micah St. Pierre tomorrow morning left her breathless. "I don't think talking to him will work," she said quickly. "So..." She swung her thumb over her shoulder.

"I need to get home and to bed. It's an early morning tomorrow."

He nodded.

And they stood there for a long moment. Staring. Surprised. Uncomfortable.

Before she walked away.

Chapter Eleven

Micah didn't sleep on Tuesday night. Toxic childhood memories and his obsession with Ashley kept him tossing and turning. In the morning, he called Jude to check in. Daddy was scheduled for a bunch of tests, and Jude promised to call him once the results were in.

Since it was Ash Wednesday, Micah had to beg off a family get-together at the hospital, which suited him fine, if Mom was going to be there. And staying busy would keep his mind off what had happened last night with Ashley.

Thank goodness she'd walked away from him; if she'd stayed any longer, he might have done something truly stupid, like expose his deepest emotions. He'd been aware of her in all the wrong ways from the first moment he'd met her—that day she'd been directing a crew of amateur painters frantically trying to get the long-neglected rectory ready for him.

He could picture the day perfectly. She'd been standing

in the middle of the living room with splotches of white latex all over her dark-brown hair. A smudge of it ran up her arm and shoulder, as if she'd leaned against a freshly painted wall.

Her sad, puppy-dog eyes had widened in surprise when he'd strolled into the rectory a day early. He'd thought they were adorable and kind. But in the years since, he'd come to learn all about the sorrow behind those remarkable eyes.

He'd also discovered the steel rod running right up her backbone. The same one he'd leaned on last night.

The Imposition of Ashes services at 8:00 a.m. kept him on track and distracted. But Mom showed up at the 11:00 a.m. service, reminding Micah that, recovering addict or not, Mom had been a regular at Heavenly Rest once. She'd brought her boys to the Sunday school here.

He'd found something within these walls. In truth, Mom had helped him realize his calling, and he ought to be thankful instead of resentful. But when she knelt at the altar rail to receive her ashes, he found himself wondering if she was truly penitent, or had merely used Ash Wednesday as a reason to get up in his face.

The thought was unworthy. He obviously needed much more prayer to find his way through this emotional minefield. Thank goodness Mom didn't stick around after the service.

But when he returned to his office to eat the peanut butter sandwich he'd made for lunch, he found Colton pacing the floor. This time, Micah was prepared. Colton had been upset last night with good reason. None of them had seen Mom for years. Her return brought up a lot of crap no one wanted to deal with. But Colton had a special reason to be here. No doubt, by now, he'd have heard all about Micah's date with Kerri.

Well, there was no time like the present to get to work on Colton, and maybe do a good service for Danny Beckett, who wanted to become a carpenter.

"I told you to stay away from her," Colton said before Micah even had a chance to sit down and find his brown paper lunch sack.

"You want a PBJ?" he asked. "I made two."

Colton stopped pacing and stood before Micah's desk, the picture of an angry sibling until he wrinkled his nose. "Dude, do you eat PBJs often?"

Micah shrugged. "It's cheap, easy, and has protein."

"Damn. I need to take you to lunch more often."

"That would be nice. I take it you're not terminally ticked off with me, then."

Colton slumped into the chair. "You're going to marry her, aren't you?"

Micah chuckled. "I took her to dinner, Colton. I didn't get down on my knee. And trust me, if I ever propose again, it will not be in public."

"But you like her. Don't you?"

"I do. She's a very nice woman. But I'm not going to take her out on another date."

Colton's rigid back seemed to melt with this news. He let go of a long breath. "Thanks, man. 'Cause you marrying her would be awkward." Colton looked away, his troubled expression nearly transparent. "I wish Mom would leave. Daddy is sober now, and..." His voice trailed off.

"Daddy's going to do what he wants to do," Micah said. It was nothing short of the truth. Daddy had been the one who stayed when Mom left. Daddy, for all his faults, had been there to drive Micah to college. Daddy had been there when Colton ended up in jail. Yes, mostly Daisy and Charlotte and Old Granny had been the backbone of the family, especially because Daddy worked long hours, but Daddy had been there. He'd had a fondness for booze, though, which got worse when Mom left. And now Daddy was sober. And Micah figured they all were worried about Mom's reappearance.

Colton looked up but said nothing. In the silence, Micah got the feeling that his brother expected him to come forth with some theological or philosophical wisdom on the subject of Mom. And for the life of him, he couldn't. He was just as worried as his brother. And he sure wasn't about to tell Colton to pray about it.

"That's all you have to say?" Colton asked, an edge to his voice.

"I don't know what to do about Mom either. I wish I did. I'm as angry as you are."

Colton nodded and pushed up from the chair. "Come on, I'll take you to lunch."

Micah shook his head. "I can't today. I'm too busy. It's Ash Wednesday. I've got services every few hours. But there is something you can do for me. And for Kerri, if you're interested."

"For Kerri?"

Micah nodded. "You remember that accident out in the inlet last year? The people who drowned while they were fishing?"

"Yeah."

"They had a son. He's seventeen maybe. Troubled. Angry. Probably feels as if he's been abandoned. Anyway, after his parents died, he came to live in Magnolia Harbor with his grandmother, who I've learned is diabetic with a lot of health issues. Kerri has given him a couple of odd jobs. But he wants to become a carpenter."

"He should apply for an apprenticeship. There are plenty—"

"He can't. He dropped out of high school."

"Oh."

"Yeah, so I was thinking you could get in touch with Kerri, get the boy's contact information, and give him an internship or something. And at the same time, you could encourage him to go back to school. Ken Nyberg says he could repeat his senior year if he wanted to. If he does that, he could apply for a real apprenticeship."

"You want me to give a high school dropout a job?"

"Don't be a snob. Someone gave you a second chance." Micah delivered this line with a raised eyebrow in a bald-faced attempt to mimic Aunt Daisy, who could make anyone feel about three inches tall with one look.

"And Kerri wants me to do this? Or are you just jacking me around?"

Micah grinned. "Listen, Kerri and I had a frank conversation before I had to run up to the hospital. She knows that I know that you and she had a romance of some kind. And she says that she might reconsider going out with you if you give this kid a chance."

Colton blinked a few times. "Wait. Are you matchmaking?"

Micah let go of a belly laugh that warmed him up from the inside out and made him forget about Dad's illness, Mom's return, and Ashley's forbidden hug. This was what he loved about his job. Surprising someone by pointing out a solution.

"Well, I guess I am matchmaking. I'm trying to match

up a troubled kid with a mentor, and maybe that will change a certain woman's mind about your character."

"Well, damn," Colton said, shaking his head as he turned toward the door. When he got to the threshold, he stopped and looked over his shoulder. "Thanks, man."

"No problem."

* * *

Ashley walked into Rafferty's at twelve thirty, at the height of Wednesday's lunch hour, but since it was a cold day in February, the crowd was thin. Jenna St. Pierre sat by the window, pensively staring at the bay.

"A penny for your thoughts," Ashley said as she took the facing seat.

Jenna smiled. "Oh, I was just thinking about baby names."

Ashley grinned. "Are you and Jude still fighting about that?"

She nodded. "I'm afraid so, especially since we found out that it's a girl. I'd love to name her Samsara. It means 'flowing' in Sanskrit and is the word used for continuous life and death. Jude still wants to name her Daisy. I understand why, but I think she should have her own unique name. I'm not a huge fan of family names." She sighed.

"I'm rooting for Samsara," Ashley said.

"So"—Jenna took a sip of water—"when you called this morning, you sounded slightly frantic. Is something wrong?"

Was something wrong? Oh boy, everything was wrong. She'd slept poorly last night, agitated by the moment in the rectory's driveway. Memories brought a flood of sensations that ranged from hot to embarrassed. Mostly though, an army of butterflies had invaded her stomach and pitched a permanent camp there.

In short, she had rediscovered lust, and she didn't know what to do about it. Which was why she'd called Jenna. Jenna was so sensible and calm about everything. She'd become Ashley's best friend, in addition to the silent partner in her business.

"I want your advice about something... personal."

Jenna's eyebrow rose, and she leaned in a little closer but said nothing.

"The thing is..." Ashley's voice trailed off. Heat crawled up her neck and back and probably blossomed into a bright-red blush. How was she supposed to talk about this? How would she answer if Jenna asked too many questions?

"What?" Jenna said with some urgency.

"Well, it's been five years since Adam died, and I..." Thank god the waitress came to take their orders. It gave her a moment to regroup.

"So," Jenna said, picking up the conversation after they'd both ordered shrimp Caesar salads, "I take it you're thinking about reentering the dating pool."

"God, that sounds like swimming with sharks," Ashley said, wishing she'd ordered a glass of wine and not a Diet Coke.

"So what? You want my blessing?"

"Well, no. But maybe advice. I was thinking about joining one of those online dating services."

"What? No. You should not do that."

"Why not? People do it all the time."

"Yeah, young people. People who aren't widows who own a business. Ashley, there are predators out there preying on lonely widows who have nice savings accounts."

"Wow, I didn't expect you to be so negative about this," Ashley said, her unsettled stomach twisting. "When did you become so conservative? I mean, you traveled the world all by yourself, and you have more money than God."

Jenna blinked. "Yikes. I guess I have become conservative." She paused a moment and continued. "You know, I don't want to discourage you going out on a date. I just think maybe you should look closer to home for companionship."

"Like who?" Ashley asked and then immediately regretted her question. She did not want Jenna to suggest the man living across the street from Howland House. That would be no help at all. The whole point was to find someone other than Micah, because, well…

"I don't know," Jenna said with a fake-nonchalant shrug. Holy crap, did Jenna realize Ashley had a crush on Micah St. Pierre?

The waitress came back with their salads and paused the conversation. After a few minutes of silent munching, Ashley broached the subject again. "You know, there aren't a lot of single men in this town."

"That's not true. Colton's single and so is—" Jenna stopped talking and stared down at her food.

Crap, crap, crap. "Am I that obvious?" Ashley asked.

"No, honestly, not at all. Really. But, um…" Jenna studied the bay, which was calm today.

"I can't." Ashley didn't specify what she couldn't do. Because saying the words *I can't date Micah* would make the whole situation more real. And she could not afford that.

Evidently Jenna didn't need her to be any more specific because her gaze zipped back. "Why not?"

"He's the pastor at my church. There are rules." Crap, this was getting way too specific, wasn't it?

Jenna opened her mouth and then shut it again. The silence swelled for a moment before she said, "Oh shit."

"Right."

"You could become a Buddhist. We could start a temple."

Ashley rolled her eyes.

"No, huh?"

"No."

"Well, you could, I don't know, go to church in Georgetown."

"I guess. But, you know, it's not clear that my sudden interest in him is returned. And even discussing this with him would embarrass the crap out of him. So, really, there is only one thing I can do. Besides what I've already done trying to match him up with Kerri Eaton."

"You're trying to fix him up with Kerri?"

Ashley blushed. "It's defensive matchmaking or something." She laid her fork across her plate. She wasn't very hungry anyway. "This is silly. It's me having some kind of midlife crisis. Or maybe it's, well, a lack of sex that's addled my brain. I don't have to get serious, you know. I could go out and have some fun. I never did that in college."

"I see." Jenna put her fork down and studied her food.

"You don't really think those online dating services are dangerous, do you?"

Jenna didn't answer right away, and Ashley didn't press. Jenna was one of those people who always thought before she spoke. She had a calm wisdom Ashley admired.

"Well," Jenna finally said, "I think you should be careful with your heart, Ashley. And I doubt that you'll find what you're searching for by posting a profile on a dating service. But I don't think it's dangerous per se. And really, compared with the stuff Aunt Patsy does, a dating service seems pretty straightforward and tame."

* * *

It was Kerri's turn to host the Stitch and Bitch at her house. The girls had gathered in her kitchen, peppering her with questions about Micah St. Pierre.

"Honestly," Shawna said, "I can't believe your date ended that way. Did he promise to call you?"

"To hell with promises. Did he call you?"

Kerri upended the third margarita glass into the salter and poured her own drink. Should she tell the truth?

Nah.

"He did call me this afternoon," she said. It wasn't a lie. Of course he hadn't called to ask her out again. He'd wanted Danny Beckett's contact information because he'd spoken with Colton about giving the kid a job. And that was the difference between Micah and Colton. Micah could be depended upon. Colton, not so much. She was waiting to see if Colton did anything about Danny.

She would not be holding her breath.

"So when's the next date?" Marcie asked.

"I don't know. He's busy. Today especially. Ash Wednesday, you know? And his father's in the hospital."

"Right," Marcie said on a long breath. "This is why dating a minister is problematic. I personally want a man who will put me at the center of his world."

Kerri had wanted that once too. And she'd discovered

it did not exist. Pining away for some kind of Prince Charming was foolish. A girl was much better off looking after herself. Besides, she didn't want to be at the center of anyone's world. She wanted a true partner and companion.

"Come on, girls," Kerri said, "let's forget about my disastrous first date with Reverend St. Pierre and go knit."

She picked up her drink and headed into the living room. Her house was a small cottage built back in the woods. She'd gotten it for a pittance four years ago because it had resembled a shack. But the shack had been built in the mid-1800s and had hand-hewn siding and wide-planked floors. She'd finished restoring the place a few years ago, adding a new kitchen and bedroom to the back of the original historic structure, and now it fit her like a glove. A small dream house, off the beaten track, but all hers, with beamed ceilings in the living room and a small fireplace, where a real wood fire crackled.

She was no Cinderella in need of rescue. No sir. She was competent and in command of her life.

"I don't want to forget your date with Micah St. Pierre," Shawna said. "What happened before he had to rush off to the hospital?"

Kerri dropped down into the corner of her small couch and put her drink down on a coaster. "Nothing happened. We'd just gotten our food when he had to leave."

Shawna gave Marcie the evil eye and then said, "Come on, honey, us single girls want to know the details."

"Well, he's very nice. And we talked about—" Kerri almost jumped out of her skin when a knock sounded at the front door.

"Were you expecting someone?" Marcie asked in a humorous tone.

"No. Certainly not Reverend St. Pierre." She got up and peeked through the peephole.

Holy crap. Colton stood on the other side of the door, shifting from one foot to the other as if the porch planks beneath his feet were hot coals.

She must have telegraphed her surprise because Shawna said, "It's him, isn't it? He's surprised you. Did he bring flowers?" Shawna got up from the couch to peek through the front window.

"Oh," she said, then turned and stared. "Not Micah, then."

Not to be outdone, Marcie crossed from the side chair to look as well. "Is that Colton out there?"

"What are you waiting for, girl? Open the door," Shawna said.

She opened the door onto a cold night. She didn't invite Colton in because she didn't want her girlfriends to hear their conversation. Instead she stepped onto the porch and wrapped her arms around her middle to keep warm.

Colton wore a brown leather bomber jacket with a shearling collar, which accentuated his bad-boy good looks. She wanted to gobble him up for dessert.

"What are you doing here?" Kerri asked.

"Um..." He studied his feet, shod in his usual leather work boots. His fit-like-a-glove, worn-in-the-knees jeans molded to his thighs and butt. Suddenly it didn't feel so cold out here. She was pathetic.

"Spit it out," she said her voice turning hard. "It's cold out here."

"We could go inside."

"No. I have company."

"You have company?" He raised his head.

"Yes."

Marcie and Shawna had their noses pressed up against the inside of the window, taking in the scene with avid interest. Great.

"I came to apologize," he said.

Again? Last time he tried to apologize, he didn't even know what he'd done. She folded her arms across her chest. "Oh really? For what?"

"Uh, well..."

Silence hung for a moment, and their gazes met. And her knees wobbled despite her best intentions. Dammit. Strong sexual attraction was her weakness. She had to remember that sex and love were not the same. And she wasn't letting him off the hook.

"Well, that's the thing, see? I mean..." Colton started, stopped, and then began again. "I like you a lot, Kerri, and I never really understood why you got so angry with me that time. You know, right after I took you on the sunset cruise."

"You mean the cruise where you got free tickets from your brother so you could help fill out the crew."

"Come on. You loved that cruise."

She had loved that cruise, especially when Colton had climbed out on the ship's bowsprit to set one of the sails. He'd been graceful, and manly, and sexy as hell. But she wasn't about to admit that to him.

Nor was she about to remind him that he didn't call her for days and days after the sunset cruise. It was as if she'd never existed. And when he finally stopped by the store, days later, he'd come out of concern for Jessica Blackwood, the woman who rented the upstairs office from her.

She wasn't admitting anything or blaming. Instead,

she looked him in the eye and said, "Colton, if you don't know what you're apologizing for, then don't try, okay? Is that the only reason you're here?"

He shook his head. "No. I'm here because of Danny Beckett. Micah told me all about your deal. I'm willing to help, but I have some concerns about his character."

"I'll vouch for him, but I have to be honest. I caught him shoplifting one day. He was trying to take a coffee mug that wasn't worth much. He told me it was for his grandmother and he didn't have any money to buy it because he needed a job."

Colton nodded and appeared to be listening. "So I heard. And you gave him a job."

"Just some sweeping up and unpacking. But he worked hard. I'm trying to get him to help with the harbor cleanup day too. But, you know, that's just volunteer work so no money's involved. He's got issues, Colton. I'm not saying he's a saint."

She met his gaze, and to her surprise Colton nodded. "Yeah, well, it's been pointed out that neither was I when I was seventeen."

She didn't have a rejoinder for him. He seemed oddly self-aware. Maybe he'd grown as a human being in the last few years.

He huffed a big breath, which escaped in a cloud of steam. "All right, Kerri, I'm going to offer this kid an internship. But here's the deal. I know from firsthand experience that just giving him a job isn't going to be enough. So I'm going to one-up you. I'll be his mentor. And I'll do it whether you want to go to dinner with me or not."

"You will?"

He nodded. "I will. And if you think getting him to

participate in the cleanup day is important, then I'll make sure he gets there."

"Does that mean you'll volunteer to help too? Because we could sure use a man with some carpentry skills."

He dug into the pocket of his jacket and pulled out a business card. "Okay. Just in case you deleted my number, here it is again. Just call me and let me know what you need."

He held out the card. She took it from him, their fingers brushing in the exchange. It was freezing out here, but Kerri didn't notice. Her core had gone right into meltdown mode.

Chapter Twelve

After the last services of the day, Micah made the pilgrimage to Dad's hospital bedside. The old man was feeling better. The docs seemed to have his heart arrhythmia under control, and he had a bunch of appointments with cardiologists over the next few days. He was going to be discharged in the morning.

Unfortunately, Mom was there, which cast a pall over the good news.

She sat in the chair beside Daddy's bed, pale as the bed linens, a smudge of ash on her forehead that Micah had placed during the midmorning services. The mark was a sign of penitence, and yet for Micah, it seemed to underscore his own failings and guilt. How could he possibly become his mother's pastor when he couldn't find the way to forgive her? How could he continue to serve, given his feelings for Ashley?

These questions cut deeply, right to his soul, and left him enervated, unable to sit down and visit quietly with his own father. So he stayed for less than twenty minutes before the tension inside him drove him away. He gave Dad a kiss on the cheek and bolted.

He'd gotten halfway down the hall to the elevator when Mom called him back.

"Micah, wait."

He stopped and turned. She came down the hallway with the grace of a dancer. She was thin and sinewy with a long neck and birdlike collarbone. She wore a long, shapeless India print dress exactly like the ones she'd worn when he was a child. She hadn't changed much in appearance. The hair had gone gray, the skin around her lips and eyes had grown lines, but otherwise, she was his mother. *Momma.*

"What do want?" he asked, his voice hard.

"A minute of your time?" she said softly.

Her tone shamed him. "All right." He crossed his arms over his chest. "Say whatever it is you have to say."

"I want to apologize."

"I don't want your apologies."

"I know. But I need to give one. And I've been trying to talk to you."

"No, you haven't."

"I sent you letters. You sent them back."

This was true. He had returned the letters the navy had done its best to deliver to all sorts of duty stations.

"Okay. You did send letters," he admitted. "But you also abandoned us. I didn't feel the need to read them."

She drew her hands around her ribs as if hugging herself. "I wanted you to know I was proud of you."

"Thanks."

"And also..." She paused, cocking her head and

capturing his entire attention with her bright, blue eyes. "I know I failed you."

"Right." His throat clogged.

"I loved booze and drugs more than I loved you. And I know it damaged you. And if I could do it all over again, I would try harder. But I can't do that. I can't go back. I can only move forward. But I can atone for my failures. I can make restitution."

"How?"

"I don't know, Micah. But I can start by saying that I understand how hard you worked to expunge the shame I brought on the family. In AA, we call children like you heroes."

"I'm not a hero."

She shook her head. "I don't mean like Batman or Superman. I mean that you took it upon yourself to bring honor back to our family. You did this by assuming my role as caregiver, by getting good grades and a scholarship that took you to a better place. You should be proud of all that. And I want you to know that I understand how you've spent your whole life thinking that if you could just be good enough, you could change things. But it doesn't work that way. I broke things. And you could never have fixed what I broke."

He stepped back, her words piercing his breast like the sharpest of bayonets. Mom had apologized countless times. Her apologies were always honest. This one was brutally so, and it underscored his problem. How could he possibly allow her to come to his church?

His church? No, it wasn't *his* church. Clearly he needed to rethink...everything.

"I'm going now," he said in a hard but professionally

polite voice. "It's been a long day." He walked away. She didn't come after him.

When he got to his car, he put the ancient thing to the test, racing it down the road to the bridge spanning the bay. He drove like a reckless idiot, but it helped him regain some control.

It was almost nine thirty by the time he turned the Forester into the rectory's driveway. The arc of his headlights swung over the pines in the front yard and came to rest on a small boy, bundled up in a puffy down coat, sitting on the house's front steps, knees drawn up and head resting on them.

Damn.

The last time he'd spoken to Jackie Scott, he'd come perilously close to damaging a relationship he'd come to value. His mother's words came back to haunt him.

What the heck was wrong with him, anyway? The kid had an imaginary friend and had asked for help in giving up the ghost, so to speak. And all Micah had done was spout theology at him.

Shame on him.

He got out of the car and came over to where the boy sat. "Hey," he said.

The carriage light by the front door limned the boy's face with yellow, giving him a ghostly glow. Micah stomped the urge to scold the kid for being out so late. His mother would do that if she ever found out. Jackie had a good mother who was justifiably protective.

"Hi," Jackie said, the lamplight catching the steam of his breath.

Micah hiked his pants and sat down beside him. "What's up?" he asked.

The boy huffed. "A lot."

"I'm listening."

"Mom and Granddad are fighting all the time."

"Oh. I'm sorry."

"Mom doesn't like Granddad messing with the computer..." Something about the way Jackie stopped talking suggested he wanted to say more but was holding back.

Micah didn't press. He just said, "Uh-huh," and waited.

"And then there's Nadia."

"Ms. Kovic?"

"She says I should call her Nadia. I'm pretty sure Mom wants to kick her out of her room but she's a paying guest. And that's my fault. I never should have called her, but I had questions about stuff."

Micah could imagine what stuff Jackie had called about. Stuff he'd scolded the boy about a few days ago. "You mean about how to get the captain to go into the light?"

Jackie looked up at him. "You don't believe that, do you?" He sighed. "At least Nadia believes there could be ghosts, even though she doesn't really believe in the captain."

"Look," Micah said, throwing caution to the wind and draping his arm over Jackie's thin shoulder to give him a friendly embrace. "I need to apologize. The last time we talked, I said some dumb things about ghosts. What can I do to help?"

Jackie shrugged. "I don't know. The ghost is fading."

"Fading?"

He nodded, biting his lip. "He doesn't come around as much."

Micah said nothing. Maybe Jackie would grow out of the ghost on his own.

Beneath Micah's palm, the boy's shoulders stiffened a fraction. "I know what you're thinking," Jackie said. "You think the captain is made up. But you're wrong. I think only kids can see him, and then they get talked into thinking he isn't real. And the problem is that, when I can't see him anymore, he's going to be stuck here all alone with no one to talk to. That makes me sad." Jackie's voice wobbled a little.

Maybe the ghost wasn't real, but the boy's emotions about the ghost were very real indeed. A sudden longing seized Micah to hug the kid and tell him everything would be okay. But Jackie was too world-wise. He'd lost a father in a war; he understood that sometimes things don't work out.

"I'm sorry you're sad," he said. "What can I do to help?"

"I don't know." Jackie shook his head. "Well...there is something Nadia asked me to do."

"Really? And what is that?"

"Nadia doesn't believe in the captain, but she's sure there is a spirit of some kind, maybe even a demon, in Mom's coffee machine. And tomorrow morning, she's going to force Mom to confront it."

"What?" The word exploded from Micah's mouth.

Jackie tilted his head and gave him a squinty look. "You aren't going to call Mom up and tell her about this, are you? 'Cause, you know, this conversation is private."

"You want your mother to be forced to face a demon?"

The kid rolled his eyes. "Do you think there's a demon in the coffee machine?" he asked in a surprisingly wise tone.

"Well...it seems far-fetched." He didn't mention his views on Captain Teal because clearly Jackie made some mental distinction between his imaginary ghost and some random demon in the coffee machine.

"You think so?"

"Yeah. I mean there's a real ghost out by the ruins of Rose Howland's cabin, but Nadia refuses to go investigate that spot." He paused for a moment. "You think she's scared of ghosts?"

Micah tried very hard not to react to this because it would undermine Jackie's trust. But clearly Nadia Kovic wasn't interested in investigating an imaginary friend. The woman was probably a fraud, more interested in exposing Ashley for trying to market the inn as being haunted, which Ashley had never done.

But if that was true, what about the coffee machine? Maybe the woman was just bat-crap crazy. "So, you said Nadia wanted me to do something. What is it?" he asked.

Jackie sighed. "She said it would be helpful to have a priest around when Mom confronts the demon. But before you say no, I told her you couldn't do it."

"Okay, so why are you here?"

"She kind of insisted. She said it would be for Mom's protection."

"And you still think it's okay not to tell your mother about this plan?"

"I know. I should tell her. But then what? I mean, Mom hates to have arguments with guests. And..." He paused a moment, his head bowed. "This is all my fault."

"No, it's not. An adult has taken advantage of you and your mother. Come on, let's go across the street and have a word with your mom."

"No. You can't. She'll be totally ticked off if she finds out that I'm not in bed where I'm supposed to be. And Granddad will have a cow. He'll ground me for another ten years. I'm in deep trouble, here. And nobody gives a crap about the captain. It's not right."

The boy's pain arrowed through Micah.

"So what can I do?" Micah asked, while mentally making a note to give Ashley a call ASAP.

"Well, I was thinking... maybe you could, you know, come for breakfast again. I think Nadia is going to try to get rid of the demon in the coffeepot tomorrow morning. And then she told me she was going because there were no other ghosts at Howland House."

Sometimes the Lord had a not-very-funny sense of humor. Earlier today, Micah had promised God that he'd give up breakfast across the street, not just for Lent but forever. And now here came Jackie needing an advocate.

He needed to put a stop to this coffeepot exorcism before it happened. And if he couldn't do that, it sure looked as if he needed to be there for it. Not to protect anyone from demons but to show Jackie that he had someone in his corner.

"Okay," he said. "I'll come for breakfast."

"You will?"

He nodded without explaining his reasons, or his plans, or promising to make it a regular thing.

He walked the boy back across the street and watched him from the garden as he used his key to slip through the back door. Ten minutes later, he called Ashley's cell phone, but it was well after ten o'clock, and his call went straight to voice mail.

Ashley regularly got up before dawn to make breakfast, so naturally she went to bed early. He would try to get there early tomorrow morning to head this thing off at the pass.

* * *

On Thursday morning, Ashley rolled over in the bed and squinted at the alarm clock. Ever since she'd opened Howland House as a bed and breakfast, the alarm had sounded at precisely 4:30 a.m. But today, for some reason, it sounded like a shrieking Valkyrie in her head. She batted it to silence and buried her head under the pillow.

It didn't help. Her head continued to pound as if she'd gone out last night and tied one on. Which she hadn't. But she hadn't slept well because she kept dreaming about that hug she'd given Micah St. Pierre on Tuesday.

She groped in her bedside table for an Excedrin. She popped a couple and chugged them down with the mouthful of water left in her bedside glass. She burrowed under the covers in the hope of avoiding dawn. The sunrise would hurt.

This wasn't an ordinary headache. She was having one of her migraines. They only came when she was stressed about things.

She curled up and waited for the pills to kick in. She'd learned to negotiate the headaches because breakfast had to be cooked and served regardless of the state of her head. Midweek in mid-February wasn't a busy time, but she had two guests, one of whom was a huge problem. Regardless, they expected biscuits.

And maybe Micah would show up for breakfast. So oatmeal needed to be started. It took forever to cook the Irish oats that The Rev liked so much.

Ha. Clearly this headache had affected her rational thinking. Micah wasn't going to show up. Probably ever again. Which was a good thing because she'd been working on her dating profile.

She tossed onto her back, the foggy painful buzz in her head fading a bit, replaced by the jangle of the caffeine in the headache pills. She waited until it was safe to roll out of bed. When she hit the shower, her head was only pounding like a regular anvil instead of Thor's mighty hammer in the sky.

Twenty minutes later, she made it to the kitchen, the earlier pain fading to dull discomfort above her right eye. Luckily, Dad had heeded whatever call motivated him these days. He was already in the kitchen, getting the bacon out of the fridge, when she arrived and donned her apron.

Breakfast would start in an hour so she didn't have to rush with the biscuits. But just as she pulled the butter out of the freezer, Nadia Kovic came sailing into the kitchen, the tails of her blouse trailing after her like a kite string. "Good morning," she said, her words thundering through Ashley's head.

The woman had boundary issues that had challenged Ashley's temper on numerous occasions. Nadia had poked her nose into every nook and cranny of the house and gardens. Looking for nonexistent specters or demons or whatever. Thank the lord, her reservation ran only through today, so she'd be gone by the noon check-out time.

This time, it took all of Ashley's fortitude not to growl at the woman. But then growling might have vibrated her skull, and that was to be avoided at all costs. Instead, Ashley gave her a thunderous look that should have reminded Nadia the kitchen was off limits to guests during breakfast hours.

But Ashley's stare of death bounced off the ghost hunter like bullets off Superman's chest. In fact, Nadia didn't even see Ashley's stare of death. Instead, the ghost hunter's catlike gaze focused on the coffee machine, which sat silent this morning on the gleaming kitchen counter.

"So, coffee machine is difficult," Nadia said, her gaze flicking from Ashley to Dad and back.

Dad nodded, muscles working in his square jaw. "I couldn't get it to turn on this morning," he said in a low voice.

"I thought you had it figured out. You just have to talk to it and wake it up gently," she said before realizing this sounded crazy.

"I know," he said. "But it scalded me yesterday." He extended his arm to show her a nasty-looking burn on his wrist.

"You didn't say anything."

He shrugged. "It's fine."

It didn't look fine.

"Is haunted," Nadia said with authority. "Is why you talk to it, yes?"

"Ah, n—" She cut off the negative word because Jackie chose that moment to come clumping down the stairs like a herd of buffalo. Boy, he was up early this morning. Why?

And then the front door opened, and Micah's voice wafted down the hall. "Good morning," he said, his footsteps sounding down the hallway. He entered the kitchen, which wasn't his usual MO. Usually, he went directly to the dining room, and he never arrived this early. But there he stood, looking big and handsome and priestly in his gray suit and black shirt and Roman collar.

Her girl parts reacted in a strange way.

But then Nadia turned to Jackie and said, "Ah, good boy. You got priest. We start now."

"Start what?" Ashley asked, the warmth in her core turning back to headache queasiness. "What is going on? Micah, why are you here so early?"

"Nadia wants to get rid of the demon in the coffeepot," Jackie blurted.

Ashley turned toward her son. His expression seemed dark and maybe even worried. What the hell had Nadia been saying to him? Ashley should have booted this woman out days ago.

"There are no demons in the coffeepot, Jackie," she said, and then turned toward Nadia. "I do not appreciate you filling my son's head with a lot of baloney about ghosts. I want you to leave, right now."

"I will leave, soon. But is duty to help you get rid of problem coffee machine."

"The coffeepot is not haunted. It's just old. I never asked for your help."

"No. But you live with demon machine. You need help. Tell me about this pot."

Ashley decided to stop arguing. Maybe if she played along, she could get the woman out of her B&B. "I purchased the machine from a restaurant in Charleston. I couldn't afford a new Bunn, so I bought the secondhand one. I got a good deal on it. The owner of the restaurant had just died. He'd had a massive coronary right in his kitchen, and..." Ashley's voice faded out. Wait a sec. Was it possible?

She looked toward Micah. "You don't think the coffeepot is haunted, do you? Please tell me you're not in on this."

Micah started talking a little too quickly. "Not exactly.

I mean, I did hear that some kind of exorcism was scheduled for this morning. I tried to give you a heads-up last night, but you must have had your phone on do-not-disturb."

"You promised not to tell her," Jackie said in an accusatory tone.

"Okay, everyone stand down," Dad said as if he were commanding a brigade or something. "Nadia, you're out. Jackie, you should know better than to go blabbing our business around town, especially to the minister. Go to your room. And—"

"Dad, shut up," Ashley said.

And, wonders of wonders, Dad stopped speaking. Ashley stared at her son. "You don't have to go to your room. I'm glad you talked to the minister about this." She didn't say the rest of what was on her mind. Clearly, Jackie had sought out Micah because no one here was listening to him.

"I think we need prayer, Father," Nadia said. "And then we talk to machine and solve problem. No need to worry. Will be quick."

Ashley glanced at the butter sitting on the counter and then up into the troubled face of her little boy. She hadn't been listening, or hearing, or paying attention to him. Maybe for his sake, she needed to go along with this insanity.

Maybe that's why Micah was here. Not to help with some stupid exorcism but to have Jackie's back.

"Okay, let's do this thing," she said. "But we need to make it snappy. My butter is melting, and I have biscuits to make."

"You're going along with this?" Dad asked.

"Yes, Dad, I am. Now be quiet."

The ghost hunter turned toward Micah. "A prayer please, Father? Nothing special needed."

Micah glanced at Ashley, as if asking her permission. Or maybe giving her a gut-check that this is what she really wanted. She nodded.

"All right," he said aloud. "How about this one?" And then he began to recite the Serenity Prayer. "*God, grant me the serenity to accept the things I cannot change; the courage to change the things I can; and the wisdom to know the difference.*"

It seemed apt given the circumstances.

"Now what?" Ashley asked when they'd all said "amen."

"Now you speak to machine. Tell spirit or demon to make less trouble."

"That's it? We aren't lighting candles or—"

"No need for that."

"Really?" Jackie asked.

Nadia nodded. "Is little-known fact. Demon or spirit needs to hear from person in charge. You tell it to go, and usually it does."

This was stupid on so many levels. But for Jackie she would go along with the play. She turned toward her Bunn coffee machine. "Coffeepot," she said, "I have a bed and breakfast to run, so be nice today."

"Really?" This from Dad.

"What?" she asked, glancing at her father, ready to go toe-to-toe with him.

"You need some assertiveness training," he said as if he thought this would actually work. It was almost hilarious. Except it wasn't funny at all.

She took a deep breath, put her hands on her hips, and was about to address the pot again when Nadia spoke.

"And talk to spirit, not pot."

"What spirit?"

"Of dead chef."

Oh great. This *was* dumb, and Ashley felt ridiculous as she sidled a little closer to the machine and started speaking. "Listen, Chef, you're not in your restaurant anymore. You're in my bed and breakfast, and when you screw up the coffee machine, my guests have to go without the elixir of life. I'm trusting that, as a person in food service, you understand what not having coffee can do to an establishment's reputation. Believe me, I've had a couple of very bad Yelp reviews about the coffee here. So either go into the light or shut up and get with the program, okay?"

"Now. Turn on machine," Nadia directed.

She leaned forward and flicked the tomato-red switch. The coffee machine came to life without any gurgles or noises or weirdness. It behaved entirely like a good-quality, commercial-grade drip coffee machine was supposed to.

"Spirit is gone," Nadia said.

"How do you know?" Jackie asked.

"I just do," Nadia said and then turned toward Dad with a hard stare. "No need to pay me for my services. Is what I do." She turned and exited stage left, leaving everyone in the room looking at one another, wondering what the hell had just happened.

* * *

Well, his fears were laid to rest. Nadia wasn't into some deep occult thing that he'd have to discuss with the bishop or the vestry. She was a fake. Jackie had called that one correctly.

But now Micah had an entirely different problem. He stood in the kitchen, his palm resting on the cool quartz countertop, studying the curve of Ashley's back, the flare of her hip where her long-sleeved T-shirt tucked into her jeans, and the shape of her backside. His mouth watered. His pulse climbed.

He needed more than the Serenity Prayer. He'd been praying for restraint and serenity for a while, and it wasn't helping.

It hadn't helped him make a relationship with Brooklyn. It hadn't forced Ashley out of his thoughts. It hadn't helped him forgive his parents.

But prayer had always provided solace. This failure put him on a collision course with his faith.

"Well," he said, "I should be going. It's—"

"You aren't staying for breakfast?" Jackie asked, longing in his voice.

That emotion triggered his guilt. He had to leave, which meant abandoning Jackie. But it couldn't be helped.

"I need to be going," he said.

Ashley nodded. "The minister is a busy man," she said.

And just like that, something changed. A few months ago, Ashley would have insisted on him staying for breakfast. Now she avoided his gaze, and the red in her cheeks gave her away.

He'd been battling his desire for a while, but Ashley had always been so wrapped up in her grief for Adam that she'd never noticed. There had never been a chance for him to cross any forbidden boundaries.

But things had changed. They'd danced at Daisy's party. They'd hugged on Tuesday. And now she wouldn't look him in the eye.

Dammitall. The walls seemed to be closing in on him. He needed out of this house.

"Sorry, Jackie, I'm really busy today. I'll see you at church," he said and hurried back down the hall and through the door.

He got into his Forester, his belly grumbling, but Bread, Butter, and Beans was off limits too. Annie served breakfast, but if he showed up there, he'd have to talk about the situation with Mom and Daddy, which would be like enduring a root canal.

He laid his head on the steering wheel as the hard truth dawned. Magnolia Harbor was haunted by ghosts and demons, and none of them could be so easily exorcised as the fake spirit in the coffee machine. He couldn't just address them and tell them to leave.

Mom could apologize, but he would have to forgive her. Brooklyn would always be embarrassed when he set foot in her coffee shop. And Ashley…

He heaved a long sigh. He hadn't done any damage yet, but if he stayed, he would. And then what? He'd lose everything.

He might have spent years in the navy traveling the world, but Magnolia Harbor had been home. He'd come back, so confident that he could bury the past. Sure he could find peace with the things he regretted.

But it wasn't possible. He'd found his limits.

How on earth could he minister to the mother he could never forgive? How could he be Ashley's pastor when he had to guard himself in her presence? And then there was Jackie. He hadn't kept his word to Jackie. He'd failed the boy too. It was impossible. It was wrong.

He fired up the SUV and drove all the way across town to the Starbucks, where he got himself a breakfast croissant and some coffee. The anonymity of the chain restaurant suited him. He found an easy chair and began surfing the webpages where Episcopal churches published job openings and calls for clergy.

Four years ago, he'd found the listing for Magnolia Harbor on this website and had decided that God had called him home. Now it was time to move on.

Chapter Thirteen

Ten days later, Magnolia Harbor hosted the interfaith youth service day, which every year focused on cleaning up the public marina and harbor, getting it ready for the summer that would soon be upon them. Every faith-based organization on Jonquil Island participated in the event.

Ken Nyberg, Heavenly Rest's youth ministry coordinator, had handled most of the heavy lifting for the event, but Micah and Rev. Pasidina from Grace Methodist had volunteered to be the clergy on-site, to help in whatever way was needed and to say the opening blessing and prayers.

Micah arrived at the public marina at seven thirty. Water droplets clung to the railings along the boardwalk, and the rain-soaked pier gleamed in the thin morning light. Lucky for the kids and volunteers, the rain had ended early in the morning and the skies had cleared. Even now, the early-March sunshine was beginning to warm things up. Spring was arriving as it always did, just in time for the rush of college kids that would descend upon them in a few weeks. As if to welcome them, the green tops of Jonquil Island's daffodils were beginning to show. In a few days, they would be in full, glorious bloom.

If only Micah's mood matched the fine spring weather. Instead, he seemed to be living under a dark, gray cloud most days, as he perused the various calls for clergy from around the country and dusted off his résumé.

There had been a job announcement in San Diego that had looked interesting. The weather there was beautiful all year round. But the rest of the offerings were not nearly as attractive. He'd sent his CV off to several churches from California to Maine, including a church in a tiny parish right smack dab in the middle of South Carolina.

That particular church, located in an out-of-the-way town with the improbable name of Last Chance, was probably his last choice. But it had the advantage of being close enough to drive home from time to time.

He didn't really want to leave Magnolia Harbor. But he needed to. For himself and for his parish. Last Sunday's fellowship hour confirmed it; he'd had to carefully negotiate the crowd to avoid spending time with either Mom or Ashley. He didn't want to spend the rest of his days doing that. And besides, it was dishonest and wrong.

He parked his SUV in the town lot and headed to the staging area by the public boat launch. A crew was already on the scene, hanging a big welcome banner that Bethel's Sunday school children had made for the event. And to Micah's surprise and pleasure, Colton was there directing a teenager on a ladder who might be Danny Beckett.

Micah had yet to meet the boy, although he had heard

that Colton had given him an internship of some kind. Not that Colton would admit out loud that he was doing a good deed in order to win the approval of a certain shopkeeper in town.

Kerri was on the scene too, looking a little harried and carrying a clipboard as she issued orders to the volunteers. Every once in a while, Colton would look in her direction with longing in his eyes. And, to Micah's amusement and satisfaction, Kerri sometimes returned the look. A little of his personal gloom vanished. Not everything in his life was coming apart at the seams.

Just then, Patsy Bauman materialized behind him carrying a plate of cupcakes. "Oh, Reverend St. Pierre, I need you."

"How can I help?"

"Ashley has a carload of cookies and cakes and whatnot that needs to be brought up here." She spun toward the parking lot, nodding. "She's over there. Go help her."

Micah took Patsy's commanding nature in stride most of the time. But for once in his life he wanted to say no. He couldn't help Ashley. And besides, what the heck was she doing here? Didn't she have a breakfast to make?

"Well, what are you standing there for?" Patsy said, clearly annoyed by his hesitancy. "We have a boatload of cakes to carry."

He appreciated the kick in the pants. He needed to get over this and manage his emotions until he found another church. And here was a perfect opportunity to prove that he could be an adult.

He belatedly headed toward Ashley's SUV. She'd raised the tailgate and was lifting some kind of sheet cake from the truck bed.

"Hi," he said with a lame wave. "I've been pressed into

service. Here, let me take that." Micah reached for the sheet cake, their fingers brushing in the exchange. The spring day turned suddenly hot and sultry, and his collar got two sizes too small. Sweat broke out on his brow.

He had to look down at the cake or get lost in her big brown eyes. The scent of peanut butter filled his nose. This must be one of Nancy Jacobs's famous peanut butter sheet cakes, a stalwart favorite at fellowship hour.

He tried to keep his gaze locked on the cake, but he failed. When he looked up, Ashley's cheeks had grown pink as if she too felt a sudden swell of heat. Was she having the same internal meltdown?

Not good. And yet, a part of him—the one he had no control over—regarded the idea of Ashley in meltdown as good news. This part of him wanted her to move through her grief and find happiness again. Having a meltdown would be progress, wouldn't it?

"I didn't think you'd be here today," he said. The words almost a confession.

"Oh, uh, well, Jackie is participating, and Dad's perfectly capable of managing breakfast on his own. So I agreed to run the bake sale when Ken twisted my arm."

"Right. Well, I'm here for the invocation and whatever anyone needs me for."

Her lips rose in a not-quite-full smile right before she said, "Oh good. I could use some help hauling cakes."

"No problem."

He turned, his arms filled with sheet cake, and headed toward the folding table under the welcome banner. He could not get roped into helping Ashley. It was clear he couldn't be an adult.

He set the cake on the table and looked down the boardwalk searching for someone else he could nominate for this job. Kerri and Colton stood farther down the dock consulting a clipboard, their heads closer together than was necessary.

He approached and said, "Hey, I could use some help. Ashley's got cakes and stuff out in her car. She needs a bucket brigade."

"Oh hey," Colton said with a gigantic smile. "I can't. Kerri needs help unpacking the trash bags and protective gloves. Danny and I are heading there now. We don't have a lot of time before the kids show up."

"I'm sorry, Reverend. I've got nineteen things on my to-do list. I'm sure you can manage a few cakes," Kerri said right before she grabbed Colton's arm and practically dragged him up the boardwalk toward Rafferty's, where a bunch of cardboard boxes had been dropped. The young man Micah had seen on the ladder was there opening them with a box cutter.

Great. This was a game of tag, and he was it.

So he turned around and went back to Ashley's car. In the space of the next ten minutes, he hauled a batch of Barbara Blackwood's lemon bars, Brenda Killlough's pecan brownies, and Jessica Martin's toffee squares. He'd given up sweets for Lent (along with inappropriate thoughts of Ashley Scott). The Lord was sure finding a way to tempt him this morning.

Especially when he ended up spending the next forty-five minutes with Ashley, arranging the pies, cakes, and cookies, writing out price tags, and counting the small bills in the cash box.

"I'm sorry, I thought Jenna was going to help me, but she's got morning sickness."

Of course she had. And besides, Jenna didn't belong to any of the faith groups hosting this event, so she didn't really need to volunteer. Except, of course, she always did volunteer.

He was there to serve and provide assistance as needed, so he tried his best to focus on the work instead of Ashley. But she'd shown up this morning like the epitome of the attractive church volunteer. She'd put her dark hair up in a ponytail that swished seductively and provided an unimpeded view of her adorable ears and long, graceful neck.

Her blue jeans took his breath away. They hugged her backside. They gave him impure thoughts. Even the arrival of Brooklyn hauling several portable containers of coffee didn't cool his jets. In fact, having a moment to compare the two women side by side proved deadly.

Brooklyn didn't stay long, thank the lord. Afterward, he focused on keeping his head down and his eyes straight ahead. Unfortunately, he kept bumping into Ashley in the confined space behind the counter.

After about fifteen minutes of this torture, Jenna finally arrived with a bright smile and a slightly green tinge to her face. "Hi, guys," she said, her gaze whipping from Ashley to Micah and back again. Something about that look set him off. Did she suspect?

The thought left him feeling as queasy as she looked. He gladly slipped from behind the booth. "Well, it looks like the cavalry has arrived. I need to go anyway. It's getting close to starting time, and I'm supposed to say the blessing."

"Thanks," Ashley said as he escaped.

"You're welcome," he replied mechanically.

But as he walked away, he heard Jenna say, "Boy, that must have been awkward."

"A little."

"So what did you decide?"

And Ashley said, "I'm going to meet him at a coffee shop on the mainland."

* * *

Ashley answered Jenna's question and watched Micah hesitate as he walked away. Had he overheard the conversation?

Well, maybe that was a good thing. After the last forty-five minutes, during which she'd nearly melted down every time he brushed against her, he needed to know that she was going out for coffee—*with someone else.* Someone named Ryan Balfour who had responded to the dating profile Ashley had posted a few days ago.

"I'm sorry I stranded you," Jenna said, her gaze following Micah as he walked down the pier. "How long were the two of you trapped here together?"

"Too long," Ashley muttered. "But I'm fine. Really."

Jenna gave her a disbelieving look.

"Okay, I'm not fine, but I will get over this," Ashley said.

Jenna opened her mouth and then closed it, as if she'd decided not to speak whatever she was thinking. Good. Things were hard enough without her best friend calling her out on her BS.

The crowd at the refreshment table began to thin as the time for the invocation and prayer arrived. Kids and adult volunteers moved down the boardwalk to the staging area. Jackie was down there with the group from Heavenly Rest, and Ashley was glad she had volunteered for the bake sale. She could remain right here and not have to deal with Jackie's sullen mood.

The boy had been increasingly incommunicado since the incident at the school several weeks ago. He was back in class but not happy to be there. And of course, he was upset about the whole ghost hunter thing. Nadia had mailed them a report on her investigation, which had concluded that there were no ghosts at Howland House. She had the gall to ask for a recommendation that she could use on her webpage.

It was bizarre. Almost as if the woman was on a mission to debunk every myth about haunted inns or something. In any case, Jackie was both humiliated because he'd fallen prey to the woman and ticked off that Dad seemed to think Nadia's report was the end of the conversation about the ghost of Captain William Teal.

So things were bad all the way around. They really couldn't get much worse. So why not go out on a date?

"So tell me about this online guy?" Jenna asked.

"He's a dentist."

"Oh." Jenna sounded less than enthusiastic, which was saying something because Jenna was a dewy-eyed optimist about everything. "Is he cute?"

"He's okay," she said, not quite telling the truth. The dentist wasn't all that cute, but at least he'd posted a real photo of himself. And he seemed to have a sense of humor, which was always good. But she doubted he was Mr. Forever. Not that she was looking for that. She wasn't exactly sure what she was looking for.

Just not a fling with her own minister.

A sudden influx of hungry customers abridged further discussion of her upcoming date with Dr. Ryan Balfour or her inappropriate crush on Micah St. Pierre. She and Jenna worked the booth until all the goodies were gone.

"I'd hang around, but to tell you the truth, I'm starving.

Jude said he'd meet me at Rafferty's for a cheeseburger," Jenna said when the last cake slide had been sold.

"Go. Eat. Don't throw up." Ashley said, with a smile.

When her friend had gone, Ashley eased herself down into a folding chair and started counting up the receipts while the kids and the other volunteers continued to scour the boardwalk and bayside beaches for trash.

"You have a minute?"

Micah's voice startled her. She stopped counting money and looked up at him. He leaned on the table, towering over her and invading her space in a not-entirely-unpleasant, but certainly unnerving way.

She dropped the bills back into the cash box and stood up, folding her arms across her chest, mostly so he wouldn't see how her nipples had reacted to the sound of his voice. She wore a padded bra, but still, folding her arms seemed like a wise thing to do. It kept her hands from reaching out and touching his face, or his hair, or any part of him.

Her heart started to dance the rumba in her chest.

This was utterly pathetic and adolescent.

"I've got a minute. I'm all sold out."

He mirrored her stance, arms across his chest. "Is it true that you posted a dating profile on Flirty and Forty?"

In a million years, she had never anticipated him asking a question like that. "Well, I don't see as how it's any of your business."

He took a little step back and broke his gaze. His arms came down as well. He rested his hands on his hips, the stance conveying his annoyance. Or something. What? Jealousy?

Oh god. No. Micah could not be jealous of her posting a profile on a dating app. No way. No how. Not good.

"You did, didn't you?" he asked.

"Well, yes."

"Why?"

"Oh for goodness' sake, Micah. For years, you've been pushing me to jump back into life. I can't even remember how many sermons you've delivered about moving through the hard times in life. So I'm on the move, okay? Although you do realize that it's not like I'll ever stop loving Adam. But why not go on a date now and again?"

He leaned on the table, shoving it back slightly. Ashley held her ground but tightened her grip around her ribs. Telling the truth would surely send him away, but it would also ruin so much.

The community's faith in him. His career. Her reputation. Everything. She could not tell the truth about her feelings. Ever.

"Is this about what happened the other night?" he asked, his voice low and husky.

She pressed her lips together.

"It is, isn't it?"

"Micah, really. It's none of your business."

He leaned a little closer until she caught the scent of his cologne or shampoo or whatever gave him that faint scent of vanilla bean. "It is, if I'm the reason. Those dating apps are dangerous."

She appreciated his worry, but really. "Micah, this is the twenty-first century. Everyone uses dating apps these days. Maybe you should too."

Before he could respond, someone down the boardwalk yelled, "Mrs. Scott, you better come quick. Jackie's gotten into a fight."

Chapter Fourteen

Jayden Walsh, who had spent the whole day calling Jackie an asswipe, finally struck. He'd waited until Jackie was on the beach picking up some really gross-smelling garbage from a spot not far from the public boat launch.

That was Jackie's first mistake. He'd allowed himself to get separated from the other kids and the supervising adults. The boat launch hid him from view, and Jayden chose that moment to exact his revenge.

Jayden hit Jackie from the blind side, knocking him down onto the sand and then giving him a couple of kicks to the ribs. When Jackie tried to get up, Jayden punched him in the nose and followed up with another blow to his eye socket. The pain burst in his head like fireworks on the Fourth of July. He collapsed back and ended up facedown, bleeding into the sand while Jayden cussed at him.

Sand and blood worked into his mouth, leaving his

tongue gritty and coppery with the taste of blood. He was going to cry. It hurt so much, but he held back, the pressure building in his chest, as he curled into a ball and waited for the next blow.

"Get off him, you dirtbag," someone said, and there were no more punches. He tried to open his eyes except the one Jayden had hit—that one was puffing out like a toasted marshmallow.

Someone—that Danny kid who had been helping out—had punched Jayden in the face and followed up by pushing him down to the sand while yelling at him for picking on someone smaller. It happened fast. One minute, Jayden was standing there, and the next, he was down on the sand, crying like a stupid, little baby.

Which made Jackie feel better about himself until he realized that Danny was probably going to get into big trouble for this. So he scrambled to his feet and yelled for help.

But he could have saved his breath because Mr. Colton had already seen what happened and came running down the boat ramp screaming Danny's name.

Mr. Colton was way bigger than either Danny or Jayden. So when he put himself between them, the fight ended. He grabbed both of them by their T-shirts and hauled them across the sand. He seemed really ticked off at Danny.

Which was really unfair. He was about to tell Mr. Colton that it wasn't Danny's fault when his knees kind of folded under him, and he collapsed to the sand and started throwing up.

Some time later—Jackie was a little fuzzy about how long—Ms. Kerri came, and she yelled for some ice and for someone to find Dr. Killough. And for a few minutes, the world was kind of a blur as grown-ups circled him, asked him questions, and pressed ice to his face. The doctor came and examined his eyes and told everyone that he didn't have a concussion, but he was going to have "one hell of a shiner" and would need an X-ray to tell if his nose was broken.

And then Mom arrived, and the pressure that had been building in his chest moved up into his throat. He was gonna cry. In front of everyone. And Mom would probably tell Granddad, and then Granddad would think he was a sissy.

"Oh, Jackie," Mom said, in *that* voice. She was angry. He was going to end up grounded for the rest of his life.

Jackie stared past his mother, refusing to meet her gaze. Across the sand, another knot of grown-ups had circled Jayden. He didn't look so good, either.

Danny, on the other hand, didn't looked damaged at all. He was standing with Mr. Colton, who was right up in his face, yelling at him.

Which was so unfair.

"Jackie, you look at me. You know how I feel about fighting. What is *wrong* with you?" Mom said in that salty voice. "I don't think violence solves problems. We talked about this."

The Rev came to stand behind her. He looked funny. Not exactly angry, though. Which was good, because getting on the wrong side of the preacher would probably be bad. He didn't really want to go spend any time in hell.

But he decided, right then, that he wasn't apologizing. Jayden was a bully who had destroyed a library book, gotten him suspended from school, and attacked him when no one was looking. He was not going to apologize for being beaten up by that jerk.

So he turned his back on his mother and The Rev, crossing his arms over his chest to keep the tears back. He had nothing to say to anybody *because no one listened to him anyway*. They would ground him and make him do chores and all that stuff. He'd do it. He didn't care. But he wasn't ever going to talk to Mom or The Rev again. He was angry with them for being stupid.

The knot in his throat got hard as ice, and the tears started in spite of his best efforts to hold them back. And then Mr. Colton turned away from Danny and came over and stood in front of him. For a second, Jackie thought he was about to get yelled at too, but instead, Mr. Colton gave his shoulder a big squeeze that almost hurt. "It's okay, little man. Danny told me the whole story."

"What story?" Mom demanded.

"Uh, Ms. Scott, this was not Jackie's fault. That kid, Jayden, started it. Danny saw it all. Jayden waited until Jackie was far away from the adults. I blame myself for that. But when Jackie got separated, Jayden jumped him and was giving him a beating before Danny broke it up."

"Colton, it doesn't look as if Danny broke up a fight. It looks as if he made a bad situation worse," Mom said.

Mr. Colton stared at Mom over Jackie's head. "Danny may have saved Jackie from being hurt worse than he is. Jackie is the victim here. You need to know that."

"Well," Mom said. "Maybe so. But he and Jayden got into it once before, and—"

Something snapped inside Jackie's head, and he turned on his mother. "I didn't start that fight either," he yelled, tears streaming from his swollen, burning eyes. "I was just reading during recess, and Jayden stole my book and tore it up, and I got mad. And I hit him. And I'm not sorry. And I'm not sorry for what Danny did to him either. He's a total asshole who picks fights with people for no good reason."

He screamed the last few words.

Mom stepped back, eyes wide. But The Rev stepped forward. "I guess that sucked big time," he said.

Jackie nodded, tears trickling down his face. Great. Now The Rev would know he was a sissy who couldn't even end his own fights. And he was really sorry he'd just yelled at Mom too. But he wasn't going to apologize.

He wanted to run away and hide. But The Rev took him by the shoulder and then pulled him, hard, into a big hug. His head came to rest on the minister's shoulder, and that's when he completely lost it. Sobbing like a stupid baby.

"You're going to be okay," The Rev said, his voice rumbling through his chest.

If only Jackie could believe that.

* * *

Kerri tried to keep her disappointment and worry in check. Never before in the history of the interfaith service project had kids gone home with black eyes and bloody noses. It was her fault. She should have taken that snot Jayden aside and put him in time-out or something.

The kid had a potty mouth and wasn't at all interested in the purpose of today's service project. He'd avoided work. He'd called several of the kids names. If Danny was to be believed—and she wanted to believe him—Jayden had singled out Jackie Scott for a thrashing when no one was looking. And a fight between six-foot Jayden and little Jackie, who was small for his age, was not a fair fight.

But the adults should have stopped it before it happened. *She* should have stopped it. And maybe it had been a mistake to bring Danny here today. He wasn't quite an adult, and he wasn't as young as the other kids, although Jayden Walsh and Danny were nearly the same size.

Kerri was worried about Danny's violent outburst. What had driven him to that? Had he been picked on as a child? Had he been abused? Or was this grief coming through as anger? It didn't matter. He should have called for help, not taken matters into his own hands. And certainly not that way.

All of it suggested that he needed more than the job Colton had given him. Although, in truth, over the last couple of weeks Colton had done more than give him a job. He'd been mentoring him. Making sure he got up on time, teaching him skills, and pushing him to go back to school.

Right now, Colton was down the pier doing an amazing job of supervising Jayden, who was sporting a split lip and a black eye. But Dr. Killough said the injuries were minor. Colton seemed to be having a heart-to-heart with the boy. She only hoped he was suggesting that maybe Jayden had brought this upon himself.

But she couldn't hear what Colton was saying. The boy seemed to be listening. Meanwhile Danny was nowhere to be found.

She couldn't go look for him. She had to supervise the kids until their parents picked them up, and of course there were several kids who had been upset by what had happened. She was giving them all a little talk about violence when a car door slammed in the parking lot and someone yelled. "Where is that little shit who beat up my son?"

So much for conversations about non-violence.

Everyone turned to watch Teddy Walsh, who had once played tackle for the Clemson varsity football team, sprint across the parking lot, heading right for Kerri.

Oh boy. This was not good. Teddy Walsh was a hometown hero for some people in this town, which probably explained why his son felt so entitled. He owned a lot of pricey oceanfront real estate and hobnobbed with all the right white folk, including all the snobs at the yacht club. He was a steward at Grace Methodist.

But if the gossip was to be believed, he was cheating on his wife. He reportedly had a girlfriend on the mainland who was twenty years younger than him.

Kerri had no sympathy for men like Teddy Walsh, no matter who he thought he was. His kid was a brat and a problem. And so was he. So she straightened her spine and got ready to be verbally tackled by a former defensive lineman for the Clemson Tigers.

He came barreling down the boardwalk, yelling as he approached. "My wife just called me and told me that Jackie Scott went after Jayden again. It's time for someone to take that boy over his knee and teach him a good lesson. I'm sure his daddy would do it if he were still here, but I'm ready to stand in. Where is that little brat?"

"Mr. Walsh, we've already had enough violence. Your son has broken Jackie's nose and given him a black eye. I think that's enough of a beating, don't you?" Kerri said in the mildest of tones.

The man stopped. "Well, good for Jayden. But my wife says he's got a split lip and worse. Let me tell you,

I'm not above suing Bethel Church for what happened here. I should never have allowed him to come to this thing this year with y'all in charge. This would never have happened if Grace Church's youth minister had been supervising."

Add racist to the list of Teddy's endearing qualities.

Colton must have heard Teddy's complaints because he sprinted up the boardwalk and intercepted the man, almost as if he was trying to protect her or something. "Whoa, now," he said in the calmest of voices. "There are lots of kids here, so you want to watch your language."

Teddy was a good two inches taller than Colton and much bigger around the chest and belly. He got right on him and pointed a finger in Colton's face. "Get out of my way."

Colton didn't move. Instead, he calmly said, "Mr. Walsh, with all due respect, Jayden hurt Jackie pretty badly. And while I understand they had a fight a while ago, Jackie was suspended from school and has provided restitution to the library for the book that was damaged. Now, you know and I know that Jayden damaged that book, don't we? Because Jackie would never damage a library book. So your boy had no cause to attack Jackie."

"You know that's not how it went down. Jackie tore up that book, and Jayden tried to stop him. And he got hurt for trying to do the right thing. I know my boy; he did not pick this fight. Where is Jackie Scott? I need to have a word with that kid."

Colton shook his head. "No, Mr. Walsh. Jayden beat Jackie bloody. Jackie didn't land one punch on him. Someone else broke up the fight."

"Who?"

"I'm not at liberty to say. But this could have been avoided if you'd teach your child some manners."

"Get the hell out of my way." Teddy pushed Colton back, and for an instant Kerri feared the adults might start throwing punches. But Colton kept his cool. He stepped back a pace and folded his arms over his chest, but he didn't turn away.

Right then, Rev. St. Pierre came up the pier to stand at his brother's side. "There are children here. Let's be adults," Micah said.

"Reverend," Teddy said with a modicum of respect that he hadn't shown to Colton. No doubt the man was smart enough to realize that verbally or physically assaulting a member of the clergy was beyond reason.

"Where is my son?" Teddy asked again.

"He's down the boardwalk with Dr. Killough."

"What are you going to do about this, *Reverend*?" Something about the way Teddy said that word made Kerri's nerves jangle.

"I'm going to escort you down to where Jayden is being taken care of."

"I don't need an escort." Teddy gave the word a nasty twist.

"Yes, you do."

At that moment, Jude St. Pierre came running down the boardwalk from Rafferty's, where he'd gone to have lunch with his wife. He came to stand shoulder-to-shoulder with his brothers. "I heard that y'all needed help," he said a little breathlessly, right before giving Teddy a solemn look. Jude, one of the most successful businessmen in Magnolia Harbor, was a member of the yacht club board. A positive sign these days, given that the yacht club had once been a bastion of whiteness. Jude crossed his arms over his chest and stared at Teddy with a solemn poker face.

Teddy Walsh was a lot of things; stupid wasn't one of them. Faced with overwhelming odds, a man of the cloth, and someone from the yacht club board, he backed down and allowed Micah to escort him down the boardwalk to get his child. They left without further incident.

And then Micah insisted on driving Ashley to the hospital to get Jackie's nose x-rayed, and Jude returned to Rafferty's, where his wife was watching the events from a table on the back patio.

The crisis was over. But Kerri still felt responsible. It should never have gotten so ugly. The rest of the event unfolded smoothly. All the kids were returned to their parents. The trash was bagged and loaded into a truck that hauled it away to the dump. Most of the other volunteers went home, leaving Colton and Kerri to fold up the bake sale tables and load them into Colton's pickup truck.

"How are you doing?" he asked as they rolled up the banner. It was the first moment they'd had to discuss what had happened.

"I'm worried. Do you know where Danny went?"

He shook his head. "After I spoke with him, he got on his skateboard and took off. I wanted to follow him, but..."

She nodded. "I know. It's probably a good thing he left. I wish he'd called for help instead of taking matters into his own hands. I guess I'm also a little disappointed in him."

"Disappointed?" Colton seemed surprised. "I caught the tail end of the fight," he continued. "And let me tell you, that Jayden kid had Jackie facedown in the sand and was kicking him in the ribs. I'll bet they find bruises all over his body. I don't know what might have happened if Danny hadn't stopped the fight."

"Yes, but he—"

"I know. He gave Jayden a black eye, but from what he told me, Jayden swung first."

"Yes, but. He should have just pinned him on the sand or something. And honestly, I heard what he was yelling at Jayden. Everyone heard. He seemed a little out of control."

"Okay. Maybe so. But he stopped Jackie from getting hurt. I don't think he hurt Jayden that bad, despite the way the boy wailed and carried on. That kid is a first-rate actor, Kerri. Doc Killough said he got away far less injured than Jackie. The doc is the one who suggested that Ashley take Jackie to the ER to be checked over."

Kerri shook her head. "It's all my fault. I should have put that brat into time-out or something. And I probably shouldn't have invited Danny."

"This was not your fault. Or Danny's. He's a good kid, Kerri. You're the one who told me that. So don't lose faith in him. He's going to need some protection because Teddy's going to find out what he did."

"You don't think Teddy would go after him, do you?"

"I don't know. I think Teddy is an—" He bit off the word, and a muscle flexed in his jaw.

She loved the fact that he'd swallowed down whatever cussword he'd been about to say. And she admired the way he'd stood up to Teddy Walsh. Not to mention the way he'd just taken Danny's side. Just because Colton had a reputation for being a player when it came to the ladies, it didn't mean he was all bad.

"It's going to be okay," she said, even though she didn't quite believe it.

Colton nodded. "It's going to be okay because we're going to keep an eye on Danny and make sure that jerk doesn't hurt him."

She inwardly shuddered at the thought that Danny might be in danger. Especially since there would be no possible way to keep tabs on the kid 24/7. But the intensity of Colton's words had her looking up into his intense gray-green gaze.

Her core melted. She could fall for him. Heck, she already had fallen for him. But this was more than mere sexual attraction. She could get all emotional about him. And that scared her and drew her toward him like a moth to a flame.

"What?" he said suddenly with a frown.

"I didn't say anything."

"No, but you cocked your head like you were *looking* at me." He gave her the tiniest of smiles, just a little hitch on one side of his beautiful mouth.

"And so what?" she asked in an altogether-too-flirty tone. "You're kind of pretty to look at."

"Pretty?" He sounded offended.

"What, too macho to be pretty?"

The smile blossomed into a wide grin. "Okay. I'll take that as a compliment. You're more than pretty, Ms. Kerri. And I was thinking just now, as I folded up that table, that I would dearly love to take you to Annie's for lunch."

"Ah, no. I need to get back to the store. Maybe some—"

"How about some other night? Dinner at Cibo Dell'anima."

Her heart danced, dammit. "Are you asking me out on a date, Colton?"

"I am. I'm hoping that I have redeemed myself."

She was tempted to quiz him to see if he understood why she had gotten so angry with him two years ago. But her heart wouldn't be in it. Because today, and for the last couple of weeks, he had redeemed himself.

By mentoring Danny. By committing to protect him. By quietly facing down Teddy Walsh, the most notorious bully in town.

Yeah. He had redeemed himself. But she had to remember that no man could totally live up to the whole Prince Charming thing. Colton still had a justly deserved reputation for being a player. So she had to guard her heart.

"I'll think about it," she said.

* * *

Hours later, after a long wait in the ER, X-rays, and a boatload of anxiety, Ashley slumped in the passenger's seat of Micah's ancient Forester. Jackie dozed in the back seat, zonked out on some pain meds. He had a big ugly splint on his nose where the doctor had done his best to reset the broken nose. Thank god, the X-rays showed no evidence of broken or cracked ribs.

Jayden Walsh had given Jackie a severe beating.

Ashley's eyes ached in their sockets from the tears she'd cried when she saw the bruises on her son's side. And within her, a deep-seated rage burned. How dare that little creep do this to her son.

Even worse, a deep pool of guilt threatened to drag her right into its depths. This was her fault. She had not listened to Jackie about the library book. Instead, she'd tried to maintain family peace and tranquility by allowing Dad to impose his own idea of punishment.

She should have fought for her son, instead of trying to maintain peace.

And wasn't this something she often did—failing to assert herself just to get along?

"You are not to blame," Micah said after many long minutes of silence. He was inordinately good at reading minds. But then Micah was familiar with her MO when it came to conflict. He'd called her out on it once or twice.

But he'd been mostly silent in the ER, which had been fine. She didn't need words. His steady presence had been a blessing and a comfort. Just as he'd been for Jackie in that moment right after the fight when Jackie had needed a shoulder to cry on.

But Jackie had cried on Micah's shoulder, not hers. She was grateful for his presence, and yet mortified that her little boy had needed to turn to someone other than her in that horrible moment of need.

"I know I'm not directly to blame," she said, her voice rusty and hard. "But I—"

"No buts. He's a small boy, and bullies love to torture small boys who like to read books. It's not your fault."

"You say that like it's a rule or something. Small boys shouldn't be bullied."

"No one should. But it's always the bully's fault, Ashley. Always."

"I should have listened to him."

"You are a good mother." He said the words like some kind of declaration.

If only she could believe it. Right now she felt like a failure in the one aspect of her life that really mattered—raising Adam's child.

They lapsed into silence for the rest of the drive back

to Howland House. When Micah pulled into the drive, he said, "If you give me your car keys, I'll arrange to have someone pick up your car at the town lot and drive it up here."

"You don't have to—"

"Yes, I do." His words had an unexpected intensity that cut off her argument. And right then she remembered the conversation they'd been having right before the fight. Her insides went into free fall. Maybe her adolescent attraction to Micah St. Pierre wasn't a one-sided thing. After this afternoon at the hospital, she could see how easily she might slide right into...

What? A relationship with him?

She stopped and imagined how things might have played out today if she'd had to face this crisis alone. And she knew. Yes, it would be nice to have that kind of rock-solid support and comfort on a daily basis.

It wasn't possible, of course. She couldn't allow it to happen. In fact, she needed to run away from it as fast as she could because the damage to Micah's career could be catastrophic.

She glanced his way as he set the parking brake. "Thanks. For everything. I wouldn't have wanted to be alone." And then she spoke to Jackie in the back seat. "Come on, buddy. We're home. Time to wake up."

When Jackie didn't immediately respond, she narrowed her gaze and watched his chest to make sure he was breathing. He was, thank god.

"He's zonked on the pain meds," Micah said. "I'll carry him up to bed for you."

"No, it's not—"

"I'll carry him up."

Ashley didn't want to argue with his tone of voice.

The minister carefully unbuckled the sleeping boy, hefted him into his arms, and carried him up three flights of stairs without even breaking a sweat or breathing hard. He laid Jackie on the bed in his garret room with such tenderness that it made Ashley's throat ache and tears threaten.

Memories played like a photo reel in her mind. Micah, playing catch with Jackie. Micah, teaching him how to shoot a basketball. Micah, helping him build a tree house in the back. Micah, coming to breakfast and giving Jackie his complete attention.

How had she missed this? Micah had been standing in for Adam. For years. Of course, he was a minister. He did those sorts of things for people. He even used his own pocket change to feed the new parking meters on Harbor Drive.

She should not read too much into this, and yet, how could she not?

Once Jackie was tucked into bed, she followed Micah back out onto Howland House's front portico.

"Before we were interrupted, you suggested that we needed to talk," she said. "I think maybe you're right. Let's take a walk in the garden. The daffodils are blooming."

She awkwardly took him by the arm and tugged him through the side gate into the rose garden, down the path past the rental cottage where Dad was staying, and out into the backyard.

Ashley had installed landscaping lights in the yard so guests could see their way out to the small beach at night. Tonight, some of the lights illuminated the daffodils, which grew in wild abandon all along the tree line near the ruins of Rose Howland's cabin. Ashley didn't know for certain, but rumor had it that these bulbs had been planted by Rose and Henri St. Pierre. They were beautiful, and despite all the worry and anxiety about Jackie, the sight of them lifted Ashley's heart a tiny bit.

"This spot always takes my breath away," Micah said, his voice low.

"Me too." She faced him, reaching for his hand. She'd never actually held his hand before. He had warm hands. Big hands. Rough hands. She forced herself not to compare them with Adam's. That would be stupid. But it was impossible. Adam was woven so tightly into the fabric of her life.

"So," she said, "you wanted to talk."

He pulled his hands away, jamming them into his pocket. "We can't do this, Ashley."

"What is this?"

"You know what I'm talking about..." His voice faded away, and his lips pressed together. He turned his back on her, and suddenly the warm day turned chilly. There was a cold breeze coming off the bay tonight.

She hugged herself to stay warm. "What, Micah? That you have feelings for me?"

"If I say the words aloud, then everything changes. Then I will have to—" He bit off whatever he'd meant to say.

But she understood. If they acknowledged whatever attraction had suddenly sprung up between them, then Micah would have to stop being her pastor. She wasn't entirely sure what that meant. Would he have to leave?

Her chest ached at the thought. So many people would be hurt if Micah had to go away to some other church. Pursuing this *thing* between them would be selfish and destructive.

And what if it didn't work out? She cringed at the thought. The altar guild had gone into matchmaking hyperdrive after Brooklyn refused his proposal. God help her if she dated him and they decided to break up later.

No. She couldn't deal with that.

"I understand," she said, but the words were not entirely true. She did understand on some cool, rational level, but her heart was cracking into little pieces. Her voice wavered as she continued, "You can't be involved with me. And to be honest, I'm not sure I'm ready to be involved with anyone. Not seriously, you know. That's why I've been exploring online dating. I need to have a social life. You know, get out and meet people."

Oh, the lies. She was ready to be involved with Micah. But it was impossible.

"Yeah, I guess that's true," he said, but the words fell flat. Maybe he didn't really believe her lies. Maybe he saw through her. They stared at each other. His face was in shadow, so she couldn't read the emotion in his eyes. But that was probably for the best. And she hoped he couldn't see the tears that had started to smear her vision.

The truth was heartbreaking.

She would never be able to give him another hug. She could never again safely invite him in for cookies and coffee. Breakfast oatmeal was off limits. She would have to forever keep her distance. She would have to let him go.

She didn't want to give up Micah St. Pierre.

But sometimes you didn't get what you wanted. Sometimes life handed you lemons. Sometimes people died. Sometimes things didn't work out.

She was strong. She'd learned how to swim the tides

of grief. She could weather this. She would go on. One day, she would be able to laugh about this. Or smile at least. That was the way loss worked.

But not tonight. Tonight she would have a real good cry.

"Good night, Micah. Thank you for everything," she said, her tone studiously cool as she fought back the tears.

He nodded and then walked away.

Chapter Fifteen

On Tuesday, Jackie kept watch out of his bedroom window, which provided an eagle's view of The Rev's house on the other side of the street, as well as the inn's parking lot. He'd been waiting all morning for Mom's regular Tuesday grocery store run. It was well after eleven before she finally left the house.

Once she pulled out of the lot, Jackie tiptoed down the stairs, snarfed up the cookies Mom had left on the kitchen counter for the guests, and then escaped through the front door because Granddad wouldn't even notice someone opening and closing that door. The guests came and went all day.

It was warm outside, making him dream of summer, when there would be no school for weeks and weeks. He'd stayed home the last few days, letting Mom fuss over him. But tomorrow he had to go back. And Jayden would be waiting for him.

He couldn't refuse to go back, otherwise Granddad

would probably send him away to a military academy on the mainland. He'd overheard Mom and Granddad taking about this last night. Granddad had been talking really loud, but then he did that 'cause he was deaf as a stone.

So life sucked. He didn't want to think about tomorrow and all the ways Jayden was going to make his life a misery. He just wanted to get out of his bedroom and forget about all the bad things that were going to happen at school tomorrow.

He headed down Rose Lane to Palmetto Street and one block over to Lavender Lane. His feet had brought him here, right to the corner where the library stood.

But he couldn't go in the library. He didn't have a card anymore. And Mrs. Wilson hated him now because Granddad had made him apologize for the book. Of course he was really, really sorry about the book, but Mrs. Wilson thought he was the one who had ripped it up. Almost everyone did.

Not The Rev, of course. And maybe not Mom. She'd said something about it yesterday that suggested she had never believed Liam's lie about the book. But Mrs. Wilson, the librarian, believed it.

The thought left a lump in his throat. He stared up at the library, a deep longing surging through him. But he couldn't go in. So he crossed the street and headed into the park, past the ball fields and down to the terrain park.

Last Christmas, he'd asked for a skateboard, but he'd gotten a new bike instead. Mom thought skateboards were dangerous. She wouldn't even let him go to the skateboard derby at the church a couple of weeks ago.

If he had a skateboard, that's what he'd do today. He'd spend the whole afternoon practicing tricks. But he didn't have a board, so he'd have to settle for watching the other kids.

But the terrain park was quiet at eleven thirty in the morning. All the other kids were in school. Except for...

Wait, the kid doing tricks looked familiar. It was Danny. The one who had kicked Jayden's ass.

He was wicked good, riding the board up and down over the terrain, popping the board up like it was nothing. Jackie found a park bench and watched while he ate Mom's cookies.

After a little bit, Danny noticed him and came over.

"Want a cookie?" He offered the last one. "They're homemade."

"Yeah, sure. Thanks. Boy, you got a couple of really bad shiners," he said. "Are you okay?"

"I'll live. Thanks for kicking Jayden's ass."

"Yeah." The kid slouched back on the bench and aimed his face at the sun as he munched his cookie. "My mom used to make cookies like this," he said.

"Why'd she stop?" Jackie asked.

Danny straightened up. "She died."

"Oh. I'm sorry. My dad died. A long time ago. I don't really remember him. He was in the army."

"That sucks. Sorry. My mom and dad died in a boating accident. I live with my grandma now. She's sick all the time so she doesn't bake cookies. Doesn't even have them in the house 'cause she's diabetic."

They sat for a long time without saying much. But Jackie didn't feel like he needed to talk. Danny got him, and he got Danny. Like they were connected or something. Losing a mom or dad changed everything.

"I guess you got to skip school on account of your nose, huh?" Danny finally asked.

"Yeah. Mom doesn't know I left the house, though. I needed to get out. Hey, could you teach me to skateboard?"

"You don't have a skateboard?"

Jackie shook his head but didn't explain the reasons. Danny probably already thought he was lame, seeing as Jayden beat the crap out of him.

"Sure. Come on."

For the next hour, Danny taught him how to scoot along and pop an ollie. He fell a couple of times, busting the knee of his jeans. But it was great fun.

After a while, they walked down to Harbor Drive, and Danny bought him an ice cream. It was kind of a positive sign that the ice cream shop was open now. It meant summer was coming.

They sat on a bench looking out at the bay, and finally, between licks of rocky road, he gave voice to his biggest fear. "I don't want to go back to school. Jayden's gonna kill me."

"Yeah, well, you should stay in school, man. And Jayden isn't going to kill you. But if he hits you again, you tell someone," Danny said. "Or you can tell me. I'll beat his ass again."

"Really? But I saw Mr. Colton. He bawled you out for hitting him. It's like Jayden gets away with crap because he's Mr. Walsh's son and everyone loves Mr. Walsh 'cause he played football at Clemson."

Danny nodded. "Yeah. I know. I pissed off Mr. St. Pierre. He said he was really disappointed in me, but it doesn't matter." Danny's mouth twisted up into a funny shape, and Jackie got the feeling that maybe Danny did care what Mr. Colton thought about him.

"Come on," Danny said. "I'll show you how to jump

down the steps from Harbor Drive to the parking lot." The bigger boy picked up his board, and Jackie followed, finishing up the last of his ice cream and wiping his sticky fingers on his jeans.

Doing tricks down a staircase seemed kind of dangerous. But then again, he was a dead boy walking so maybe it didn't matter. Maybe he could break his arm or something, and then he wouldn't have to go to school tomorrow.

But they didn't get that far. As they turned the corner onto Harbor Drive, Ms. Kerri came dashing out of Daffy Down Dilly and got right up into Danny's face.

"What in the Sam Hill are you doing out here at one in the afternoon when you're supposed to be at work with Mr. St. Pierre? I went out on a limb to get you that job with St. Pierre Construction, and you not showing up for work makes me look bad. Do you understand that?"

Oh boy, she was really ticked off. And it sounded like Danny had skipped his job today, which was kinda bad. Especially since he worked for Mr. Colton, who was really nice and The Rev's brother and all. But then again, he understood. Mr. Colton was disappointed in him because he'd stopped Jayden on Saturday.

And so, really, Danny being in trouble was all Jackie's fault.

"Why aren't you at school?" Ms. Kerri asked, jolting Jackie from his thoughts.

"Mom let me stay home, you know, because of my nose," he said.

She gave him the once-over and noticed the hole in his jeans. And maybe a little bit of the blood from the scrape on his knee. "Does your momma know you're out here skateboarding without kneepads and a helmet?"

"Well..."

"Uh-huh. I figured as much. Go home, Jackie." She turned toward Danny. "And you, young man, you get your butt in here. We need to have a long conversation about responsibility."

But before Ms. Kerri had even finished speaking, Danny slammed his skateboard onto the sidewalk and escaped down the street.

"Dammit," Ms. Kerri said under her breath as she watched him sail down Harbor Drive, bobbing and weaving around pedestrians.

She turned around and frowned at Jackie. "Are you still here? Go home. You've already done enough damage."

He blinked for a moment, her words like a physical blow. What had he damaged now? He didn't know, but he was so tired of people blaming him for the book Jayden had ripped up.

Except, of course, it was his fault that Danny had lost his job with Mr. Colton.

So he turned and ran all the way back to the inn. Where Granddad was waiting.

* * *

Ashley was fit to be tied. Her son had run away, gone skateboarding, scraped and bruised his knee, and had evidently, according to the phone call she'd gotten from Kerri Eaton, been hanging around that boy Danny Beckett. Evidently Kerri had adopted the troubled kid and was trying to make a difference in his life. Good for her.

And Ashley was grateful that Danny had come to Jackie's defense on Saturday, but she was uneasy with the fact that Danny, who was six or seven years older than Jackie, would want to hang out with her son. What was up with that? Jackie hadn't once mentioned this boy's name. And today he left the house without telling anyone where he was going and was discovered downtown with this kid.

Was he good influence or a bad one? Ashley didn't know.

She was at her wit's end over Jackie. Since when did he go around picking fights with other boys? And these worries sucked away any excitement she might have felt about her date with Ryan the dentist.

Especially since their casual coffee had morphed into dinner at a fancy restaurant because Ryan had had an emergency root canal that tied him up all afternoon.

She should have said no. But she'd agreed to the date *before* she'd come home and found Jackie sitting in the library with a skinned knee, a guilty expression, and Dad looming over him.

And now here she stood in the parking lot of the Moonlight Bay Grille about to meet a strange man and have a date for the first time in decades.

The Grille, as folks liked to call it, had been a staple of Georgetown, South Carolina, dining for decades. Ashley had only eaten at the seafood restaurant once, ages ago when she and Adam had come to South Carolina for a visit. Jackie had been six months old and had stayed with Grandmother.

She hadn't remembered it being so dark inside. But then the last time she'd come to this restaurant, it had been with her husband. She remembered the evening as romantic. Tonight the dining room seemed cave-like. She could barely read the menu.

And Ryan Balfour turned out to be shorter, balder,

and fatter than his profile picture on Forty and Flirty. But what the hell. She wouldn't judge the book by its cover. She'd liked his sense of humor in his texts and emails. And he had a nice voice over the phone.

Still, a sense of wrongness settled in as she gazed across the pristine white tablecloth at Ryan. What was she doing here with this stranger? Why wasn't she home with Jackie? How had she ever arrived at this place in her life?

Where the hell was Adam? Where the hell was her happily ever after?

Served her right for believing she deserved one.

But she plastered a smile on her face and tried to enjoy herself.

"So I imagine it's hard to get away when you own a bed and breakfast?" Ryan said.

It was a good conversation starter. He was divorced, so he probably had a lot more experience dating than she did. And it was nice that he'd started out by asking about her life. It seemed kind or something.

So she explained about Dad and how he was living with her now, practically running the inn by himself. How had she let Dad get so involved? She had too much time on her hands these days. Too much time to think, and to worry.

About Jackie. And Micah St. Pierre. She'd spent a lot of time, today especially, thinking about him. How he'd been at the hospital, about their halting conversation the night of the fight.

She didn't talk about any of this to Ryan, of course, but Micah weighed heavy on her conscience when she forced a smile and said, "It's much better now that I have help. You know, when I started, a lot of other innkeepers told me it was insane for a single mother to become an innkeeper."

He blinked. "You have a kid?"

He seemed so surprised that it startled her. Had she not mentioned Jackie to Ryan? She'd certainly mentioned him in her dating profile. Had Ryan not read it all the way through? Damn. What did that mean?

A weird discomfort settled in her gut as she said, "I'm sure I told you about Jackie. He's a funny kid. He's eleven now, and sure the inn is haunted." Somehow talking about Jackie's ghost seemed safer than mentioning how he'd been recently suspended from school or the fact that her own father thought he needed to be sent off to military academy. Not that she would ever do such a thing. But still.

"Oh really? So your inn is haunted. That's handy," Ryan said, rattling the ice in the scotch he'd ordered when they first sat down. The ice-rattling was super annoying.

Ashley sipped her water, wetting her parched throat. "Handy how?" she asked.

"I'm sure you can charge a premium if you advertise that the inn is haunted."

"I don't advertise the fact."

"Why not? Is there really a ghost?" The skepticism in his voice rang like an alarm bell.

Maybe two or three weeks ago she might have simply said no, but Jackie was home with a broken nose, bruised all over, and clearly angry about a lot of things, chief among them his ghost. So she wasn't going to throw her troubled child under the bus with the stranger. She was going to back him up as best she could. "I've never seen the ghost. But my son says he's real," she said without any smile or waver in her voice.

"Really?" More ice-rattling. Ryan's voice dripped with a kind of cruel skepticism.

"Really," she said. "It's the ghost of Captain William Teal."

"The pirate?" He laughed out loud. "You're pulling my leg, right?"

Something snapped. "Look, Ryan, there's something you should know about me. I'm one of Captain Teal's descendants."

"What? Really?"

It occurred to her that she'd never once identified herself that way. She'd always thought of herself as Rose's descendant. But the captain was her great-great-something-grandfather.

The waitress came by with his appetizer. He ordered another drink, and she asked him about his dental practice, just to change the subject.

Big mistake. He talked on and on about dental implants. And when the waitress returned, he ordered another scotch.

He continued to talk about his business, giving broad hints about his net worth, the size of his house, his boat docked somewhere close by. Ashley picked at her food. The salmon was fine but she'd lost her appetite.

"What's the matter?" he asked. "Is the salmon bad?"

"No, it's fine. I just—"

"Hey." He whistled and snapped his fingers at a passing waiter—not the one who had been helping them. When the young man came by, he pointed at her plate. "This salmon is unacceptable. It's overcooked, as anyone can see. I ordered it medium rare, and this is well done. Take it back and bring another."

"No, really it's fine," Ashley said, her face flaming hot.

"If it's not right, I'm happy to—"

"It's fine, really."

"Ashley, don't be a doormat. Clearly you don't like the fish and—"

That was it. She'd had enough, so she got up out of her chair with a short apology to the poor waiter before she turned on Ryan the dentist. "Don't tell me what I think. I can think for myself. And honestly, what I'm thinking right now is that you drink too much, have a swollen head, and are rude."

She picked up her purse and marched herself right out to her car. Ryan, who clearly had not read her dating profile, didn't follow her, thank god.

* * *

Kerri had tried mightily to resist Colton St. Pierre, but after days of saying no to his dinner invitations, she finally relented. Not because he was as handsome as sin. And not because she remembered the way the man could make her body sing.

No, she relented because this afternoon, when she'd called him to say that she'd seen Danny with Jackie Scott, Colton had dropped everything and chased the boy down to the skateboard area at the park.

He'd dropped his busy schedule to sit for an hour talking to the boy. Kerri didn't know all the details of that conversation, but Colton had swung by Daffy Down Dilly late Tuesday and asked her out in person.

And she'd relented.

And now here she was, walking into the fanciest restaurant in town, on the arm of Magnolia Harbor's most eligible bachelor.

Cibo Dell'anima sat on the corner of Ash Street and Harbor Drive. Until recently, this neighborhood, on the south side of town and across the street from the fish market, had been devoid of nice places to eat. But Magnolia Harbor kept growing as more beachfront property north of town was developed into high-end rental properties.

The kind of properties Colton built. And Teddy Walsh bought and rented. Men like Colton and Mr. Walsh came from opposite sides of the tracks, but both had gotten rich on real estate. It was enough to make Kerri reevaluate her investment portfolio.

Especially when Colton showed up at her door on Wednesday evening, driving his brand-new Audi instead of a St. Pierre Construction pickup. He wore a suit and tie and presented her with a bouquet of pink roses. And now he was holding the door to the restaurant, pulling out her chair, and allowing her to select the wine.

Which was ridiculously overpriced. But by all accounts, the place did a land office business with the wealthy tourists that flocked to those new developments.

The menu billed itself as a fusion of Italian and American soul food, but it wasn't quite either of those. She ordered corn bread with spin rosso, sorghum, green garlic, brown butter, and whipped ricotta as her antipasto, and casonsei pasta stuffed with chicken and mascarpone for an entrée.

Colton ordered a steak.

When the entrées and wines had been selected and ordered, the waiter left them, and suddenly Kerri had nothing else to distract her. She had to acknowledge that she not only found Colton hot and attractive but also admired him. She admired his success, and mostly, she admired the way he hadn't given up on Danny when things had gone sideways.

She didn't want to imagine him as some kind of Prince Charming. But she could feel herself being sucked right into the romance of this situation. She was such a sucker for romance too.

"So," Colton said, breaking eye contact and staring down at his hands, which were resting on the table. They were beautiful hands. Big, masculine, with close-cropped nails. The palms were rough. She would never forget them sliding over her skin.

"So," she responded when the silence stretched into the awkward realm.

He hunched his shoulders and leaned forward a bit. "Um, look, I want to say that I'm sincerely sorry for messing up that summer when we went on the sunset cruise. I guess I didn't have my head on straight back then. I guess I didn't..."

His words faded away, leaving Kerri hanging. She waited for him to finish, but the silence hung like a cloud.

Dammit. He still didn't understand, did he? She needed to watch her heart with this man.

"I'm curious," she said. "Of your last few relationships, how did each of them end?"

His head moved back. "What?"

She shrugged. "It's a simple question. How did each of your past relationships end?"

"Well, uh..."

She leaned forward. "Have you ever had a long-term relationship?"

He leaned way back and rubbed his hand over his close-cropped hair. "Well, uh..."

"No?"

The waiter arrived with the wine and saved him. She decided not to quiz him again. He didn't have a clue.

But when the waiter left, he picked up his wineglass, took a healthy gulp, and then leaned forward. "I haven't done relationships. But you know this already."

"Yeah, I do, Colton. Because you ghosted me after you took me on that romantic sunset cruise. You didn't call or text. Nothing for a week or more."

His gaze roamed to the window, which provided a dark view of the lights at the commercial pier where the shrimpers sold their daily catches. "You're right, I didn't call. And I guess that is my usual MO. I'm sorry."

This time the apology sounded sincere, but unfortunately, she was a sadder, wiser girl.

"On the other hand, you never called me either," he continued, his gaze zipping back to hers. Oh boy, those green eyes of his could really shine with intensity.

"Uh, well, I guess—"

"No guessing. I didn't call you for a few days. I was going through some things at the time, and I was a little confused. But you didn't call me either. I thought, well, hell, she doesn't like me much."

"You thought that?"

"Yeah, actually I did. I kind of felt dumped. I walk into the shop one day to talk to you, and you just took after me for no apparent reason. So yeah, I figured you were not interested. Are you interested?"

Once again, the waiter's timing was flawless. He arrived with the antipasti, giving her a moment to regroup.

When the waiter finally left, she gazed down at her perfectly presented plate and had trouble finding her appetite. She studied the food for a long time without eating until she finally worked up the nerve to raise her head and ask, "Why didn't you, I don't know, come back and try again? Did you think I was more trouble than I'm worth?"

The corner of his mouth lifted a fraction. "No. Not then and not now. I thought..." He stopped talking.

"What?"

"I thought I wasn't good enough for you." His voice was low.

Holy crap. "Why?"

He shrugged. "I was a screwed-up kid like Danny once. And I made a bunch of gigantic mistakes that have kind of followed me around. And you're... Well, you're beautiful, and smart, and you have a master's degree in business. And here I am, like Danny. I had to earn a GED and pull myself up by the bootstraps."

"Oh, Colton. You're a huge success." She slid her hand over his, the touch igniting her. "I should have called you," she said, her heart thumping hard in her chest. "I..."

"What?"

"Well, if we're going to be honest about past relationships, my marriage ended when I caught him in bed with my best friend. So I'm a little gun-shy, okay? And sometimes I judge too quickly."

"You were married?"

She nodded. "Yeah. I don't talk about it. I was young and just out of college, and I married a Morehouse Man and I thought I was set for life. But it didn't work out that way. So, for the record, your college education is not necessarily an indication of your worth."

He smiled. "Thanks for sharing that. You know, it's kind of crazy. When you first asked me about my relationships, I thought I was in deep, deep trouble. But right now, I'm thinking that maybe it's better to get all that stuff out of the way right at the start. So we can be honest."

Her mouth went dry as she stared into Colton's gray-green eyes. Who was this man? He was doing a great job of sounding reasonable and mature and exactly like the man of her dreams. If only she could trust that he was real and not some fantasy she'd made up in her own mind.

Chapter Sixteen

Micah stood in front of his mostly empty refrigerator contemplating dinner. Unlike Mondays, Tuesday evenings were mostly free. He'd even escaped the paperwork at the church office this afternoon and had gotten in a workout at the gym. He was freshly showered now, wearing his civvies, and feeling proud of himself for actually getting in a few push-ups.

It would be stupid to go to Rafferty's for a steak after all that work. Besides, he had plenty of TV dinners in the freezer. He just wasn't enthused about any of them. He wasn't enthused about much, really.

Life had been difficult the last few days, especially Sunday. For the first time in forever, Ashley had been missing at services. Patsy had told him she was staying home to be with Jackie, which made sense. But he missed her with an urgency that demanded action on his part.

But Mom *had* come to services, slinking into the back

pew and slouching down as if hiding from him. That made him feel even worse. She shouldn't feel that way about church. And whose fault was that? Not hers.

He needed to give her forgiveness. He preached forgiveness all the time. It was at the heart of his faith. But he couldn't forgive his mother. He couldn't escape his attraction for Ashley Scott.

And that meant he couldn't continue as the rector of Heavenly Rest. The best thing for everyone would be for him to tender his resignation, allow the vestry to form a search committee, and continue his job search.

To that end, he'd sent his résumé off to no less than six church search committees in the last two days. Most of these churches were out of state, including the one in San Diego and another in Bangor. Maine sounded beautiful but cold.

He opened the freezer drawer and contemplated his choices: Salisbury steak, lasagna, or a pint of Ben & Jerry's. The ice cream called to him, but he settled on the lasagna.

He had just popped the dinner into the microwave when his phone rang. This happened with great regularity. He picked up his cell. He didn't recognize the number.

He connected the call.

"Rev? Are you there?"

It was Jackie Scott, whispering. "I'm here," he answered. "What's wrong, Jackie?"

"I only have a second. Granddad went to the bathroom. I'm using the office phone. I need to talk to you. Can you come over? Now?"

He pushed the button on the microwave, stopping it. "I'll be there in a minute."

"Don't tell Granddad I called. Bye." The boy rushed

the words at the end, suggesting that his grandfather had just finished in the bathroom.

Micah threw on a jacket and crossed the street. It was after seven in the evening, so this would be okay. Ashley was clearly at her regular Tuesday-evening Piece Makers meeting. The coast was clear.

He hesitated at the inn's front door. Should he knock or just walk in and tell Andrew Howland that he'd come to have a chat with Jackie? He opted for the latter course and opened the door.

Andrew was in the inn's small office on the ground floor. The one with the landline that Jackie had just used for his mayday.

Micah walked down the hall and peeked into the office, where Andrew sat with his back to the open door watching a video on his laptop. Ashley's father had evidently not heard him, and he remembered something Ashley had said about him being hard of hearing.

Old home videos played on the computer screen, and Micah stepped forward, recognizing a young Ashley, maybe nine or ten, her dark ponytail swaying as she tugged at the arm of an older woman with the same dark hair.

"Come on, Mommy," she said with a bright, happy laugh. "Last one in is a rotten egg." She let go of her mother's hand and raced down the path to the small beach behind Howland House. "Come on, Andrew," the woman said.

Andrew stopped the video just as the woman was turning away, a smile on her face, the wind in her hair. Ashley's mother had been a beautiful woman. Just like her daughter.

He swallowed down an aching sadness. He couldn't

say he understood Andrew's grief, because Micah had never loved anyone that way. He'd had a few girlfriends over the years, but nothing permanent. The life of a navy chaplain had been hard on relationships.

He knocked on the doorframe loud enough for Andrew to hear it. The man bolted upright in the office chair and shut the laptop as if he'd been caught doing something embarrassing.

"Sorry," Micah said. "Didn't mean to intrude."

Andrew swiveled around. "I didn't hear you come in."

"Stealth priest," he said, leaning into the doorframe.

"If you're looking for Ashley, she's not—"

"I know, it's Tuesday. She's off quilting. I—"

"Oh, she's not at the Piece Makers meeting. She went out on a date. With a dentist named Ryan." Andrew smiled. "She needs to get on with her life."

Whoa, what was that? A warning? Or was his own guilt reading something into Andrew's words that wasn't there? Obviously, Ashley needed to move on to whatever was next in her life.

It just wouldn't be him. And besides, this house call wasn't about Ashley at all. "I stopped by to talk to Jackie."

Andrew's face grew tight. "He's in lockdown."

"Lockdown? Really?"

Andrew's jaw tightened. "Yeah. The kid sneaked out this afternoon when he was supposed to be recovering from his injuries. He didn't ask permission, and Kerri Eaton discovered him hanging out with that Danny Beckett boy. Now what the hell does an almost-grown teenager want with my grandson? That's what I want to know."

"Maybe Jackie was simply thanking Danny for coming

to his defense," Micah said, his concern over Jackie's phone call rising.

"Yeah, well, I told Ashley she should enroll the boy in a self-defense program. He needs to grow a backbone, that boy."

Micah had to bite his lip not to argue. It was not his place to argue. But if Andrew Howland thought Jackie needed a backbone, he'd missed something. Jackie was tenacious, and curious, and funny, and kind. "Well, maybe I can help. I came by to see how he was feeling. May I speak with him?"

"Of course you can. He's up in his room. You know the way."

Micah turned toward the stairs but hesitated a moment. "You know, Andrew," he said, "the church has a bereavement group for people who have lost their spouses. It meets every Thursday evening at six. The door's always open."

"I don't need any of that crap," Andrew said, and Micah didn't argue.

Instead he headed up the stairs to Jackie's room. The boy was waiting for him.

"What's the matter?" Micah asked. One look at the boy's battered face made something break inside Micah's chest.

"You have to help Danny," he said, his voice agitated. He was pacing back and forth.

"Okay. I've been trying to help him. But what especially can I do?" he asked.

"He lost his job because of me. And all he did was keep Jayden from killing me. And honestly, I don't know what I'm going to do tomorrow. I'm going to die. Will you bless me or whatever. 'Cause—"

Alarm shot through Micah like a jolt of electricity. The child's words were so stark and disturbing. Of course Jackie was terrified. Jayden had broken his nose and sent him to the hospital where he'd been poked and prodded. Why hadn't Micah seen this coming? He should have. But he'd been too wrapped up in his own problems.

"Whoa now, Jackie, no one is going to die tomorrow," he said. "I can see you're scared. And you have a good reason for that. So let's sit down and talk about what we're going to do about it, okay? I promise you I'll keep you safe."

The kid nodded, his chin quivering as he flopped down onto his bed. Micah picked up the desk chair, moved it to the bedside, and sat down in it backward. "I'm listening, Jackie," he said.

And Jackie started talking, the words flowing from him like a river, as tears leaked from his bruised eyes.

* * *

It was barely eight when Ashley arrived back at the inn. No doubt Dad would be waiting in the office with a million questions about the dentist, especially since she'd left her date early. Maybe she should have gone to the Piece Makers meeting instead of coming home.

No. They would have grilled her too. Dad had blabbed his mouth about the dentist during fellowship hour. So the quilters were well aware that they'd been ditched for a man.

They'd also give her dating advice, as if the over-seventy crowd had any meaningful relationship tips for her. Oh, lord help her, she didn't need a dating app now.

Now that the church ladies had whetted their appetite with Micah, they'd get busy working on her too.

Would they add up two and two? Heaven forbid.

She parked the car in its reserved spot and sat there for a long moment, thinking about taking a walk across Lilac Lane and having another talk with Micah.

It was an insane idea this time of night. And besides, he was probably off at a meeting, or dealing with a crisis, or visiting a troubled soul. The man never rested.

A familiar concern filled her heart and mind. Back in the days when Micah had come to breakfast a few times each week, she could make sure he got some decent nutrition. But he'd been eating Brooklyn's croissants for nine months, and it showed around his waistline. She was willing to bet there were some nights when he ate ice cream for dinner. She'd caught him doing that once.

Dammit. If he didn't take care of himself he would end up with diabetes or something. The urge to cook him a decent meal and leave it on his doorstep became almost overpowering.

She almost got out of the car and went right into the kitchen. But halfway to the inn's door, she reconsidered. Cooking for Rev. St. Pierre would probably be unwise, even though Grandmother had gotten away with cooking for old Rev. Ball. But by then Grandmother and Rev. Ball were in their seventies, and…

Wait.

Holy crap, had Grandmother and Rev. Ball had some kind of wild senior citizen secret love-thing going?

The thought left Ashley queasy. Dad was always telling her she was too much like Grandmother. Was she really?

Maybe.

But she was not going to have an affair with her minister, even if the attraction was mutual. And besides, she couldn't exactly have a secret love-thing going with Micah when he wanted and needed a wife.

And she did not want to be married again, especially to a man who was required to go wherever his calling led him. She'd been there and done that and had the T-shirt, and many scars on her broken heart to prove it.

She'd traipsed after Adam like a good army wife, the same as her mother had with Dad. And she'd been happy and in love and never regretted any of that.

But that was her old life. Her new life was here in Magnolia Harbor, settled in one place, where her family had lived for generations. She loved owning her own business. She did not want to tie her life to another man.

So cooking for Micah was out. As were all other thoughts about any kind of secret assignation, affair, or relationship. He could lose his job, and she could lose the life she'd built. No. It would be stupid.

With this resolution firmly in mind, she headed through the inn's front doors and down the hall. She looked in on Dad. As expected, he was in the office, watching old movies again.

It broke her heart, but she said nothing about it. Everyone had their own way of grieving, and this was Dad's way.

"Hey, Daddy," she said in a louder-than-normal voice.

He closed the laptop and turned. "Wow, you're home early."

"The dentist was a bust."

"Oh? What did he do?" Dad leaned forward, wanting details.

"He was his own biggest fan," she said. "And he was

rude to the waiter, which ruled him out as second-date material. So, everything quiet?"

Dad's mouth quirked. "I guess some of what your mother and I taught you has rubbed off. Good choice on dumping the dentist if he was rude to a waiter," he said with a little nod. "Everything is quiet with the guests, but the minister came by. He's upstairs talking to Jackie."

"Micah is here?"

"Yeah. I figured maybe he could straighten the kid out. He's been up there for…" Dad checked his military-issue watch. "Wow, it's been almost forty-five minutes."

Ashley cocked her head. "Did you ask him to come, Daddy?"

"No. He just came by to see how Jackie was doing. I figured it couldn't hurt." He pushed up from the desk. "I'm going to turn in. I'm tired."

He looked tired. And older than he had a few months ago. She might be annoyed with him, but her worry about him trumped everything. She wished she could make it better for him, but that was not possible. He would have to walk this path himself and figure out how to live without the spouse he'd loved for almost fifty years. She'd been down that way herself, and it took time to get to the other side.

She watched him shuffle out the door and then headed up the stairs to the third floor. She was huffing and puffing a little when she reached Jackie's open door. Micah, dressed in jeans and a T-shirt, sat backward in Jackie's desk chair, his head cocked a little as he listened to Jackie.

Her son, who was sitting on the bed, sneakers and all, was talking a mile a minute.

"And then, I don't know, we could tell him that

he's dead or something. And maybe that would work. I was reading in the book Jayden tore up about how some ghosts don't realize they're dead. They have to be convinced, you know. Like that movie *Sixth Sense*."

"Since when have you seen *Sixth Sense*?" Ashley asked. She had expressly forbidden him from watching that movie because she was afraid it might encourage him, or scare him, or something. Had she been wrong?

Jackie turned a pair of deep-blue eyes on her. They were Adam's eyes, and right now she could read the annoyance in them. She was losing Jackie. He was growing up and away from her, and she didn't know what to do about it.

"I saw it over at Justin's house. And there was nothing scary in that movie, Mom. You know I'm not a baby."

Right. That was certainly true. And here sat Micah listening to him about the stuff he would no longer talk to her about. It made her angry. And sad. And lonely all at the same time.

She shifted her gaze toward the minister. He met her gaze, but his dark skin turned a little ruddy. Was he blushing? "I thought you were out on a date," he said. Something about the tone made heat flow right through her.

No doubt her own cheeks had just blossomed like the red roses in her garden. "I was, but I left early. The guy was a jerk. And you've been here talking about Captain Teal, I see."

Jackie rolled his eyes. She probably deserved that but she didn't give him any grief about it. Maybe she should take a clue from Micah and just listen for once. Unfortunately, right now she was listening to dead silence.

It stretched out for several moments before Micah

finally said, "Uh, well, our conversation is kind of private."

"What? With the door open?"

Micah gave her a long, hard stare. "I follow a door-open policy all the time. But the door doesn't matter. This conversation is private."

Ashley shifted her gaze toward Jackie, who was giving the minister this adoring look. The expression on her son's face raised a flock of conflicting emotions. She was overjoyed that Jackie had a man like Micah in his life, but deeply jealous that somehow it was okay for Jackie to be open in his admiration when she had to keep all her emotions under wraps.

And, of course, it was far too easy to compare Micah to the idiot she'd had dinner with. The man who hadn't bothered to read her profile all the way, who'd been surprised and even troubled by the fact that she had a young child, the man who was seriously unkind to people.

Yeah. It was way too easy to make that comparison.

"Okay, but can I interrupt for a moment? I'd like to have a word with the minister in private." She pointed over her thumb into the hallway.

"Great," Jackie said with another eye roll. "I knew you were going to ruin it. You always ruin things."

The words hurt. She hated to think that he might grow up like Dad, angry with his own mother the way Dad had been all his life. A knot the size of a peach stone lodged in her throat.

And then Micah said, "That was unkind, Jackie."

Ashley's son sank his head onto his knees, the picture of misery.

"I'm sorry," she said, but Jackie was not in a forgiving mood.

Micah followed up with, "Hang tight. I'll be back in a minute. Let me handle your mom."

She probably would have exploded except that Micah had put one long finger to his lips as if he'd known exactly how she'd react to the idea of him "handling" her.

And he winked.

Chapter Seventeen

Micah followed Ashley out into the hallway, closing Jackie's door behind him. He expected Ashley to turn on him with a sharp tongue that he probably couldn't handle. At least not emotionally. He didn't want to be a wedge between Ashley and her son. He wanted to help them.

But instead of giving him a piece of her mind, Ashley headed toward the door at the end of the hallway. Where did that door lead? He'd only been to the third floor of Howland House a few times, and only to visit Jackie, and sometimes the person staying in the attic guest room.

Never to this end of the hall. It had to be Ashley's bedroom.

"Uh, this is inappropriate," he said.

"I would like a private conversation too. I don't want Jackie listening at the door, which he will do. We're adults. I think we can manage."

It was still inappropriate. In fact, the bright-red cover

of the pamphlet the diocese had published on boundary issues flashed through Micah's mind like a stop sign. But he blew right past it.

The bedroom smelled like her: lavender and roses, with a flowered bedspread and a brass bed. The ceiling angled, and a couple of dormers with window seats piled with lacy cushions underscored the over-the-top femininity of the room. No man regularly ventured into this territory.

And no guest either. Unlike the public rooms downstairs, this room was lived in. Clothes had been draped over a wing chair, the bedside table had a prodigious number of books piled on it, and the dressing table was blessed with a variety of pots and bottles and all sorts of womanly stuff.

He should run, but he longed to stay and explore every nook and cranny, examine the book titles, and poke his nose into her dresser drawer and inhale.

She turned to face him, shoulders tight, face a mask, her lips bearing the remnants of the bright-red lipstick she'd put on for some other man.

"What are you doing, Micah?" she asked.

He was tempted to ask her the same. After all, she'd invited him into her boudoir. The pamphlet had a whole chapter on this kind of thing. The bottom line: Avoid at all costs.

"I'm breaking the rules," he said.

She frowned. "Come on, this isn't about you and me. It's about Jackie. I'm his mother, and—"

"I'm not talking about that rule," he said in a low voice. "I'm talking about the one about ghosts." Good grief, they were skating close to the edge here. He needed to steer this conversation back where it belonged.

"There's a rule about ghosts?"

"It's not a rule, exactly. It's more like a theological holding. While you'll find plenty of Anglican priests who regularly exorcise ghosts, it's more or less frowned upon here in America. We tend to hold the view that any paranormal manifestation is caused by something evil and not the spirits of the dearly departed. I think Jackie's ghost is an imaginary friend that he's struggling to let go of. But entertaining his thoughts about how to send this ghost into the light is technically something I'm not supposed to do. Assuming I thought the ghost was real.

"But for the record, I didn't come here to talk to him about his ghost. I came because he called me."

"He called you?"

Micah nodded, wondering how to convey the fear Jackie had expressed about returning to school. He didn't want to criticize Ashley. "Yeah. He called me to ask if I would help Danny Beckett, the boy who protected him on Saturday. He wanted me to talk to Colton and make sure Danny didn't lose his job because of the fight. The situation with Danny is a great deal more complicated than Jackie realizes, but I told him I would help. And after I put his mind at ease, I just sat and listened to him. He's worried about his ghost. He's completely terrified of returning to school and facing Jayden Walsh. And he's overheard your father talking about sending him away."

"Dammit," she said on a harsh breath. At the same time, her eyes began to glitter. "I'm not sending him away. That's just Dad talking."

"I know. You would never send him away, Ashley. And the thing is, Jackie is almost as worried about Danny and his job as he is about Jayden picking another fight. And his concern about the ghost comes from a deep altruism and empathy. He's a really fine boy, Ashley. You've done a good job with him. But he needs our help right now."

She blinked, and a tear escaped her eye. She wiped it away as she nodded. "Thanks. I think I needed that affirmation. I've been feeling like a failure. I don't know what to do, Micah. I know he's frightened."

"Well, for starters, I think we need to find a way to help Jackie let go of his ghost. I don't know if that's some kind of fake exorcism or a ceremony or what. But I think we can help him with that. I'm going to do what I can for Danny Beckett. And finally, I think you need to go talk to the principal at the school and Mrs. Wilson, the librarian, and make it clear just who destroyed that library book. We both know it wasn't Jackie."

She pressed her lips together and nodded. "I should have done that. But I didn't want to pick a fight with Dad. He's so sad."

"I know. But he's upset the boy, Ashley. Talking about military school is not helpful."

She nodded, biting her lip. "Of course it's not. And you've laid out a sensible plan. Thanks," she said, her voice shaky. She turned away to pluck a tissue from the box on her nightstand. She dabbed her eyes, but the tears were coming at a steady drip now.

Micah crossed the rug, suddenly anxious to provide the same comfort she'd given him the night Dad went into the hospital. Maybe he was required to be careful about following the rules, but Ashley and her family were facing a crisis. She was a mother deeply worried about her son, a daughter trying her best to ease her father's pain. She was, like her son, a good person. An altruistic person. And her pain moved him.

"It's going to be okay. I promise," he said, closing the distance between them.

"How can you promise?" Her voice was tight.

"Because we're going to help Jackie and we're also going to do our best for Andrew. And we'll do it together, okay?"

"Are we?" she asked.

He nodded.

"But..." She looked away, her lower lip quivering. He could almost read her mind. Just like Saturday night, when they'd danced around it.

He should go. Now. But he couldn't move. Giving in to his deepest yearning, he raised his hand to her cheek and brushed away one of the tears with his thumb.

She closed her eyes, her lips parted, and she let go of a small breath that feathered across his skin.

He lost his restraint.

He leaned in, capturing those slightly parted lips, drinking in the bouquet of flowers that was her taste. Not merely the subtle taste of rose petals, but something darker and more complex that filled his mouth and intoxicated him.

He halfway expected her to retreat, or slap his face, or cry out or something—anything—to stop him. But instead, she leaned into the kiss, pressing her body up against his until he bore some of her weight. Her arms left her sides and sneaked up to his shoulders and then to the nape of his neck, where her fingers traced a line of fire.

He deepened the kiss. She followed his lead, and time hung suspended as they explored this forbidden carnal intimacy.

He almost drowned in it, until she gently disengaged.

Now her lipstick had been kissed away, leaving only

swollen flesh a hundred times more inviting. Several passages from the Song of Songs passed through his mind.

"Jackie is waiting for you," she whispered, taking a tiny, reluctant step back.

Good god, he'd crossed over a line, and he could never go back. Not because he'd tasted the forbidden, but because he'd made a promise. To the woman and the boy.

He would not break his promise. He knew the pain of broken promises far too well.

* * *

Kerri and Colton lingered over a slice of fig and raspberry tart and a couple of cappuccinos. They'd stayed so long that the waiter had started to get antsy. But Kerri was reluctant for the evening to end.

Colton had opened up, telling her stories about his childhood, which had been both blessed and cursed. His mother had addiction issues and abandoned him. But he'd also had the support of a group of strong Black women like his great-aunt Daisy. When he talked about the renovation of Daisy's house, he spoke with such love. Not only for the kind of work he enjoyed but for the satisfaction of giving back to the woman who had helped keep his family together when everything fell apart.

"Without Daisy, I don't know what would have happened to me," he said, with love shining through his voice. His recognition of his aunt and the role she played in his life changed things. Colton wasn't some kind of player who didn't value women. Yes, he'd played the field, but maybe he'd never found the right woman.

Oh good lord, that was dangerous thinking. But she allowed it to fill her head just the same.

When they finally left the restaurant and headed out into a chilly spring night, she decided that maybe she should throw caution to the wind and make a move. Yes, she'd had a little too much wine, but life was short, and he was handsome, and they'd seemed to connect or something.

She snagged his arm and pulled him close—so close that his breath feathered across her skin, heating it. "Take me home," she whispered.

He blinked, and then his mouth twitched a bit. "Really?"

She nodded.

And then he moved in with that amazing grace she remembered from the last time. Colton's spine-tingling kiss carried hints of berry and fig and honey from the sinful dessert they'd shared, overlaid with something far more carnal. It awakened every part in her body. The kiss, like the man, was brash and sweet and kind and sensuous all at the same time.

In the moment, he became the embodiment of her secret fantasy—the lover who simply took charge and brought her to the pinnacle of pleasure.

She managed to get to his Audi, kissing him the whole way. She had to stop once she'd buckled up. And then, the foolish man headed down Harbor Drive at a ridiculous and dangerous rate of speed. Thank the lord they arrived at his house in the historic section of town without mishap.

She lost her heels the minute the front door closed behind them. Her dress hit the floor in the upstairs hallway leading to his bedroom. Her bra and panties and his pants and boxers were shed in the blink of an eye. So, by the time they hit the sheets, they were blissfully naked.

Hours later, Kerri drifted up from a contented sleep, finding herself spooned like a beloved rag doll by the most eligible bachelor in Magnolia Harbor. A player didn't cuddle like this, did he? Had she misjudged him?

Maybe she had, but she'd also broken a promise to herself. She'd been determined not to sleep with Colton after the first date.

She couldn't blame him for this situation. She'd kissed him first. She'd suggested that they come back here. It was all her fault.

Her stupid, romantic self kept making this mistake. Here she was in Colton's house without any mode of transportation. To get back home, she'd have to rely on him. She'd given up a measure of her independence. She'd done that once before, in her marriage. And it had made her miserable.

Those memories moved her from sex-drunk idiot to fully awake. She needed to go home. Now. At home she could be in control.

She called his name.

He grunted but didn't awaken.

She gave him a little nudge.

"Leave me alone," he said in a sleepy voice.

She sat up in the bed.

He rolled over, giving her a view of his back.

"Colton, I need a lift home." This time she said it in a loud voice.

"Uh-huh," he murmured.

She tried prodding him and shaking his shoulder again, all to no avail.

Okay, so that was the way it was going to be. She gave

herself up to him and he would be in control. No way that was happening.

So she left the bed and retraced her steps down the hall to the front door, collecting garments as she went. When she found her purse, right inside the door, she pulled out her cell phone and called an Uber.

Ben Lawlor was out driving tonight. He picked her up at Colton's front door and had the good grace not to say a word as he drove her home. But she was willing to bet that, by tomorrow afternoon, every person in Magnolia Harbor would know that she'd been caught outside Colton St. Pierre's house, doing the walk of shame.

Chapter Eighteen

In the wee hours of Wednesday morning, Ashley reluctantly swam up to consciousness. She didn't want to wake up. She'd been having the most wonderful dream.

All warm and sexy and...

Oh, wait.

Her eyes flew open. She had not been dreaming about Adam.

She lay there for a few minutes, the bedside clock ticking off minutes. Micah's kiss filled her thoughts.

It had been...hot. Hot enough to melt her down. Hot enough to give her erotic dreams about someone other than her husband.

What was she going to do about this? She sat up in bed and leaned her elbows on her raised knees while she thought about this problem. After several long moments, she decided she would do nothing. What could she do? She couldn't pursue the minister without creating a scandal of momentous proportions.

So kissing Micah would have to remain her secret. There would never be another kiss. There never could be.

And yet, a full-body flush ran over her skin, making her suddenly hot, despite the cool morning air on her skin. This was ridiculous. She needed to push these thoughts back into a box where they belonged and get on with her day. Kissing Micah didn't change the fact that she needed to get up and make breakfast for the guests.

She wandered into the bathroom, took a cold shower, and began her morning routine. But she paused after brushing her teeth and washing her face, right before she put on a dab of moisturizer, and studied herself in the mirror.

Time had left a mark on her. The gray in her dark hair had become a tiny streak at her temple—too much to pluck out now. Maybe it was time to start coloring it. Or maybe get some highlights or something.

When was the last time she'd been to the beauty shop?

Her hair wasn't the only thing in need of some attention. Her skin, though mostly unlined, had picked up a few seams around the corners of her mouth, probably from frowning all the time. She needed a facial. And her eyebrows were out of control.

And despite the blue polka-dot dress she'd worn recently, her closet was filled with basic jeans and T-shirts and a pair of black dress pants she often wore to church. She had become boring. A tiny bit frumpy, even.

So maybe Micah's kiss had done more than ignite her libido. It had made her take a good, long look at herself. She needed a makeover in more ways than one.

Not just the wardrobe, and the hair, and the face, but she needed to take charge of her life the way she'd once taken charge of the inn. Her grip on things had been sliding, ever since Mom had died and Dad had swooped in.

Today was a good day to assert herself.

She arrived in the kitchen with a renewed sense of purpose, only to be greeted by Dad, who wasted no time in expressing his view that she needed to force Jackie back to school. Today.

"No, I'm going to talk to the principal," she countered as she got the butter out of the freezer. "I need assurances that Jayden Walsh is not going to hurt him. And the school needs to give those assurances."

"The boy needs to fight his own battles, Ashley."

Did he? Maybe. But battles that left him bruised and bloody were over the top. He did not need to be bullied. Ashley had never seen eye-to-eye with Mrs. Thacker, the principal, who'd suggested therapy for Jackie because, when he was six, he'd gone to school and told a little girl that she needed to "walk the plank."

That language had been punished. But where was Mrs. Thacker when it came to Jayden Walsh ripping up a library book? The woman chose to believe some other boy. And Ashley had a good idea of why.

Not that she was going to express her views about Teddy Walsh and the way some people in this town worshiped the man.

"I'm his mother. He needs me."

"Jackie is fine. It's just a broken nose. Do not do what Mother used to do to me. She'd swoop in anytime anyone looked cross-eyed at me. It was embarrassing."

She ground her teeth. So much of this had to do with Dad's unhappy relationship with Grandmother. "Good grief," she muttered under her breath.

"What was that?" Dad asked, his tone challenging.

She looked up at him, no longer willing to pull her punches. "Dad. You need to go get your hearing checked because you're going deaf, and you'd be so much happier if you could actually hear stuff. And while I'm expressing *my* views, I think it would be helpful to visit the church's bereavement group. And finally, I am not Grandmother. Okay? But I am Jackie's mother. So the next time the school calls with a problem, you will forward that call to me, understand?"

She glared.

He glared back.

And they lapsed into silence for the rest of the morning.

When breakfast service had finished, Ashley called the school to let them know she'd be keeping Jackie at home until she could speak face to face with Mrs. Thacker. This didn't go over well with the school secretary, but it did get her a meeting with the principal later that afternoon.

In the meantime, she called St. Mark's parochial school, located more than half an hour north of Magnolia Harbor, and learned that Jackie could transfer in for the remainder of the school year, but that they did not recommend it, seeing as it was March already and the term ended in early May.

Well, at least it was an option. Not a good one because of the distance, but if she had to put Jackie in another school to save him from bullies, she would do it.

Then she changed into a flour-free pair of pants and a clean shirt and walked down to the public library.

Shirley Wilson was there, the way she'd been for the last forty-five years. The woman was nearing seventy and probably needed to retire. But no one was about to ask her to do that. She was a fixture. Everyone in town had endured her icy stare at one time or another. And they'd also enjoyed the many books she recommended. She probably knew the reading habits of everyone living in Magnolia Harbor.

"Can we have a private word?" Ashley asked.

The woman frowned. "Whatever you have to say to me you can say right here...quietly."

Ashley scanned the reading room. It was deserted, probably because it was lunchtime. Her own stomach was rumbling.

"I would like to talk to you about finding a way to make Jackie feel comfortable here again. He told me he doesn't want to come here anymore. To be honest, Shirley, he told me he was afraid he'd get yelled at. And yelling doesn't sound like you." Ashley used her best innkeeper voice.

The woman's frown lowered. "Is that what he said to you?"

Ashley nodded. "I'm sorry. I just have this feeling that—"

"Ashley, your father told me he was not to be allowed in the library for the next two months. Did you not know this?"

Ashley's face flamed hot as the twin emotions of anger and humiliation settled into the pit of her stomach. "I did not know this. I apolo—"

"Oh, I'm so glad to learn this. On the day the book was destroyed, Andrew brought Jackie in here and stood right behind him while the boy confessed to having destroyed it."

"What? Jackie didn't—"

"I know that. I'm the one who ordered that book for the collection, knowing that I had one particular little boy who would be over the moon when I put it in his hands.

He's been doing a lot of research on ghosts, asking a lot of questions, and seeking out resources."

Ashley nodded. "I know."

"Well, I was stunned when I saw what had been done to that book. It was destroyed. And not by accident, Ashley. Someone viciously tore the pages out. That person was not Jackie, no matter what he confessed to. It was obvious the confession was forced. And I was flabbergasted when your father told Jackie to surrender his library card."

"What?"

Shirley nodded, concern lining her face. "I thought that was cruel, Ashley. I realize that your daddy got away with all kinds of shenanigans when he was a boy because your grandmother would cover for him. And I get that he doesn't want that for Jackie. But I don't see how the two situations are the same."

"You knew my dad when he was young?"

She nodded and smiled. "I dated your dad once a long time ago."

Ashley's mouth may have dropped open.

"Not for very long, because he was kind of an idiot. But he was never cruel. And when he brought Jackie in here that day, it felt cruel. He told me, in no uncertain terms, that I was not to allow Jackie in the library for the next two months."

"Oh." The word escaped in a harsh breath. "I understand now. I'm sorry. Jackie thinks you're going to yell at him if he comes back."

"Of course not. I don't yell, never in the library. And I would have welcomed him back anytime, notwithstanding your father's demands. A child should never be denied access to a public library. Ever." She opened her desk drawer, withdrew Jackie's library card, and handed it to Ashley.

"Thank you," Ashley said. "And for future reference, my father is not in charge of Jackie's discipline. I am."

"I look forward to seeing Jackie soon."

Ashley took Jackie's card and left the library, stepping out onto the sidewalk with her head buzzing with fury. What the hell did Dad think he was doing?

Because it sure wasn't saving Jackie.

* * *

Kerri sat on the couch in her living room, sipping a Diet Coke, while Shawna and Marcie drank wine. Kerri was never going to drink wine again.

She'd been fighting a headache all day. It was starting to dissipate, but the ache in her heart had continued. She liked Colton. She kept mistaking him for the man of her dreams. But when it came right down to it, she'd asked him to drive her home, and he'd been more interested in his beauty rest.

Now people were talking about her because Ben Lawlor had blabbed to someone who had passed it right on to the town grapevine.

So hours before Stitch and Bitch, Kerri had fielded phone calls from Marcie and Shawna, not to mention the knowing looks several customers had given her today at the boutique. And then there had been Patsy Bauman, who'd dropped by and asked her, point blank, if she was messing with Micah St. Pierre's heart and mind by going out with his brother.

Oh boy. The entire female congregation of Heavenly Rest probably hated her now.

"That bad, huh?" Marcie said, leaning toward her and patting her hand. They were both on the couch in her small living room.

"I wouldn't worry about the gossip," Shawna said. "It's not as if you are the first woman seen leaving Colton St. Pierre's house in the dead of night."

"Thanks, guys." Kerri couldn't hide her sarcasm.

"Oh, honey, I wasn't dissing you," Shawna said. "I just mean that this will blow over. It's not about you, anyway. It's just the Heavenly Rest Altar Guild having a cow over Reverend St. Pierre."

"I know, " Kerri said, "but Micah and I were never an item. This has nothing to do with him."

They both looked at her as if she'd just fallen, head-first, from the turnip truck. "It has everything to do with him," Marcie said.

"No, it doesn't. Trust me on this. Micah and I went out for dinner, it's true, but…" She paused. It was now or never. She had to tell the truth.

"But what?" Marcie pressed.

"Look, you guys don't know this, but a couple of years ago, Colton and I had a fling, and—"

"What?" Her friends spoke in near unison.

Kerri nodded. "I slept with him, okay? It was just a short, little fling. And to be honest, it almost broke my heart. So when everyone started matching me up with Colton's brother, it was—"

"Awkward," Marcie said on a long breath.

"Yes, exactly. But it's more complicated than that. Evidently, Colton said something to Micah that sent the good reverend into his own matchmaking frenzy."

Her friends were so stunned their mouths dropped open. It took a moment before Shawna spoke again. "Are you telling me that Reverend St. Pierre was trying to make a match between you and his brother?"

"Yes, but then we had this—"

Kerri's explanation was cut abruptly short by a hard, fast, definitely masculine knock on the front door.

"Who could that be?" Marcie said. "I think I've heard that knock before."

Kerri rose from the couch, sprinted to the door, and opened it to find Colton on the other side. He appeared agitated. He was pacing back and forth, a deep frown on his face, his hands aggressively jammed into his jean pockets.

"Have you seen Danny?" he asked before Kerri could say a word.

His question hit her like a bolt to the heart, leaving her with twin emotions: concern for the troubled teen and an ominous sense of déjà vu. Her silly self would have been overjoyed to have him arrive on her doorstep full of apologies for what happened last night.

In fact, she'd been sorely disappointed when he hadn't called all day. And for an instant, when she'd crossed the room from the couch to the door, a stupid part of her heart had hoped he'd come to talk to *her* about *their* relationship.

But no. This visit wasn't about her or them or last night. It was about Danny. She cared about Danny, so she couldn't yell at Colton or send him away or anything like that. Colton cared about Danny because she'd insisted on it as a precondition or whatever.

So she was caught, like a spider in a web of its own making.

"What's wrong?" she asked, swallowing back all the words of hurt she wanted to hurl at him.

"This morning, I picked him up at his grandmother's like always. And we headed up to that new condo development out by the Ocean Highway exit onto Teal Road. Teddy Walsh was there, talking with the general contractor on that job. St. Pierre Construction is only doing the framing and drywall. Anyway, when we got there, the general contractor told us we had to clear out because the investors didn't want us on the job."

"Oh no, Colton. That's—"

"Bullshit. Yeah, it's stinks, and it's wrong, and we're probably going to sue for breach of contract. When I told Teddy that I would go to court, he responded that all I had to do was fire Danny and all would be right with the world. Danny heard him say it."

"Oh no." Kerri's heart twisted. This was so very bad and unfair.

"I told Teddy he could take his demands and shove them. Sideways. So we left and headed over to a build out on Redbud. I dropped Danny off and went to consult our lawyers about what legal options we might have.

"And then, about an hour later, my construction manager called to say that Danny had taken off." He blew out a frustrated breath while jabbing his hand through his close-cropped hair. "I been searching for him all day. His grandmother had no clue. But he must have gone home because his skateboard is gone. I'm worried about him. I don't want him to blame himself for Teddy Walsh being an asshole."

"I haven't seen him," Kerri said.

"You got any idea where he might have gone? His grandmother has problems, Kerri. But to be honest, I don't think she wants to be bothered with him. It's not like me, when I was a kid. I screwed up, got into trouble, but at the end of the day, Aunt Daisy and Old Granny were there for me. And I mean *there*."

"I know. I had a grandmother like that too." She smiled. "You have any ideas?"

Kerri pinched the bridge of her nose. "I think I know where he is. Danny has been frustrated that he doesn't have a car. He told me a couple of times that he needed to go to the mainland."

"For what?"

"To visit his parents. They're at Oakwood Cemetery."

"You think he rode his skateboard all the way across the bridge?"

"I really do."

"Okay, thanks." I'm going there to bring him home, right now."

"Wait, let me get my coat. I'm coming with you."

Half an hour later, they drove through the gates of the cemetery onto a gravel drive that wound through a stand of live oaks trailing long beards of moss. It took a while to find Danny. He didn't respond when they called his name. Instead they had to tramp through the graveyard using their cell phone flashlights. They eventually found him curled into a tight ball on the ground beside his parents' headstones.

Chapter Nineteen

Four days might have passed, but the taste of Ashley's kiss had not faded. Micah could recall it exactly without effort. Unfortunately, whenever his mind was not otherwise occupied, the memory seeped into his frontal lobes like a specter.

Condemning him. Reminding him. And confirming that his integrity required him to find another church. Quickly.

His prayers on that score had been answered yesterday when a member of the search committee for Christ Church in Last Chance, South Carolina, had called him. The church was about 120 miles due west of Magnolia Harbor, which made it close enough so that his family couldn't accuse him of abandoning them.

He had an interview scheduled for next week, and the moment he'd entered that appointment into his calendar, he'd accepted that he was moving on.

At least his efforts on the museum committee would

be finished by the time he left town. Tonight was the ribbon-cutting ceremony and opening reception for the town's VIPs. He wasn't looking forward to the event.

Not because he expected trouble. Although there had been some of it already, because the museum was trying to provide a fair, inclusive, and complete presentation of the island's history. From the get-go, a small percentage of the population had protested everything.

But most of those protests were in the past now. They'd worked things out.

No, he wasn't worried about people showing up with ugly signs. He was worried because Ashley would be at the reception. He hadn't seen her since that moment in her bedroom.

He drove to City Hall and headed for the front doors, swallowing back the metallic taste that came from gulping too many antacids. He prayed for strength and patience as he walked.

And then he looked up, and there stood Ashley, looking...different.

She'd cut her hair to chin length and done something to it, making it lighter and more stylish. She wore a bright-blue dress that hugged her curves, the neckline plunging a bit in a deep V that displayed more than a little cleavage where a strand of pearls lay.

His mouth went dry. She had spectacular cleavage. It was probably a good thing that she'd been hiding it for the last five years. Who was this woman wearing high heels?

Not Ashley Scott, exactly. But some supercharged version of her who appeared to have the world by the tail, and Harry Bauman at her side.

Harry was in his element, glad-handing and politicking.

Ashley's gaze caught Micah's. "Looks like our chairman has arrived. Late as usual." Her smile crinkled up the corners of her dark-brown eyes. He could remember a time when her smiles never quite reached her eyes. But today, the sorrow seemed to have disappeared.

She whispered something to Harry, who was schmoozing with the state representative. The museum unveiling had brought out the VIPs and the press from as far away as Columbia and Charleston. Harry waved and went back to talking.

Ashley came forward and took him by the crook of the arm, sending heat through his body. "I know you don't like events like this. So smile and leave the talking to Harry. He's got it all under control, and he's happy to take credit for all your hard work." Her smile deepened.

"I don't care about—"

"I know." She gave him a conspiratorial wink. "But just in case no one says this tonight, none of this would have been possible without your enduring patience."

"Thanks." He fought against the urge to pull his arm away. In truth, her hand felt great against his arm. But it seemed forbidden. Wrong.

He'd always been aware of her, almost from the first moment he'd met her in the living room of the rectory on the day he'd moved in. Now that awareness had bloomed into a raging sexual attraction that was going to burn him to a crisp.

Maybe, if the heat flowing through him had been devoid of context, he could have ignored it or brushed it aside. But this was Ashley.

Context mattered.

Well before he'd recognized this physical desire, he'd

found a refuge from loneliness every morning when he'd stopped by Howland House for breakfast, where the oatmeal was always steel-cut and served family-style. Before he noticed the curve of her backside, he'd admired the way she loved her son with the fierceness of a momma lion. This was not a woman who abandoned people.

It also hadn't taken him long to realize that she would stand up to the court of public opinion. She didn't follow Patsy Bauman around. She often told the busybodies in his congregation to back off.

He loved those Sundays when she brought hummingbird cake to fellowship hour and fed the multitudes. And when she smiled, which didn't happen as much as it should, it lit his skies. When she frowned, he worried about her.

And just like that, with a burning under his tight collar, he realized that he'd crossed a line a long time ago. Maybe not physically but in his mind.

In his heart.

He loved Ashley Scott. But the Episcopal Church frowned on their clergy falling in love, dating, or otherwise getting romantically entangled with members of their own congregations. Breaking this rule was cause for dismissal.

So he had limited choices now: Leave Heavenly Rest and find another church or leave the ministry entirely.

Was the Lord calling him to another church? Or putting this test in front of him to challenge his commitment to his faith?

He didn't know. All he could do was pray for a sign. And do the best he could.

Right now that meant focusing on the unveiling.

Micah gave the blessing, Harry and the state representative gave speeches, Ashley cut a ribbon with an oversized pair of shears, and a Gullah storyteller entertained the crowd in a language only a few could understand.

Now, a couple of hours later, the reception was winding down, and he found himself in the main gallery where Rose's diary was displayed. Across the room, Ashley was speaking with a reporter.

This new Ashley in her cute haircut and sexy dress seemed more comfortable inside her skin. Maybe this wasn't a new Ashley at all, but the old one waking up from a long sleep.

Just then, Jenna came by and leaned into him. "Nice work," she said. "I'm exhausted. I bet you are too."

"Yeah."

"In case no one has mentioned it, none of this would have been possible without your cool head."

"And your cool cash," he said with a smile.

She laughed a little. "I guess. In the great scheme of things, this museum didn't cost that much, Micah." Her gaze traveled to Jude, who was standing in the adjoining gallery dedicated to Gullah culture. He was talking to the storyteller. They were not speaking English.

"I was sorry that Colton didn't come tonight," she added.

"Me too. But I guess Danny Beckett has an appointment with a counselor on the mainland, and Colton is driving him," Micah said.

"Colton told me all about how he rode his skateboard to the mainland. I'm working on finding Danny a used car so he can drive himself to appointments, and I heard that you stepped in and worked your magic to get his grandmother some home health care." She smiled.

"It wasn't magic," he said.

"Well, I think it was. And it's good to see Colton getting involved in a troubled kid's welfare."

"I had nothing to do with that."

She laughed. "Oh yes you did. Even if you had a little help from a certain shopkeeper in town."

Micah remained silent, and after a moment, Jenna spoke again. "You know, Colton and Kerri have been seen all over town together. And everyone is wondering why the woman you took to dinner a few weeks ago is now hanging out with your brother."

He shrugged. "Easy come, easy go."

"You are impossible. You set them up, didn't you?"

"I might have." Micah shifted his gaze back to Ashley. She was smiling and nodding as she spoke with a reporter who had learned that she was Rose Howland's descendant. Earlier in the evening, the reporter had spoken with Jude about Henri St. Pierre.

"So," Jenna said, following his gaze, "enjoying the view?"

He pretended not to hear what she'd just said. He was not going to admit that he had, indeed, been enjoying the view.

"What do you think about the new, improved Ashley?" Jenna said. Jenna had a talent for poking people in their soft spots.

She would not stop until he said something. "I think blue suits her," he said, shifting his gaze to give his sister-in-law a back-off look.

Which had absolutely no impact on the woman. "I think she looks fabulous in blue. And I'm sure she bought that dress to impress the press or, you know, the next guy from Forty and Flirty that she goes out with."

"Does she have another date?" he asked without thinking. Lava-hot jealousy flowed through him.

"Maybe you should ask her."

He closed his eyes. He should have walked away from Jenna the moment she started asking questions. But instead, he'd been trapped. "And why, exactly, should I be talking to her about her social life?" he said, trying to sound disinterested in the topic.

"Because she didn't buy that new dress for the guys on Forty and Flirty. And we both know it."

"No?" He scowled at her. "Then the press, I guess."

"Can it, Micah. You aren't fooling me. You need to do something about this."

"About what?"

"About your feelings for Ashley. They show every time you look in her direction. And you're kidding yourself if you think no one has noticed."

"And what, exactly, do you think I should do, Jenna?" His voice had an edge to it. Because, when it came to Ashley, the choices were all bad ones.

"Oh for goodness' sake, Micah. What are you afraid of?"

"What?"

Jenna faced him, blocking his view of Ashley. "You love her. And more important, she has feelings for you. I know this. It's not a guess. So you need to quit messing around and ask her to marry you."

"But—"

"Don't give me a long speech about the church and the rules and all that stuff. There are no buts, Micah. You love her. And she loves you. And besides, she'd make a terrific minister's wife. She'd manage you the way you need managing. And she'd feed you something better than ice cream for dinner."

He opened his mouth and closed it again. As a technicality, the rules held that he wasn't supposed to date someone with whom he had a pastoral relationship. They didn't exactly say that he was prohibited from marrying one of them. Of course he'd have to seek the bishop's blessing. But marriage was a whole different thing from dating. It presupposed a commitment. And it was consistent with the proscription the church imposed on premarital sex.

"I can see you're thinking about it." Jenna patted his arm. "Good. Don't waste too much time in thought." She rose up on tiptoes and gave him a sisterly kiss on the cheek. "Now I'm tired, and I'm going to go play the pregnant-lady card and make Jude take me home. Nice work on all of this." She headed off toward the adjoining gallery.

At the same moment, the journalist shook Ashley's hand and walked off in the opposite direction.

They were alone in the gallery.

* * *

The reporter from the *Georgetown Times* finally left, and Ashley stopped smiling. The corners of her lips felt trembly and out of practice. Her feet hurt too.

Why on earth had she worn heels?

She could probably take them off now. Everyone was gone. Except for Harry, probably, who would still be bending someone's ear about how he had been the mover and shaker on this project. Let him have his moment of glory. The real movers and shakers had been Jude and Jenna St. Pierre. It had been his vision, and it was their triumph.

She slipped off her heels and sighed when her bare feet hit the cool tile of the floor.

"Feel good?" A low voice came from behind, startling her. She recognized that baritone.

Micah stood across the room with his hands in his pockets. Her nipples tightened at the sight of him. Did the tight fabric of the jersey dress give her away? Good grief. She'd thought she'd pushed all that out of her mind these last four days. She'd thought she'd been taking charge of her life, telling Dad to back off, giving the principal a tongue-lashing, and then going out for a spa day.

But no. One look at Micah, and it was as if the last four days had rewound. She still hadn't purged this adolescent attraction.

She managed a phony smile. "My feet are killing me. I haven't worn heels in I don't know how long. But, you know, this was a pretty big deal."

He nodded. His shoulders stiff. She should probably go before her untoward yearnings ruined this evening. Her decision to take charge of her life, redo her hair, change her dating profile photos, and maybe even go out and sleep with someone just for fun did not concern him.

At all.

And yet her fingers itched to touch him.

Harry came sweeping into the main gallery, Patsy following after him. "Everyone's gone home," he announced.

"And the caterers have cleaned up too," Patsy said.

Harry came over and gave her a kiss. "Nice work." He shook Micah's hand.

"Y'all coming?" Patsy asked. Harry was already heading for the front door.

"We'll be along in a moment," Micah said. "I'll make sure the door is locked. I've got one of the keys."

The Baumans waved, and Ashley realized, with a thump of her heart against her ribs, that Micah had sent them away on purpose. So they could be alone in an empty museum.

Not good.

"Well, I should be—" She started toward the door.

"Wait. I want to say something." His tone rang urgent, echoing in the empty gallery.

He closed the distance between them, bringing his vanilla bean scent with him. She inhaled it like a hopeless addict.

"I wanted to talk to you about something," he said.

"If it's about Jackie, have no fear. I've put Dad in his place, returned Jackie's library card, and given the principal of the school a very large piece of my mind. She assures me that Jackie will be safe, and so far so good. But I swear if—"

"I don't want to talk about Jackie."

"Oh."

Micah stepped a little closer. They were too close now. His body heat enveloped her. She wanted to sink into it.

"I think maybe we should..." He started and paused, licking his lips.

Kiss again. The thought penetrated her brain like a speeding bullet, killing all of her better intentions and higher cognitive functions.

And in that moment, she took charge. She'd been taking charge for four whole days, and it was wonderful.

So she stepped right up, raised up on tiptoes, and pressed her mouth to his.

He tasted like vanilla with a smidgen of spicy cocktail sauce that had probably come from the shrimp served during the reception. She deepened the kiss. Definitely cocktail sauce overlaid with something that was Micah's alone. Unique, earthy, hot.

She threw her arms around his neck, and he staggered back a couple of steps until he fetched up against the display case containing Rose's diary. The backstop was helpful, especially when his big hands roamed down her back and found her bottom.

Oh. Wow. She was suddenly glad she'd stopped into that fancy lingerie place in Georgetown and had scandalized herself by buying a pair of sheer and lacy panties.

All that silk loveliness threatened to burn entirely as she climbed his body, discovering that he seemed totally into her right at the moment.

She rubbed against him, and he groaned. It was incongruous and delicious and gave her a sense of power and even control.

She became aware of living in her own body: pounding heart, rushing blood, inhaling and exhaling. Her skin grew hot and sensitive, registering the texture of his hair, the worsted of his suit jacket, the stubble on his cheek.

She found the clasp at the back of his collar and was about to undo it when footsteps echoed through the gallery.

It was nothing short of astonishing how quickly two people could jump back from each other. But they managed it just as Patsy came sailing through the gallery. "Oh," she said in a funny tone. "I'm so glad I caught you, Ashley. I've been meaning to talk to you all evening.

Sally Hirsch called Brenda earlier this afternoon. She can't help with coffee tomorrow morning. I was wondering if you could come early and help out."

"Sure," Ashley said, her voice cracking strangely as the adrenaline rushed through her body, replacing the flush of desire with the fear of being discovered. What the hell had she almost done? Seduced The Rev in the museum?

Oh my god.

Then she wondered if Patsy could see how her panties were, literally, in a twist.

"Thanks. Y'all don't stay too late. Tomorrow is Sunday," she said in a chipper tone that grated.

When she left, Micah walked to the other side of the gallery as if he didn't quite trust her. Or himself.

Ashley spoke. "I'm sorry, will you—"

"You have to marry me," Micah interrupted.

"What?" Her brain, which was pickled in all sorts of hormones and adrenaline and other chemicals, had a hard time actually understanding what he'd said.

He seemed happy to elucidate. "If we get married, I don't see how the bishop or the vestry could complain. I mean, it's not as if we—"

"What?" she said again.

He stopped speaking, thank god.

They stared across the museum gallery, Rose's diary between them.

"Is that a no?" he asked in a low voice.

"Yes. Micah, I'm sorry. I like you. I'd like to date you. Hell, let me be totally honest here. I would actually like to jump your bones, which is so astonishing it knocks me for a loop. And, yes, I do understand that it's forbidden, which may be why it's so damn seductive. But I am not ready to run off and get married."

"But we—"

She held up a hand. "Look, I know what you're going to say. Adam is dead and I need to move on and we've been friends. And all that. But I don't want to get married. To anyone. I mean, I just now realized how much I enjoy being on my own. Probably because Dad has so seriously overstepped his boundaries. But honestly, I followed my husband around from place to place because he was in the army and I loved him. Because I was ready to support him in that life. But it's different now. I've settled down in one place. I've learned to be on my own."

"I..." His voice faded away, and his delicious lips pressed together firmly for a moment. He nodded as if he truly did understand, which was terrible, because the situation was so unfair. If he weren't bound by rules, things would be vastly different. They could date. They could fall in love. They could settle down and live here in Magnolia Harbor. Together.

"We better go," he said.

His words had a finality to them that made her itch.

Chapter Twenty

Micah had asked her to marry him.

Ashley lay in the bed trying to process what had happened at the museum tonight. She checked the clock on her bedside table. Two o'clock and she hadn't slept a wink. Her mind would not stop twisting and turning over what had happened.

She wasn't going to rush into a marriage. But it irked her that she was precluded from dating a man she liked and found attractive. It was so unfair.

And besides, she wasn't sure she wanted to be a minister's wife. It would be a lot like being a soldier's wife.

When she'd been not quite twenty, she'd thought nothing about sublimating her own life for her husband's career. She'd followed Adam the way Mom had followed Dad, moving every two years. Sometimes living in terrible conditions in places she didn't like much. And sometimes going places she might never have gotten to see but for the United States Army.

Jackie had been born in Germany. Germany had been fun.

Other places not so much.

But she'd loved Adam and had never really given any thought to any other kind of life until the price of being an army wife had come due, and she'd become an army widow.

Now a small ball of laughter and pain labeled "Life With Adam" would always exist inside her brain. But over the last few years, she'd built a whole new life around that grief. The grief would never leave her. Ever. But each year, this new life seemed larger and more real than the old one did.

And she liked this new life. She wasn't sure she wanted to trade it in. She didn't want to become "The Minister's Wife."

And yet...

Dammit. She liked Micah. A lot. And if she could, she would have explored a future with him. But not this way.

She punched her pillows and tried to get comfortable in bed while the thoughts played through her mind. She may have slept some before her alarm clock sounded, but not much.

She dragged herself off for a cold shower and some biscuit making. Rolling biscuits centered her. It was her yoga and her meditation, which was why she baked them every morning.

The weather was cold and cloudy, so she dressed in a sweater and a pair of jeans. She planned to swap the jeans out for dress pants before she went to church. No sense getting flour on anything but her baking jeans.

Dad was in the kitchen when she got there, even

though they didn't need a short-order cook on Sundays. He was wrestling with the coffee machine.

Evidently the ghost was back. Or more likely Nadia had taken them for a ride.

"I had trouble with it yesterday, so I went online and ordered a new one. It will arrive tomorrow," she said.

Dad gave her a bleary-eyed look and then slapped the machine, which gurgled to life. He sighed. Clearly he needed coffee as much as she did.

"Dad, next Thursday you are going to the bereavement group meeting at church. I'm going to put my foot down. You either go or move out of the cottage." She folded her arms over her chest.

He stared at the coffee machine dripping the elixir of tough mornings into the carafe and nodded. "Okay."

Hc didn't fight. So she decided not to mention the length of his hair. It wasn't important. He was starting his grief journey, and it had to be ten times harder for him because he was older and taking care of Mom had been his life.

She got busy making biscuits. The process of rolling the dough usually brought peace and tranquility, but not today. Today her mind kept turning to those few, forbidden moments in the museum.

"So how was last night?" Dad asked, after he'd poured himself a cup of coffee. He sat down at the counter.

"It was good. I'm glad that project is done, though."

She popped the first batch of biscuits into the oven and started rolling the next batch.

"So, how did The Rev like the new look?" he asked.

She stopped dead in her tracks and frowned at her father. "What's that supposed to mean?"

"You know exactly what it means. You think I haven't seen you staring across the street and sighing."

Damn. Was it that obvious?

Dad slurped some coffee before continuing. "You aren't fooling anyone."

"Oh good god, I hope so. Because..." She didn't finish. What if Patsy Bauman had seen them last night? She would tell everyone, and then Micah would be in big trouble.

She might *have* to marry him in order to save him.

The thought didn't exactly frighten her the way it had last night. Which was a sure sign that she hadn't had sufficient sleep. She didn't want anyone—not Dad, Micah, or the Episcopal Church—telling her who to be and how to act.

Dammit.

"Why are you trying to hide how you feel?" Dad asked. "I hope it's not some misguided loyalty to Adam."

"No. Yes. I don't know. The problem isn't how I feel. It's that my feelings are not allowed."

"Why not?"

"He's my minister, Dad. It's like...I don't know... fraternization rules, you know?"

"Oh." He said the word as if he'd just now figured it out. "Oh, that's bad."

She nodded. "You think?"

"Well, what the hell, you could always become a Methodist." He chuckled, his bloodshot eyes glinting as he took another sip of coffee. "That might make Mother roll over in her grave. Patsy Bauman's head would explode. It might even be entertaining."

"Dad."

"I'm serious. I've come to realize just how short life can be. And I hate to see you all alone."

"I'm fine alone, Dad. I can manage."

He cocked his head. "This has nothing to do with managing, Ash."

She stared at him for a solid minute. He was right. She could manage but she wanted more. And maybe she should stop whining about the situation and do something that might get her what she wanted.

* * *

On Monday morning, Micah blew off his usual paperwork and drop-by visits from parishioners and postponed his regularly scheduled dinner with Len Huxley, the chief warden, in order to drive west into the heart of the South Carolina midlands. There wasn't much out here between Georgetown and Orangeburg, and even less when he left Route 301 and headed toward Last Chance on the state road.

Micah drove through acres of farmland, the pale green of early spring, planted in crops he didn't recognize. He had grown up in South Carolina, but he could honestly say he'd never set foot in this part of the state.

It was a hundred miles from anywhere significant. It was isolated and rural and might be exactly what he needed. A kind of penance for his foolishness. A way to work himself back to an even keel.

He hadn't slept much since Saturday. And every time his mind returned to that moment when he'd proposed to Ashley, he cringed.

Of course she didn't want to marry him. He was an idiot. And now, since he'd crossed the line, he had to salvage his career. And find a way back into God's good graces.

He motored into Last Chance surprised to see a healthy

business district for such a tiny, rural place. The church stood on the south side of town, on Palmetto Avenue. Unlike Heavenly Rest, it had only a few shade trees in the churchyard. It had a lawn instead of pine-strewn sand and flowers growing along the foundation.

The church had probably been there since the 1930s, but it wasn't on any registry of historic buildings like Heavenly Rest. It was a plain, square, stuccoed building with a few arched windows.

He tamped down his disappointment at the church's small size. Who was he to be disappointed? Besides, he hadn't followed the call to the church because of ambition. He'd always been motivated by a need to help people.

And that's why he'd enjoyed working as a chaplain for so long. So he pushed aside the unwanted emotion and whispered a small prayer of thanks for this opportunity.

The search committee was composed of only four people: A semi-famous ex–baseball player named Dash Randall chaired the group. His wife, Savannah Randall, was also a member. The committee members also included an older woman named Lillian Bray and another man of middle years named Clay Rhodes.

They seemed like nice people, and he'd done fine during the interview. The committee seemed most interested in the strategies he had used at Heavenly Rest to improve membership. It might have been easy to take a lot of credit, but he hadn't done much except show up. Like Last Chance, the church at Heavenly Rest had gone without a minister for a long time before he'd arrived.

He handled the conversation well until Mr. Randall said, "You've been so successful in Magnolia Harbor. What's changed?"

He'd expected this question, and he'd rehearsed an answer.

"Well," he said on a long breath, "this is a bit awkward, but I asked someone to marry me, and she turned me down. She owns a business in Magnolia Harbor. And, well..." He let his voice trail off.

It was the truth. On more than one score. But if the search committee investigated, they'd discover that he had, indeed, proposed to Brooklyn Huddleston on Valentine's Day. The whole world had witnessed that proposal.

No one, thank the Lord, had seen Ashley shoot him down.

"I'm so sorry," Mrs. Randall said in truly empathic tones. She leaned forward, inspecting him out of sharp brown eyes for a long, uncomfortable moment. "If you come here, I can assure you that we'll help with that."

With what? he was tempted to say, but kept his mouth zipped.

"For goodness' sake, Savannah," Mrs. Bray said in hard tones. Micah sized her up to be the local equivalent of Patsy Bauman, if not quite as thin or as stylish. "Please don't start matchmaking before we've offered the man a position."

Oh, wait. Maybe he had that wrong. Maybe Mrs. Randall was the main busybody. Micah had come to realize that every church had busybodies.

"Well," Mr. Randall said. "Thank you for coming out here to visit with us today. I'm sure the committee will have additional questions. We'll submit them in writing. And if we decide to go on to the next phase, we'll have you back to meet the parishioners."

The interview ended. And Micah was on his way out to

his car when Mrs. Randall caught up to him. "Reverend St. Pierre," she called, "wait up."

She came down the curving walk to the parking lot, the spring sunshine lighting up her blond hair in gold. "Did you have another question?" he asked.

She shook her head, and then gave him the oddest of looks. "I know this is going to sound very strange, but I don't think you belong here."

He blinked.

She smiled. "Oh, I don't mean that you aren't qualified, or that you wouldn't make a wonderful priest for us. In fact, I think everyone liked you before they met you. Not to mention that it would be good to have a person of color as our minister. But that's not what I'm talking about."

"Um..." He was at a loss for words. The woman came off as slightly ditzy.

"I know," she said with a wild gesture. "I won't try to explain this. Sometimes I see things. So please listen, okay? You're being haunted, and I think if you dealt with the ghost or ghosts you'd be able to—"

"Oh, there you are, darlin'," Mr. Randall said, coming down the walk from the church. He hurried over, as if perhaps he realized that his wife was saying something both crazy and, well, essentially true.

He *was* haunted. By his past and every damn one of his mistakes. But that was hardly unique. Everyone could say the same thing.

"Mighty glad you could come," Mr. Randall continued, clearly trying to end Micah's conversation with his wife. "If you have time, you might want to go south on Route 70 a few miles and check out Golfing for God."

What had the man said? *Golfing for God?* Maybe

Micah should get out of his own head and listen. "Excuse me. Did you say—"

"Golfing for God," Mr. Rhodes finished. He had also come down the path from the church. "It's a putt-putt place dedicated to Bible stories. Old and New Testament. My daddy owns the place. And yes, he is very eccentric."

Mr. Rhodes didn't stop to say more than that. He crossed the parking lot and climbed into a big Ram pickup truck.

"No," Mr. Randall said. "He was not joking. And believe it or not, the putt-putt place is hugely popular. Tourists come through here looking for it."

Micah, who had grown up in a tourist town, doubted this. But he decided he might check it out. He also decided that the people living in Last Chance were a bit quirky, like maybe there was something funny in the drinking water.

"Now don't forget," Mrs. Randall said, affectionately elbowing her husband to one side. "You need to deal with that ghost."

Wait, what? She said *ghost* singular. "Excuse me, Mrs. Randall, why did you say ghost?"

"Because there is one, isn't there? And I also know that if you deal with it, then everything will be fine."

"Savannah"—Mr. Randall's voice was low—"I don't think he fully understands what you're saying."

"They never do," she said with a sigh.

"Why don't you go wait for me in the car, honey," Mr. Randall said.

"Okay, but please don't talk him out of it."

"I think you already have."

She waved as she crossed the parking lot toward a vintage candy-apple-red Cadillac convertible.

"I have to be honest with you, Reverend St. Pierre. We have a matchmaking problem in Last Chance," Mr. Randall said.

"Wait, what?" He was now thoroughly confused and a little alarmed.

"My wife is a matchmaker. A professional one. She would tell you that she isn't anything of the sort. She'd say she's a match finder. I have no idea what that means. But sometimes she says weird things, and people in this town take them literally. My old aunt was the same way, rest her soul."

"You mean like what she just said about the ghost?"

"Exactly. If I can interpret. Some people in this town would tell you that you need to go find a ghost to exorcise, and once you do, then voilà—you will find true love. Of course it never quite works that way. Actually what she said could be interpreted as meaning that you should go talk to that woman who refused you and see if maybe there's a chance for reconciliation before you decide to move out here to the sticks.

"And honestly, that would be good advice. We will probably have you back to meet the parishioners. You're exactly the kind of priest we need here. But, obviously, we would want you to be happy and stay for a long time. It's hard for little places like ours to keep a priest. So, Savannah is right. If you're only leaving Magnolia Harbor because of a broken heart that could be mended, well..." His voice faded out.

For the third time, Micah was rendered utterly speechless.

* * *

On Monday morning, right after breakfast service, Ashley headed off to Grace Church with the determination of a woman who had spent the previous evening listing the pros and cons of changing congregations.

On the pro side: Micah St. Pierre. On the con side: Patsy Bauman would probably hate her for deserting the church Grandmother had loved so much, but maybe all would be forgiven if folks knew she was doing it for Micah.

So really what would be the downside?

And besides, after the last week or so, she'd made a solemn vow to go after what she wanted. And she wanted to date Micah St. Pierre, not marry him.

So she parked her car in the Grace Church parking lot and strode through the front doors, a woman on a mission.

The church was so much bigger than Heavenly Rest, and the doors led to an entry foyer. To the right, a hallway led into myriad classrooms, meeting rooms, and the ballroom regularly rented out for weddings and other parties. To the left stood a pair of large wooden doors that led into the sanctuary.

The sound of toddlers echoed down the hall. Like Heavenly Rest, Grace Methodist rented out the Sunday school space to a Montessori preschool. The place had a familiar church-school smell—some amalgam of apple juice and crayons and books. It was a nice smell, and reminded her of those September mornings when Mom had taken her into a new school.

An army brat got used to changing schools. You made new friends. It was hard to leave the old ones, but it all worked out in the end. And that's what this would be like. And in this instance, she wasn't moving to a new place, she was just changing the destination on Sundays. Grace Church had the benefit of being a shorter drive from the inn.

So she could do this thing. For Micah. For herself. Easy peasy.

But when she stepped into the church's office, the Grace Church secretary popped her optimistic bubble. Ashley had completely forgotten that Gale Walsh, Teddy Walsh's mother and Jayden's grandmother, served as Grace Church's secretary.

Gale was a good Christian woman, but on Monday morning, she greeted Ashley with something way less than Christian fellowship.

"Ashley," Gale said in an acerbic tone, "what brings you here?" She made no attempt to hide her disdain

But Ashley needed to make friends. "Gale, what happened between my son and your grandson was unfortunate. But I want you to know that I forgive Jayden for breaking Jackie's nose and ripping up his library book."

"He did no such thing." She sniffed.

"He did, Gale. And I think we, as adults, should find a way to forgive each other." She said the words, knowing Micah would approve of them, but not feeling entirely charitable the more Gale glared at her.

Clearly, Gale was not in a forgiving mood. The forced smile she gave Gale made the corners of her mouth hurt. Time to get on with the main purpose of her visit. "I was wondering if Reverend Pasidena is in?" she asked.

Gale's forehead bunched up until the groove between her eyebrows became a canyon. "What's this about?" she asked, her tone snippy.

"It's a private matter."

"You don't have an appointment."

"I know, but if he's at all like Reverend St. Pierre, he's used to folks showing up unexpectedly. Especially on Mondays."

"Really? I am surprised. It's a wonder your minister gets any work done."

Yes, actually it was a wonder. And sometimes, on Mondays, Micah didn't get back to the rectory until after eleven p.m. His headlights would often light up her bedroom ceiling right before she fell asleep.

She kept her mouth zipped about Micah's comings and goings, and instead she said, "Well, if an appointment is necessary to speak with him, then I'd like to make an appointment. When might he be available?"

Gale swiveled in her office chair and tilted her head back, studying the computer screen. The posture suggested that Gale didn't use the computer for much.

Ashley resisted the urge to cross her arms over her chest or tap her foot while Gale fiddled around for the next few minutes without actually offering her an appointment time.

And then, almost as if in answer to Ashley's silent prayer, the inner office door opened and the minister stuck his bald head out and said, "Gale, can you get me the report from—" He stopped mid-sentence and opened the door all the way, giving Ashley one of his winning smiles. "Ashley, hello. What brings you here today?"

The frown over the church secretary's eyes got deeper. Not even Botox could help those grooves. "I was trying to schedule an appointment to speak with you," she said.

"Appointment?"

"Now, Reverend Pasidena, you know you have a mountain of—"

"Come on in, Ashley," the minister said, giving Gale

a meaningful, what-is-wrong-with-you glance. "I've got a few minutes right now, if that's convenient."

Holy crap. She'd done it. She was here. She was going to talk to Rev. Pasidena about changing churches. Unexpected adrenaline rushed through her.

The pastor gestured toward one of the side chairs. His office was big enough to hold a sizable desk, a credenza, a couch, and a couple of chairs. It had a window with a view out over the lawn that stretched all the way to Dogwood Street.

"So, what can I do for you?" he asked.

"Well..." Ashley reflexively clutched the arms of her chair as nervousness set in. "I was wondering what would be involved with moving Jackie from the Heavenly Rest Sunday school to the one here?"

He blinked. "You want him to come to Sunday school here? Why? I would think you'd want to stay far, far away. You do know that Jayden is enrolled in our Sunday school. Teddy makes sure he comes every week."

Something in the minister's tone seemed off, as if he was saying that Jayden needed the religious instruction. Or something. But his point was well taken. Jackie couldn't come to Sunday school here.

Oh crap. Maybe Dad could take him to Sunday school at Heavenly Rest. Would that be good enough to satisfy the rules? She didn't know, but she was committed to this now, so she decided to be a bit more truthful.

"Well, actually, I was thinking about changing churches," she said in a rush.

Rev. Pasidena had light-brown eyes with flecks of amber and green in them. They widened in surprise, and she let go of the chair's arms and dropped her hands into her lap. She forced herself not to look down. Somehow, looking down might convey the wrong message. As if kissing a priest was a terrible sin when it wasn't.

"Ashley," the minister said in a solemn tone that yanked her mind back from a clear, sweet memory of Micah's hands roaming over her backside, "what's going on?"

She huffed out a breath. "For reasons I don't wish to discuss, I—" She stopped herself before she said the word *need.* Need would imply something that wasn't there. She didn't need to stop going to Heavenly Rest. She *wanted* to. So she could kiss Micah. On the lips, with some tongue preferably.

Her face heated. Not with embarrassment as much as pure, unadulterated want. "Well, I would like to come worship here," she said in a firm voice. Of course this didn't answer his question.

"But—"

"I just wanted to find out if, you know, there were any restrictions or forms or something," she blurted before he asked her about her motives a second time.

Oh boy, maybe she should have thought this through. It might not be possible to do this on the up-and-up without going into specifics about her feelings for Micah. She wasn't ready to discuss that with anyone. She hardly knew her true feelings. He was a friend. She'd kissed him and danced with him. And now she'd like to see if there was more to it.

"Restrictions?" the minister said. "Ashley, if you want to join us on Sunday, or any day, the door is always open. For you and Jackie. But why? I mean, I'm always interested in growing our congregation, but your family practically built Heavenly Rest."

No "practically" about it. The Howland family had

given the land to the Episcopal Church and had almost single-handedly funded the church's construction back in the 1890s. Thomas Howland V's name was memorialized on the cornerstone. And of course there were dozens of Howlands buried in the churchyard.

That's why the church had been named Heavenly Rest. Howlands had been buried there before the land was given to the church. Yeah. History. It was a bitch. So she didn't actually respond to this comment from the minister. She sat there like a lump, not sure what to say next.

"What's wrong?" he asked.

Everything. Nothing at all. Dammit, Micah St. Pierre had proposed marriage and she'd said no. And she didn't want to send him away. No. She wanted to… Well, best not get into that right now. She wanted to date him. And kiss him again like she'd kissed in the museum. And maybe some other stuff. Did they still call it necking these days?

But saying this out loud to a man of the cloth seemed like a violation of Micah's trust. So she nodded and smiled. "Well," she said in a breezy tone, "it's good to know that I don't have to fill out forms. Now, I need to be going." She got up and prepared to flee.

"Whatever you say to me is confidential. If something has happened that you need to talk about. I'm here. I'm listening."

Oh crap. He'd jumped to the wrong conclusion. "No, no, no, *nothing* has happened. I'm just looking to make a change," she said, turning for the door.

"Ashley," he called her back. "I want you to know that my door is always open. I'm concerned. If something is amiss, then you shouldn't keep it a secret."

"Nothing's amiss," she said in a too-urgent tone that probably rang false. "Thanks," she added and escaped into the outer office.

Where she ran smack dab into Donna Cuthbert, who had probably been listening at the door.

Chapter Twenty-One

Micah had stopped by Golfing for God yesterday. The putt-putt hadn't been exactly on the way back to Magnolia Harbor, but he figured it would be best to know what he might be getting himself into if he was ever offered the job in Last Chance.

To his surprise, he had stayed at the mini-golf place for quite some time, chatting with Elbert Rhodes, the proprietor, who was indeed very eccentric and thoroughly entertaining. Elbert had goaded him into playing the putt-putt's front nine, which featured holes from all sorts of Old Testament Bible stories. His personal favorite was the plague of frogs, where overgrown fiberglass frogs spit water in an arch across the fairway. If you messed up your putt, you got wet.

Elbert had assured him that the frogs were, by far, everyone's favorite.

As a result of this detour, Micah didn't get home until quite late Monday evening. He'd gotten up at dawn the next morning to deal with the mountain of paperwork on his desk, left over from the day before. He hated paperwork, but it was the least of his problems.

He'd rescheduled his usual Monday dinner with Len Huxley for this evening. No doubt, Len would want some explanation of his whereabouts yesterday. Micah ought to tell the church's warden the truth. It would be best for the congregation if they began the process of searching for new clergy earlier rather than later.

So, he was at the Rubicon's edge. When he told Len, there would be no going back. But he wasn't ready to cross the river.

Or to be more precise, Savannah Randall's words kept echoing in his head, making him think about having a long chat with Ashley. Maybe she would reconsider.

Or maybe God was calling him to do something else.

Or maybe he was losing his mind.

Any of these possibilities was plausible.

He shoved the troublesome thoughts to the back of his mind, where they percolated, surfacing every once in a while despite his efforts to concentrate on the financial reports he needed to review before tonight's meeting with Len.

The numbers in the spreadsheet were beginning to blur when Colton burst through his office door, clearly agitated.

Micah's acid stomach clutched. Every nuance of Colton's body screamed trouble. "What?" Micah asked, his heart wrenching at the wild look in Colton's eyes. "Is it Daisy?"

Colton shook his head and plopped into his chair. "I need your help."

Colton asking for help and advice was starting to

become a regular thing in Micah's life. He liked playing the older brother, and he was pleased that his little gambit seemed to be working out. Kerri and Colton had been seen having dinner around town. And Danny seemed to have found a couple of guardian angels.

"What can I do?"

"Teddy Walsh is trying to put me out of business."

"What?"

He nodded and braced his elbows on his knees. "Teddy is popular in this town, and he has a lot of investment money behind him. He's gotten St. Pierre Construction fired from several subcontract jobs we had. If that were the limit of it, I'd be okay. But he's running around to other developers telling them not to hire us. And it's like they all meet up at the yacht club and suddenly I'm getting all kinds of pushback from people I've been doing business with for years."

"This is about Danny, isn't it?"

He nodded. "Teddy wants me to fire Danny. I can't do that."

"Well, I think we need to get Danny back in school. That would probably solve the problem."

"Easier said than done."

"No. You just have to be the father figure and lower the boom on him. He will listen to you, Colton. I've watched him with you. He adores you."

Colton rolled his eyes, clearly uncomfortable with the notion that anyone would adore him that way. "I'm just afraid that, if I insist on something, he'll bolt again. He's really fragile, Micah. I'm really worried about him."

Micah studied his brother for a long moment without saying anything. It truly seemed as if Colton might be more worried about Danny than he was the business. And of course, Colton was not a man who felt comfortable expressing his emotions.

"What does Kerri say?" Micah asked, somewhat unartfully. He wanted the inside story on how the romance was faring.

Colton huffed a breath. "She says the same thing you do. She's a huge proponent of tough love. I think she's employing the same tactic with me."

"Oh?" Micah tried not to sound too interested.

"She's backed off. I don't think she approves of me, entirely. I don't know." He got up and started pacing. "I gotta figure this out, Micah. I could lose them both."

Whoa. This was interesting. "What do you want me to do?" he asked mildly.

"I don't know," he said in a raised voice. He pounded on the edge of Micah's desk in frustration, sending a pile of papers flying.

"Oh shit, I'm sorry," Colton said in a voice laced with remorse. He sounded like the boy he'd once been. Prone to outbursts and then remorseful. Raging out of control because...

Because he was scared of losing someone he cared about. Like all of them, Colton had been scarred by Mom's addiction.

And right then, Savannah Randall's words came back at him. Mom was the ghost in the room. Not Captain Teal. And not Adam Scott.

Colton was afraid of losing these new connections in his life. Micah was afraid of losing his church, which had been his rock for so long. They were scarred. They were both afraid.

Colton started gathering up the papers that had fallen to the floor while Micah tried to figure how he could help his brother. When they'd been little, Micah had been the stand-in parent when Mom was not emotionally available and Daddy was too busy. Was that what Colton wanted now?

The thought of being his stand-in parent unsettled Micah. Not now. Not when—

"What's this?" Colton interrupted Micah's thoughts.

Micah looked up to find Colton reading one of the papers he'd just picked up.

"Are you planning to leave?" Colton asked, dropping the paper in front of Micah. It was a printout of the email Dash Randall had sent him last evening, thanking him for interviewing for the rector's position at Christ Church. It also contained several additional questions that the search committee wanted answered, which was why Micah had printed it out. Micah wanted to write out his answers carefully and thoughtfully using a pen and paper. He always thought better with a pen in his hand.

"I've been considering it," Micah said honestly.

"You're doing this because of Mom, aren't you?"

"No, it's—"

"Yes, it is. Don't lie. Shit. She comes back and everything falls apart." Colton turned and headed for the door.

Micah raced after him, through the door and into the hallway. "Wait, Colton. Nothing has been settled, and this isn't really about Mom." But that was a lie. Maybe his attraction to Ashley Scott had triggered his search, but Mom's reappearance had confirmed his decision. He could never be Mom's pastor.

"Forget it," Colton said with a gesture of finality. "I don't even know why I came here. It's not like you have any kind of real relationship with Danny." He turned away and stalked down the hallway and out of the building.

Micah didn't follow him. This was something he could not fix.

* * *

Ashley seriously considered ditching the Piece Makers meeting because Donna Cuthbert was going to interrogate her about her business with Rev. Pasidena yesterday. She needed to have a viable cover story, but she just didn't have the bandwidth to come up with one.

She was an idiot for rushing in without giving the issue some thought. Micah had asked her to marry him, although as proposals went, it left a lot to be desired. He had not suggested that she run off to the Methodists and give them a reason to gossip about her. But unless she could be honest about her decision to change churches, that's exactly what would happen.

And that would be ten times worse than getting caught kissing Micah without having made a grand announcement.

Of course she could marry him. But the thought scared her silly. What if it didn't work out? What then? Would she be excommunicated from the church? Would she be persona non grata during fellowship hour? Or would the burden fall on Micah?

Bottom line: She was not ready to get married. To anyone. She was attracted to Micah, and she regarded him as a fine man and a friend. But this was a gigantic leap into the dark. And besides, she had just realized that she could be in charge of her own life, instead of playing second fiddle to a husband.

Her thoughts were entirely valid. And yet they raised such guilt because only she could make Micah an honest man. And she was the impediment. Oh sure, the church's rules were a problem. But when all was said and done, she wasn't ready for a second marriage.

And she couldn't tell any of the Piece Makers the truth. Indeed, the only people who actually knew the truth were Jenna and Dad. And they would keep their mouths shut. She hoped.

She arrived at Patsy's house on Tuesday evening equipped with a scratch-made sheet cake even though it wasn't her week to supply refreshments. Chalk this offering up to stress baking and a lame attempt to divert Donna Cuthbert by appealing to her sweet tooth.

"Hey," she said with false brightness as she set the cake down on Patsy's kitchen counter. "I brought a surprise."

"Is that your coconut cake?" Donna asked, right on cue.

"It is," she said. "I felt guilty about missing last week's meeting."

"Must have been a good date," Nancy said, helping herself to a slice. "If you're feeling guilty."

Ashley refrained from saying a word about the obnoxious dentist. If Ryan Balfour hadn't been so obnoxious, she wouldn't have come home early, and she wouldn't have invited Micah into her bedroom, and she wouldn't have kissed him.

So, yeah, it was the dentist's fault.

Ha.

"Donna says she saw you over at Grace Church yesterday," Patsy said, pouring out glasses of sweet tea.

When Ashley said nothing in response, Barbara said, "Why were you over there anyway?" She spoke in a proprietary voice, as if no member of the Howland family was allowed to set foot in Grace Church.

"I was there to talk to him about..." Her mind blanked for a second before she blurted, "...a party." It seemed reasonable. People were always renting out the party room.

"Oh really?" Donna said. "What's the occasion?"

"Um, my birthday. I thought I'd give myself a party."

"But your birthday is in November," Cousin Karen said. Karen never missed an opportunity to send birthday cards.

"I know, but the room gets booked, you know?"

"You didn't need to talk to Rev. Pasidena to book the room," Donna said, frowning.

"I know. But he was there, and I thought I'd chat with him." Donna knew she was fibbing.

Thank god Patsy saved her by putting down her cake plate and saying, "Y'all, I think it's now well-established fact that Kerri Eaton and Colton St. Pierre are dating." Patsy assiduously avoided making eye contact with Ashley.

What did that mean? Did Patsy blame her because Micah and Kerri hadn't been a match made in heaven? Ashley experienced a tiny moment of vertigo in which she had to stifle the urge to howl. Or maybe fall to her knees and make a tearful confession of her desire to...

Well, the idea of telling these women she wanted to get naked with Micah St. Pierre *would* make their heads explode. Too bad Dad wasn't here to witness the event.

She stomped on the errant thought, her pulse rate climbing. A sudden, unbidden desire to find the front door and run came over her.

"I saw them kissing on the front porch of his house. Yesterday morning," Barbara Blackwood said. No doubt Barbara had been spying on Colton from her front room.

Barbara lived right across the street from Colton and was almost as bad as her younger sister Donna when it came to minding other people's business.

"We need to go to the next name on the list," Patsy said, picking up her cell phone and reading. What the hell? Did she have a real list? On her phone?

Oh good grief.

Ashley sank down onto one of the kitchen stools when her legs went all rubbery.

"Who is the next, then?" Sandra asked.

"Marcie Harvey."

"Oh, she's nice. She handled my loan paperwork when I bought my condo. And very pretty too," Nancy said.

"And one of Kerri's friends," Patsy said. "According to Louella Pender, Kerri and Marcie are learning to knit together. Which is helpful because we can maybe get Kerri to act as the go-between. We just need to ask her."

Patsy swung her gaze toward Ashley and said, "You were so good at arranging that date for Micah and Kerri, maybe you could talk to Kerri about Marcie. You know, enlist her to help or something."

Someone's cell phone dinged with an incoming text, but the noise almost underscored the absurdity of it all.

"Patsy..." Ashley began and then lost the ability to string words together. Good thing Sandra jumped in right at that moment.

"Wait!" Sandra said, holding up her cell. Evidently the text had been for her, and she was reading it with a deep frown on her long face. "We have a much bigger problem."

"What?" several of them asked in unison.

"My old college pal just sent me a text wanting to know my opinion of Reverend St. Pierre."

"Any of your old college pals would be too old for him," Patsy said, deadpan.

"No. She wasn't asking about him romantically. She was asking what I thought about him as a minister. Evidently he interviewed with the search committee for her church. Just yesterday."

She looked up, her face grave. "Ladies, Micah is thinking about leaving Heavenly Rest."

"But... we can't let him do that," Patsy said. "The last time we made a call for clergy it took two years to find someone we liked."

"I think," Nancy said in her small voice, "we need to find out why he's considering leaving us. Maybe he just can't bear to be in the same town as Brooklyn. Maybe his heart is really broken."

"Maybe we need to talk to Brooklyn and find out why she said no," Karen said.

Patsy turned toward Ashley and failed to notice that she was turning blue. Drawing breath had become impossible. This was her fault, not Brooklyn's.

"What should we do?" Patsy asked.

Damn. Patsy didn't have a plan for this. Well, that wasn't surprising. Who would?

"Well," Ashley managed to say, pushing the air through her throat, "I guess the first step might be to talk to him."

"You think?" Karen said, sarcasm lacing her tone.

Chapter Twenty-Two

When Micah met Len Huxley for dinner on Tuesday night, he chose to say nothing about his interview the day before. It wasn't honest, or fair, or even by the book of rules. But he could not bring himself to sever his ties to Magnolia Harbor.

If Christ Church ever offered him a job, he'd have to provide some kind of transition period for the congregation at Heavenly Rest. It wasn't fair for him to keep this a secret from his church. But he did.

After Colton's outburst earlier in the day, he found it impossible to pull the trigger. He had been thinking about himself again. Not anyone else. And yet keeping it a secret would harm the congregation. If he was going to leave, they needed to make their own call for clergy.

So he was guilty either way. Guilty of abandoning his family. Guilty of not being honest with his congregation. Guilty of having feelings for someone he shouldn't.

When he pulled into the rectory's driveway around

eight p.m., he was exhausted and heartsick. He left his Forester and paused a moment before going inside. The weather had turned warm, and the earthy scent of springtime hung on the air.

He stared across Lilac Lane at the inn. The place was ablaze, suggesting that bookings were beginning to pick up. Soon, the inn would be awash in guests and remain that way until schools went back into session in August.

He lifted his gaze to the third-floor dormer windows. Ashley's bedroom window was dark because she went to the Piece Makers meetings on Tuesday. She wouldn't get back home until after ten o'clock.

Funny how he knew her comings and goings. But then he'd been living across the street for several years.

Jackie's window shade was drawn, but the light was on, and he watched the boy's silhouette as he crossed from one side of the room to the other.

For an instant, the pressure in his chest lifted a fraction. And just like that he decided. Tonight was the night, while Ashley was at her meeting. He wouldn't have to run into her, and he could help Jackie the way he'd promised.

He hurried into the rectory and found the cardboard box where he'd been collecting various items that might come in handy for an exorcism. He stared down at his equipment: a chasuble and some dried sage, a Bible, the *Book of Common Prayer*, which might not be terribly helpful since the section on exorcism admonished priests to call their bishops before attempting one. But he was not about to call the Rt. Rev. Readdie about Jackie's ghost, especially after a ghost hunter had certified the inn ghost-free.

He doubted that he was being called to send any demons back where they belonged, but he was a man of faith. And so, he'd also done a little theological research on the topic and had printed out a well-known Catholic prayer, adopted by Pope Leo XIII in the late 1800s, which asks for the intercession of Michael the Archangel against all sorts of spirits and demons.

As a Protestant, he wasn't all that into the practice of praying to Catholic saints and archangels. But for the purpose of convincing a young boy to let go of a ghost, the prayer might be helpful.

He hefted the box and headed across the street. This time he rang the bell, and a red-eyed Andrew let him in.

"What's up?" Andrew asked.

"I'm here to help Jackie with his ghost."

Andrew's gaze hardened, but he ushered Micah into the foyer. "There is no ghost."

"No?" Micah said, turning the word into a question.

"No. And you know it. Coddling the boy is not the solution." Andrew folded his arms over his chest.

Well, this was a fine situation. Micah had come tonight because Ashley was off with her quilting club. The coast was clear. Except for this determined gatekeeper. He had a sense that Ashley and Andrew had been caught in a struggle over Jackie. He needed to convince Andrew that going along with Jackie might just solve the problem.

So he met Andrew's glare with priestly patience. He had spent years of his life talking to stubborn people. He had a knack for convincing folk to change their minds.

"Andrew, you stand there with a pair of red eyes and tell me it's not possible for the departed to haunt a person?" he said in his kindest voice. "I'm not here to get rid of a ghost or a demon. And I'm not here to coddle

Jackie. I'm here to help him take the last step he needs to lay his father, finally, to rest."

"What does Adam have to do with any of this?" Andrew said.

"Everything. You know as well as I do that every psychologist Ashley sent Jackie to see has told her that the ghost is an imaginary friend Jackie invented to get over the grief of losing his father. You know how hard it is to lose the life you thought you were living and find yourself in a new one entirely. You're going through it now. Jackie has been going through it for most of his life. He's ready to lay the past to rest. I'm here to help him."

Andrew blinked, eyes watering. "Yeah, well..." His voice faded off. "Whatever. Do what you want." He waved a hand in dismissal and turned, stoop-shouldered, to walk back to the inn's office.

It wasn't a wholesale endorsement, but Micah would take what he could get. He walked down the hallway, dropped his box of equipment on the kitchen counter, and took the stairs two at a time. When he reached the top floor he was a little out of breath, suggesting that the extra pounds he'd put on in the last year were starting to weigh him down. He needed to eat better.

Jackie's door was closed. He knocked.

"Go away," the boy said.

"It's Reverend St. Pierre. I've come to help you talk to the ghost," he said. He told himself to put his doubts aside, for Jackie's sake.

The door swung open a moment later, but one look at Jackie told Micah he was not welcome. Something had changed. The room. It looked as if someone had scrubbed it clean.

The pirate books had disappeared from the shelf. So had the poster of famous pirate ships. The worn-out *Pirates of the Caribbean* bedspread had been swapped for a Mandalorian comforter.

Micah was evidently a day late and a dollar short.

Jackie confirmed this by saying, “I don’t need help.”

“Oh?” Micah leaned in the doorframe. “So you talked the captain into leaving?”

The kid rolled his eyes. “Come on, Rev, you know there never was a ghost. I mean, right? So I’ve just given him up.”

He’d just given him up. How?

And the more important question. *Why?*

“I don’t need you. You can go,” Jackie said, and then slammed the door in his face.

What the—

Something was seriously out of whack. Jackie hadn’t actually let the ghost go. He’d simply turned his back on it, as if he’d come to some decision that he needed to accept the prevailing view about ghosts. As if he’d decided to conform instead of being his own beautiful self.

And who had taught him this lesson?

He stared at the door with its KEEP OUT sign scrawled in crayon. He itched to open the door to talk with Jackie. But it wasn’t his place. And besides, he was too close. It was all too important. And Ashley wasn’t here, so he needed to back off, and keep his distance, and stay on his side of Lilac Lane.

He went downstairs, his heart breaking with each step.

Andrew was waiting for him. “Where’s Jackie?”

“There isn’t going to be an exorcism. Evidently Jackie’s decided the ghost isn’t real.”

"Well, hallelujah for that. Things will be so much easier around here without that hanging over our heads."

Micah didn't want to rain on the man's parade. Micah didn't think the relationship between Jackie and his grandfather was going to get any easier at all. Call him a student of human nature. Jackie had ripped a page from his mother's book. Instead of standing up for himself, he'd simply given up the fight.

Ashley did that all the time.

"Good night, Andrew," he said, and headed toward the front door.

"By the way, have you heard the latest?" Andrew asked to his back.

He turned. "You are the last person I would expect to be listening to gossip."

"Why? I discovered a long time ago that listening to the gossip among enlisted ranks can be enormously beneficial to improving morale. As a navy chaplain you should know this."

Spoken exactly like a bird colonel. Micah agreed with him. One of his duties as a chaplain had been to help the navy brass learn what was on the minds of sailors. "I guess that's true," he said.

"Well, in this case I think you'll be interested. Evidently Ashley has been overheard talking to Reverend Pasidina. The scuttlebutt is that she is thinking about changing churches." Andrew gave him a wink and a wave. "Good night, Reverend St. Pierre. You have a good evening."

* * *

Ashley left the Piece Makers meeting early, claiming a nonexistent headache in order to escape the conversation, which had devolved into a debate on whether Micah was leaving because of Brooklyn's rejection or Kerri's obvious preference for his younger brother.

Oh, if they had known the truth…

But she had no intention of confessing or continuing to lie by omission. So leaving seemed like the smart alternative.

But when she reached to top of the hill, she turned up the drive to the rectory and knocked on Micah's door. He deserved to know people were starting to gossip.

He came to the door dressed in a navy T-shirt and a pair of athletic shorts.

Yummy. Her skin prickled with reaction.

She took a moment to inspect the parts of him that were on display—parts he usually kept under wraps, like his quads and calves and biceps. Although sometimes in the summer, he did wear short-sleeved shirts, but they were nothing like this muscle tee. Yeah, he had nice pecs. She wanted to rest her head against them, but obviously that was not the reason for her visit.

"We need to talk," she said.

He nodded and stepped out onto the stoop.

Damn. The days of casually stepping inside the rectory were gone, weren't they?

"I heard you interviewed at a church in some remote section of South Carolina," she said, wrapping her arms over her chest, not so much as a barrier but to keep from throwing herself against him. Her libido and girl parts were threatening her sanity. Five years of celibacy had obviously left a burning need in its wake.

"How on earth did you hear about that?"

"Evidently one of Sandra's old college sorority sisters is a member of this church. Someone named Lillian Bray?"

He crossed his arms over his chest, mirroring her own stance.

"I take it you know this person?" she asked when he'd said nothing.

He nodded. "She's a member of the search committee."

"You were going to leave Heavenly Rest?"

He nodded.

"Because of me."

His dark eyes grew darker in the light cast by the front-door lamps. "No. It's not your fault. It's just what needs to happen."

"Why?"

"I've told you. I crossed a line. I'm crossing one right now standing here having this conversation with you. I don't want to go, Ashley. In fact, I should have told Len Huxley at our dinner this evening. I guess now I'll have to explain why I wasn't honest with him." He sighed. "I guess, now that people know, I don't have the choice to wait and see whether I can land the job in Last Chance."

"What?"

"Last Chance. It's a tiny town in the middle of the state."

"You can't leave."

"I have to. Especially since you evidently visited with Reverend Pasidena."

"You heard about that?"

"Come on, Ashley. Someone overheard you."

Donna Cuthbert or Gale Walsh. She could take her pick. "I didn't say one word about you, Micah. I merely asked the minister what might be involved in switching churches."

"And Reverend Pasidena is probably trying to figure

out why you feel the need to switch. Especially given your family background and its ties to Heavenly Rest. He probably thinks I harassed you or something."

"But you *didn't*. Micah, no one has driven me away from Heavenly Rest, unless it's the rules the church imposes on you. I was trying to solve a problem. For both of us."

"I know. You didn't intend to create a problem. You thought you could just go to the Methodists and we could come out of the closet, so to speak."

"You make it sound so terrible. Look, I would really like to date you. There, I've said it. Out loud."

"We can't date. I thought I made that clear."

"Okay, now you're just being stubborn. If I'm a member of Grace Church, the problem is solved."

"No, it's not. You can't ignore the fact that you left your church because of me."

"So you think the only solution is marriage?"

"It would probably get us around the rules."

"Oh for goodness' sake. You want to marry me because of the rules?"

"Look, I'm trying to save my career here."

Her pulse beat at her temples, and the headache she'd lied about had now become a reality. "Micah. I am more than willing to explore a mature relationship with you. I'm willing to forgo premarital sex. For you. But I'm not rushing into marriage. And I'm not moving to some town named Last Chance."

"Then we have nothing to discuss."

And suddenly the headache was the least of her problems. The pain had moved right into her chest, as if he'd driven a knife into her heart. This new hole existed right next to the one labeled "Adam."

It shouldn't be possible. She'd resisted this attraction. She'd told him no when he'd proposed. But Micah had been her friend for years, and when he moved away, she was going to miss him.

Was it possible to grieve a love that never was?

Maybe. It was as tragic as a rosebud losing its petals before it came fully into bloom.

But there was no getting around the facts: Two kisses weren't a good reason to jump into marriage. Especially if it meant leaving Magnolia Harbor and Howland House and moving to a place named Last Chance.

For his sake, and her sake, and Jackie's sake, she had to say no. She and her son were not interested in starting over someplace new. She'd started over so many times in her life. She just couldn't do it again.

"I'm sorry," she managed to croak through the thick place in her throat. She ran across Lilac Lane and all the way up the stairs to her bedroom. Where, for the first time in some months, she cried herself to sleep.

Chapter Twenty-Three

Ashley's head pounded—thud, thud, thud—like someone was trying to pound the door down.

She cracked an eye.

Oh wait, someone *was* trying to pound the door down. She'd locked it behind her last night when she'd come up here to cry.

Crying herself to sleep had earned her this headache, which was bad, but not as bad as the burn in her eyes. Wait, sunlight was streaming in through the window. She hadn't bothered to draw down the shades last night. The clock on her bedside table said it was nine in the morning.

She'd missed breakfast.

"Ashley, if you don't answer me, I'm going to take an ax to this door." Dad's voice.

"I'm okay," she said, her voice rusty in her throat.

"Open the door, dammit," Dad commanded like a bird colonel.

She climbed out of the bed, grateful and embarrassed that she didn't need to throw on a robe, because she was still wearing yesterday's clothes. She opened her door.

Dad took one look at her face and some of the military starch melted out of him. "Are you okay?" His gaze traveled over her rumpled clothes.

She could lie to him and tell him she'd been crying over Adam. But she was finished with lying to people. To him. To everyone.

"I'm in a state of utter humiliation," she said.

He cocked his head. "Why?"

"Because I followed your advice," she said without anger. Although maybe she should be angry. Not at Dad. Dad's advice seemed reasonable. But Micah's reaction to her decision had not been reasonable. Instead of saying thank you for making this sacrifice, he'd gotten all stiff with righteous indignation.

She could not win. It would be better to swear off romance for the rest of her life. Unfortunately, her libido was not down with this plan. It tweaked somewhere in her midsection and sent her a graphic image of Micah St. Pierre in that T-shirt. Frustration mounted. She could never have him on her own terms.

"What advice?" Dad asked.

"Oh, come on, Dad. I went to see Reverend Pasidena. First, I had to get by Gale Walsh, and then Donna Cuthbert dropped by the church office and evidently listened at the keyhole while I was talking to the minister. I didn't exactly tell Reverend Pasidena why I wanted to change churches. But, you know, people are wondering."

"So."

"Well, it's only a matter of time before they understand the reason."

"So?"

"Dammit, Daddy. According to Micah, I am not allowed to join the Methodists so I can date him." Her annoyance came through loud and clear. Good. Better to be annoyed and angry than heartbroken.

"What?"

"That's what Micah said. I can't just join the Methodists without creating a big problem for him. And you know, as much as I hate to admit it..." Her voice wobbled as the heartbreak reasserted itself. "He's right on some level. Oh my god, the gossip would be cruel, and everyone would want to know if we'd been carrying on behind their backs. And—"

"Stop. The people in this town should mind their own damn business."

"But Micah is their business, Daddy. And this will end his career, which is why..." Her chest became so tight she could hardly breathe. It took a moment before she could force the words from her lips. "He's going to resign and move someplace in the middle of nowhere called Last Chance."

"Shit."

Well, that cussword pretty much summed up the situation. "Yeah, he's been interviewing at some other church. And I'm not going to follow him, Dad. My life isn't in Last Chance, it's here. And when people figure out why he's going, I'm going to be ostracized or whatever. It's going to be bad. I can't win. I should never have—" She couldn't speak one more word without falling apart. So she sucked it all back down and started building another internal wall to keep this sorrow from overwhelming her.

"The people in this town often have their heads up their butts. Actually, it sounds like Micah does too."

"Daddy, that's unfair."

"Is it?" He blew out a big breath. "Honestly, honey, I think you should sell this place and move on. You could do so much better than this narrow-minded town."

Suddenly she'd had enough of him. She punched the doorframe with the heel of her hand. It hurt. "Dammit to hell and back again. Daddy, if you want to go, don't let the door hit you on the way out. Go travel the world the way you and Mom were planning. Because honestly, you've been nothing but a pain in the butt. And I should never have listened to you about the Methodists. What's happening here isn't funny. It's not about Patsy Bauman's head exploding or getting some weird vindication for something Grandmother did way in the past. This is my life we're talking about. It's my heart. And it's breaking right now."

The tears flowed, and it took a minute, gazing into the raw hurt on Dad's face, before she realized she'd gone too far.

His shoulders sagged, and he headed for the stairs.

"I'm sorry, Daddy. I didn't mean it. I—"

"No, actually," he said, turning back, "I think you did mean it. I'm sorry you're so unhappy." He headed down the stairs with a kind of military precision.

She didn't follow him. She needed to talk to him, but maybe she needed a shower and a moment to calm down before that happened. She didn't want to lose her father the way Daddy had lost Grandmother. She needed to bridge the gap. Find some way to coexist. That's what she always did.

Independence was great, but she loved Daddy, warts and all.

It occurred to her that, maybe, she felt the same way

about Micah St. Pierre. But did she love him enough to give all this up? She didn't think so.

She headed back to the bedroom, passing the open door to Jackie's bedroom. Evidently Dad had gotten Jackie off to school today without any help. Or maybe the boy had managed by himself, which was a chastening thought.

She glanced through the open door. Something wasn't right. She stopped and peeked into the room.

The old *Pirates of the Caribbean* comforter was gone, replaced by the one she'd bought for him almost a year ago. The one he refused to put on his bed even though it was covered with images of Baby Yoda.

The comforter wasn't the only weird thing. The posters of tall-masted ships, the books on pirates, his Lego pirate ship were all missing, almost as if Jackie had exorcised them from his life.

She walked into his room. Dirty school uniforms littered the floor, and the Lego blocks from his pirate ship had been scattered everywhere. Had he smashed the Lego project that had taken him so long to build?

The closet door stood ajar, the hamper empty, and behind it in the low portion that stretched out toward the eaves stood one of the cardboard shipping boxes that her coffee supplier used. OLD PIRATE STUFF had been scrawled across the lid of the box in a bright-red marker. She opened the box.

It was like a pirate treasure, packed carefully away. The posters, the books, his pirate costume from a couple of years ago. He'd put it all in this box the way she'd done with Adam's things. The same way she'd folded away Jackie's baby clothes years ago, when she'd stupidly thought she and Adam might have a second child.

Tears filled her eyes.

For years, she'd wanted Jackie to stop telling stories about the ghost in the tree. Evidently, he'd decided to listen. But maybe not by letting go of the past but by shoving it back into a closet. By burying it.

The way Grandmother had buried Rose's diary in the library.

The way Daddy buried his anger with his mother.

The way she'd been burying her feelings for Micah.

Bury it all and hope you could forget it. Hope you could expunge it. Hope you could pretend that none of it had ever existed.

Oh yeah, she'd taught Jackie very well, indeed.

* * *

On Wednesday morning, Micah had to drag himself out of bed. He hadn't slept more than an hour or two, and gravity seemed to be especially strong today. Each step down the hallway to his small office took a Herculean effort because of the weight of his guilt. And a sense of impending dread.

The heaviness bearing down on his shoulders had one other cause: Ashley. She would never be a part of his life. He should have realized the impossibility of that long before now. He'd fooled himself into thinking that God might answer that prayer. But God had not, and God could not make this situation right.

The only person in the world who could make it right was his own self. He'd made mistakes. He had to admit them. He was not his mother. He didn't skate along, avoiding the consequences of his actions. No. He had to pay a penance for them.

He arrived at his office, tidied up his desk, and then

placed a single sheet of notebook paper in front of him. It had a to-do list. A grim one.

But before Micah could begin working on his list, Len Huxley called.

"Hey," he said.

"Micah, what's this rumor going around about you leaving us?"

Micah huffed out a breath. "I'm sorry, Len. I'm going to resign. I think you will need to call the vestry together and create a search committee for a new rector."

"But why? And why didn't you say a word yesterday?"

"I apologize. I should have said something last night. But I gather many members of the congregation have heard that I interviewed at another church."

"Yes, and to be blunt, I'm surprised. I thought you were happy here. So when Sandra Jernigan called, I was surprised. I really need an explanation."

"And I can't give you one. Suffice it to say that I have decided to leave."

"Why?"

He swallowed down the truth. "I just have."

"Please don't tell me this is because the altar guild has been matchmaking. I know several of them have called me. They are worried that they might have overstepped."

"Might have?" he asked acerbically.

"I'm sure we can rein them in, Micah."

"No. It's not the altar guild. I just need a change."

Len pressed him several more times, and Micah blocked him at each turn. He was not going to throw Ashley under the bus. That would be unkind. So he scheduled a meeting of the vestry for tomorrow night and let Len do the organizing.

His phone rang again, moments after ending his conversation with Len. It was another member of the vestry. He got ten phone calls in the space of an hour and a half from concerned parishioners. This situation was blowing up in his face.

And then, at about eleven thirty, the bishop called.

Evidently someone important enough to get through to the bishop on short notice had connected the dots. Someone, he suspected, named Patsy Bauman.

Great. The bishop would not accept his dodges. She'd want the truth. All of it. But he wasn't ready to confess.

* * *

On Wednesday afternoon, Jackie didn't go immediately home from the bus stop. He didn't really care if Mom or Granddad missed him. He was in a crappy mood, so he shouldered his backpack and headed down to the ice cream place on the boardwalk. He had a few dollars in his pocket that Granddad had given him for helping rake up some leaves in Mom's garden.

He bought himself a rocky road cone and then headed off toward the park. Maybe someone would let him borrow their skateboard for a couple of runs, now that Danny had taught him a few moves.

The park was kinda crowded with kids he didn't want to hang out with. Jayden the butthead was there with Liam. So far Jayden had kept his distance at school, especially after Mom had spoken with the principal. But this wasn't school. There was no Mr. Helme there to keep Jayden in line. And Liam was a lying sack of poop.

He balled his fists and turned around, heading for the

library. He had his card back, at least. But he was still worried about Mrs. Wilson. She probably thought he was the kind of kid who ripped up books.

He sauntered along the path toward Lavender Lane with no place to go. He wished he'd had enough money to buy two scoops instead of one. He might still have some ice cream left.

Right before the exit to the park, there was a little garden that had daffodils all over it and a statue of an angel with outstretched wings.

Mom had told him once that the angel was a smaller copy of a much bigger, famous statue that was in some park somewhere. He forgot where. She was a very pretty angel with flowing robes and hair. And there was a plaque at the base of the statue with Thomas Howland III's name on it. He was Jackie's great great-something-grandfather. Anyway, he'd put up this statue.

Just like he'd built the library.

Jackie was glad his last name wasn't Howland. Since his last name was Scott, most people forgot that he was related to Thomas Howland and all the rest of them whose last name should have been Teal but wasn't. He stopped for a moment to look up at the angel's face. He may have prayed, but it wasn't a real kind of prayer. Mom always said that you should be asking for good things for other people when you prayed, not just for something you wanted for yourself.

So praying for Jayden Walsh to catch the measles and miss school for the next two months was not a worthy prayer. Praying for a skateboard wasn't either. He prayed for those things anyway.

Movement caught the corner of his eye as he turned from the angel. Danny Beckett was sitting on one of the park benches, his head bowed as if he might be praying to the angel too.

Jackie studied him for a long moment. The Rev hadn't kept his word. He'd promised to fix things with Mr. Colton so Danny could go back to work. But that clearly hadn't happened. It was the middle of the afternoon, no later than four o'clock, and Danny was not at work.

He took a couple of steps toward the older boy. "Hi, Danny. I just wanted you to know that I spoke with Reverend St. Pierre about your job."

Danny looked up. His eyes were kinda red and puffy, and he looked weird somehow. Like his whole body was tense or something.

"Are you okay?" Jackie asked.

"Go away," Danny said. His voice sounded weird too.

"Okay. But I just wanted you to—"

"Go away!" Danny jumped up from the bench and bellowed at him. And that's when Jackie saw the gun.

It was in Danny's hand. He wasn't pointing it at Jackie, but it scared him. He couldn't move or talk, even though he wanted to know why Danny had the gun.

"What the hell are you waiting for?" Danny yelled. "Go, now, kid. Get out of here."

Jackie ran. Scared and worried and confused. He ran without thinking for a while, desperate to get away from something terrible. But then his brain kicked in, and he stopped. He had to *think*. He had to help Danny.

He came to a halt at the corner of Pine and Tulip Streets. He was a long way from home, and he didn't have a phone. But Harbor Drive was just a couple of blocks away. And there were lots of people on Harbor Drive.

Ms. Kerri. She cared about Danny. He ran harder now, until he burst through the doors of Daffy Down Dilly.

* * *

It took a moment before Kerri could fully understand the little boy who came bursting into the boutique around four fifteen on Wednesday afternoon. Jackie Scott was big-eyed, breathless, and white as a sheet.

When the words "Danny Beckett" and "gun" came out of the child's mouth, she went into alarm mode.

"Where?" she asked, her pulse racing and her hands starting to shake.

"At the angel," the boy said. "You know, in the park."

She knew exactly where that was.

"You go home, you hear. Straight home. I'm calling the police now, and I will take care of this."

"I'm worried about him," Jackie said in a voice too grave for such a small child.

"I am too. I'll take care of him, I promise. Now you go home."

She ushered the boy out of the store, called the police and Colton, and then took off to the parking lot and her car.

She didn't care about niceties when she reached the park. She left her car in a no-parking zone and sprinted toward the angel statue.

When she arrived, Danny was sitting on a bench, head bowed. He looked like he might be crying. She approached cautiously, not because she thought Danny was violent but because she *knew* he was despondent. "Danny? What's wrong?"

He looked up, eyes red, tear tracks across his cheeks.

"Really?" he asked in a sarcastic voice. "Mr. St. Pierre is about to lose everything, and you have to ask that? It's all my fault."

"Of course it's not," she said, taking another step forward.

But Danny sprang up from the bench. "Yes, it is. That's what Granny says. She says I'm at fault. For *everything*." His voice broke, and he waved his right hand, punctuating his words. Yes, Jackie had been right. Danny had a gun.

"Your grandmother is wrong about all that," Kerri said.

"Is she? My parents would be alive except for me."

"Why do you say that?"

"I wanted to skate that day when they went fishing. I had a big fight with them. And I stayed home. And they went. If I'd been there, they would have—"

"No," Kerri said. "You don't know that, Danny. And besides, better sailors than your daddy have died in the inlet when the weather turns bad. Their boat capsized in the same spot where Captain Teal's pirate ship sank. So you don't know what might have happened. You're here because of God's grace."

He bit his lip and shook his head. "No. I'm not. It's a mistake. And then I got into that fight, and now everything is ruined. And Granny says it's my fault. I'd be better off dead."

Alarm raced through her. The counselor Micah had arranged for Danny had been concerned about the boy's mental health. She felt helpless and frightened. She didn't know the right thing to say, but she kept talking anyway.

"Where'd you get the gun?" she asked.

"It was my daddy's," he said, his voice breaking a

tiny bit. "We used to go to the range when…when…" He didn't finish the sentence. Instead, he turned away from her.

Just then, Colton arrived, and the mere sight of him made the tight muscles in Kerri's chest ease a bit. At least she wasn't alone with a despondent teenager. In that moment, they exchanged looks, and she knew she had fallen hopelessly in love with that man.

He'd come running the moment she'd called. He was risking his business for a troubled kid. He was exactly the man she'd been looking for all her life.

"I think he might want to hurt himself," she whispered.

And Colton nodded. They had both worried about this. Danny was so very fragile and sad.

"Danny," he said. "Look at me."

The kid refused to turn around.

"You are not a problem. Mr. Walsh is the problem. Not you. Now put down the gun, and let's go somewhere to talk about this, okay?"

"Hey," someone yelled from behind Kerri, "that kid has a gun."

She turned to find Jayden Walsh and several other boys staring at them from the footpath leading to the park's entrance. They were all wide-eyed.

"You boys get out of here," Kerri yelled.

Danny turned around and glared at the other kids.

And then, like something out of a bad dream, Ethan Cuthbert of the MHPD came racing through the park's entrance. She'd called him herself, but his arrival only made things worse because Jayden and the other boys yelled and pointed at Danny.

When Ethan saw the gun in Danny's hand, he drew his own weapon.

"Put the gun down," Colton said, his voice more than urgent.

But Danny didn't listen.

Maybe he didn't understand the gravity of the situation. Maybe he panicked. Or, Lord help him, maybe he waved that gun on purpose.

But in that horrible moment, two things happened simultaneously. Colton launched himself at Danny, and Ethan raised his weapon and squeezed off a round. Colton successfully disarmed Danny, but he also took the bullet that was intended for him.

After that, Kerri's world unraveled.

Chapter Twenty-Four

Ashley recognized the ache in her chest. It was an old friend. Odd to think of this heartbreak as beneficial, but in a strange way it was. Loss was like that. She would have done anything to avoid it but she'd come to know that grief was just the flip side of love. And grief was inevitable. A good life couldn't be lived without loss.

And the only way through the grief of losing something important was not to deny it. But to embrace it fully.

And so, she spent Wednesday in a state near tears. Not because of Adam. No, that loss had become a dull ache, akin to a little bit of arthritis at a spot where a bone had been broken. She would never forget him. Never stop loving him. Never stop missing him.

But he was not here anymore. And he would never return to her.

No, this was an acute pain created by Micah St. Pierre. He was going to leave Magnolia Harbor. And if she wanted to be with him, she would have to pull up stakes and move away. She wasn't ready to do that.

So maybe she didn't love him enough.

But, damn, it didn't feel that way today. Losing Micah permanently was a heavy blow that left her gasping and trying to find her bearings.

That would be enough for one woman to bear, especially with her guilt for having encouraged the kisses that had crossed the line. But her thoughts were divided between her own disappointment and worry about Jackie. She was losing him too. And she feared that one day, Jackie might decide, as Dad had, that he never wanted to come back to Magnolia Harbor.

Where would she be then?

Alone. Truly alone. This terrified her.

She couldn't change the church's rules, and she wouldn't convince Micah to give up his calling, but she could make an effort to change the course of her relationship with Jackie.

And so, when three fifteen in the afternoon came, she was standing in the kitchen with a batch of cookies and a gallon of milk. She intended to have a heart-to-heart with her son about his pirate, the bullies at school, and anything else he wanted to talk about, up to and including allowing him to get a skateboard.

But three fifteen came and went with no sign of Jackie. This was unusual. He always got home around that time. By three forty-five, she had descended into freak-out mode. Where the hell was he?

The scenarios playing in her mind went from benign to horrifying in a matter of moments. She almost called the police but then forced herself to put down her phone. He'd probably gone off to the library, or maybe the park.

Magnolia Harbor was a mostly safe town that a kid his age could navigate on foot.

He'd be okay. But his absence spoke volumes. He didn't want to be at home. And she was part of the problem. He would be home soon. She almost lost faith by four fifteen when Jackie was officially an hour late.

When he came sailing through the front door at almost four thirty, she heaved a gigantic sigh of relief. And then she saw his face, pale as the proverbial ghost himself. And he was breathing hard, as if he'd run up the hill.

"What happened?" she asked, her motherly intuition clanging an alarm.

"Danny," he said, his breath coming in hard bursts.

"What did he do?"

"He had a gun."

Her arms and legs grew numb, and her insides clutched when Jackie said the word "gun." "Oh good god. Where is he?" She picked up her phone, ready to call 9-1-1.

"Mom. It's okay. I told Ms. Kerri, and she's already called the police. She told me to run home, and I did what she told me to."

"Oh." Ashley heaved a long breath. "Thank God." Then she bit back the words that almost followed. Scolding him for not coming home would be the worst thing she could do. Even if she wanted to ground him right now for the rest of his life.

She could not protect him from everything in the world. She had to let him go. And it almost broke her heart because that's what every mother has to do. And letting go was very hard.

So instead of panicking and calling Kerri or Colton or 9-1-1, she forced a smile and said, "I made your favorite cookies. Chocolate, chocolate chip."

She must have succeeded in sounding calm or maybe her cookies did the trick, but in any event, Jackie scrambled up onto one of the kitchen stools and helped himself to several cookies.

Silence settled between them for a long moment before he said, "I'm sorry I didn't come home right after school."

"It's okay. You're here now. And safe." Boy, someone should give her an Oscar for this performance. She sounded calm when internally she'd gone into total freakout, her mind spinning more horrific scenarios before she reeled herself back in. Jackie was safe. That was the important thing.

He took a bite of cookie. Staring down at the counter. "Danny is screwed up, Mom."

"Why did he have a gun?" she asked, despite the fact that she didn't want to have this conversation. But hadn't she been avoiding the hard conversations with Jackie for a long time? If Micah had taught her one thing, it was that she needed to listen to Jackie.

Jackie pushed a half-eaten cookie away. He folded his arms across the counter and rested his head on them, a picture of misery. "I don't know," he said after a long pause. "I think he's very sad because his mom and dad died and his grandmother is sick. And he got into trouble because he stopped Jayden from hitting me."

Oh good grief. Jackie had always been a sensitive kid. And hadn't Micah pointed that out to her on numerous occasions? He cared about other people.

Ashley circled the counter and rested her hand across Jackie's shoulder blades. He was warm and alive under her palm. That calmed her in an elemental way. And it reminded her of those nights when he'd been small, sleeping in a bassinet beside her bed. She'd often rolled over to place her hand on his back, just to feel the rise and fall of his breathing.

She loved him with her whole soul. "Honey, I'm glad Danny stopped that fight. And I've been thinking about this a lot, and I've decided that it might be best for you to go to St. Mark's next year. What do you think? "

He shrugged, clearly not super-enthused by this idea. But at least it was a starting point for a conversation. In the meantime, it was all she could do not to pick up the phone and call the police just to find out if Danny was okay. Jackie would be worrying about him, clearly. But she held off for the moment, choosing instead to enfold her son a fierce hug. For the first time in forever, he didn't try to avoid it. At least for a few, precious moments.

When he pulled away, she let him go. "Now eat your cookies. They'll make you feel better."

He gave her a twitchy smile and then crammed another cookie into his mouth.

Maybe it was a good time for a distraction. The last thing she wanted was for him to go up to his room and brood about what had happened today. "So, did you see the box The Rev left you?" she asked.

"What box?" Jackie asked.

"He left it on the kitchen counter yesterday evening, I think. Dad moved it to the office this morning. It's definitely for you."

"Really?" Jackie swallowed down the last cookie like the proverbial monster.

"Yeah. Come on, let's see what's in it."

He followed her into the tiny office. The box sat on the credenza where she kept an upright file to store expense receipts. Jackie peered into the box. "What's all this stuff?"

"I think it's a do-it-yourself ghost-busting kit."

Her son wrinkled his nose.

"Well, there's a thingy in there for burning incense, but there's also a bunch of dried sage. So I think we're supposed to burn the sage. And there's a Bible, the *Book of Common Prayer*, and a printout of another very odd prayer."

Jackie pulled the printout from the box and read it through, his brows lowering. "Mom, this is all about angels and demons."

"I know. Leave it to The Rev to throw himself body and soul into something when he puts his mind to it."

"This just means he thinks the ghost is some kind of demon."

"Well, we have to accept that possibility, right?"

"Do we?" He looked innocent right in that moment. A champion for good over evil.

"I guess we don't. And really, I'll have to take your word on this. If you say the ghost is not a demon, then I believe it."

"You do?"

She nodded. "I know I haven't been listening, Jackie. I'm listening now. You tell me what we need to do."

"I...I'm not sure."

"Well, why don't we go out to the tree and see if we can hail the ghost and give him a pep talk about going into the light then. You know, like with the coffee machine."

"Mom, that didn't work. You got a new one, remember?"

"It worked for a few days." She smiled. "Come on, let's go ghost hunting."

"But Mom, the captain has stopped talking to me."

"He has?" This was news.

He nodded. "Yeah. He's been kind of fading away. I think it's like only kids can see him or something. And I'm not such a kid anymore. Or maybe you were right. Maybe I just imagined him."

"Do you believe that you made him up?" she asked in an urgent voice.

He stared at her for a long moment before he shook his head.

"All right then. Let's go see if we can find him."

"Right now?"

"Sure." She checked the window. It was getting dark. "I guess nighttime is the best time to go ghost hunting. How about we eat some ham sandwiches first?"

Just then, Dad walked into the office. "What's this about ghost hunting and ham sandwiches?" he asked.

She was about to tell her father to butt out of this bonding experience, but when she turned, she discovered that Dad had gotten a haircut since this morning. He'd also shaved and ironed his shirt the way he used to do. She studied him for a moment.

"For what it's worth," he said, "I called the coordinator of the bereavement group at the church today. I'm going to go tomorrow. So, you'll be on call."

She smiled. "That's good, Dad. Really good." She was still sorry for her angry words this morning, but maybe they had shaken him out of his self-righteousness.

"Mom says we should use the ghost hunting kit that The Rev left for us. Do you think the ghost is a demon?" Jackie asked.

Dad gave her a helpless glance before he said, "I don't know, but if you guys want ghost hunting help, I have nothing better on my schedule for this evening."

Jackie's gaze narrowed. "But you really think this is a stupid idea, right?"

"No. It's not stupid. I think maybe I've been stupid. I think maybe I should have stopped talking a while ago and started listening. So I'm ready to go out to the tree and see if I can hear this ghost of yours. This is your show, kiddo."

The boy blinked. "But I don't know what to do."

"Son, when that happens, and it happens all the time, just forge ahead like you have a plan. No one wants an indecisive leader."

"Right," Jackie said with a nod, while Ashley rolled her eyes.

* * *

Micah lied to his bishop. He told her exactly the same story as he'd given to the Christ Church search committee, leaving the impression that he was considering a change because his longtime *Methodist* girlfriend had refused his marriage proposal. And in furtherance of this lie, he'd also complained about his altar guild and their matchmaking attempts.

The bishop had given him a little sermon about the need to keep the congregation out of his private life. She also gave him the usual pep talk about how important it was for him to have a life outside of the church community. She'd ended the call with, "I can see why you might want to make a change, but have you considered that maybe this pastoral role isn't one you enjoy?"

If he hadn't spun the truth into such a big, gigantic lie, he might have admitted that reading financial reports, and organizing volunteers, and dealing with the endless gossip and background noise were not his favorite part of his job. But he loved helping people. And he could write a good sermon.

"I like being a rector," he said, but in that moment, a cascade of doubt filled his mind. Maybe God was calling him in a different direction.

"Well, think about it. I know you are loved, Micah, because I have gotten several concerned phone calls about you today. So choose carefully."

He got off the phone in relatively good shape, all things considered. Only his honesty was shredded. And now the die was well and truly cast. He would have to move on, either to Christ Church or somewhere else.

He left work in the early afternoon and headed home, where he subjected his out-of-shape body to a grueling workout on the stationary bike. Hunger now gnawed at him but there was nothing in his fridge except a take-out box from Rafferty's containing something—probably leftover steak—that was growing a fuzzy green science experiment.

He checked the freezer. Nothing. Not a frozen dinner or a pint of ice cream in sight. One package of frozen peas sat in the corner.

When had he gone grocery shopping last? Weeks. He'd been living on the fly, mostly eating out. Which probably explained the heartburn that had become a regular fixture of his day.

Ha. That was a lie, too. The heartburn was a sign of stress and guilt. But even the guilty had to eat. So he searched his contacts for the number of the take-out Chinese place down the street and was about to call when his phone rang.

It was Jude.

He connected the call. "Hey, what's up?"

"Colton's been shot." Jude sounded shaky, maybe near tears.

"What?" Micah's chest burn had become a three-alarm fire.

"Ethan Cuthbert shot him."

"What? I don't—"

"I don't understand either. Danny Beckett had a gun, and Colton got shot when Ethan tried to intervene. He's at Georgetown Hospital, and they say he needs surgery. Jenna and I are on our way there with Aunt Daisy. You have to come."

"I'll be there as soon as I can," Micah replied, his heart suddenly rampaging around his chest and the palms of his hands going prickly with adrenaline.

He pocketed his phone and headed for the car without changing clothes. As a result, the receptionist demanded his ID when he got to the hospital and tried to walk past her without checking in. He flashed his clergy badge, which earned him a surprised glance because the sweaty shirt and workout shorts were not exactly normal priestly attire.

Colton had been in surgery for a while by the time he arrived. The family had staked claim to the surgical unit's waiting room. Jude, Jenna, Daisy, Charlotte, Daddy, and Mom were there, along with Kerri Eaton, who sat in a corner hugging herself and rocking back and forth.

Someone had given her a hospital blanket, and Marcie Harvey, who worked at the bank, was with her.

He'd presided over family emergencies like this. Many times. But never within his own family. The priest who was so good at handing out comfort didn't even know where to start.

He suddenly wished he'd taken the time to shower and change into his work clothes. He stood there feeling naked and shaky and confused. "I'm sorry. I was working out when I got the news."

No one seemed to think less of him for showing up sweaty. And Charlotte got up and gave him a big hug in spite of it. The hug kick-started his brain, and he remembered what he needed to do. So he made the rounds, hugging each member of his family.

When he got to Mom, who had unshed tears in her eyes, he hugged her too. It felt surprisingly good for some reason. "I'm sorry," he said. He wasn't entirely sure what he was sorry for.

"You have nothing to apologize for, Micah. You were my rock when I was falling apart. And that was unfair because you were no more than fifteen or sixteen. I apologize."

He nodded, searching for forgiveness. Maybe there was a trickle of it somewhere. It was a start. A tiny one. It would take time.

He continued giving hugs until he got to Jude. "What do you know?" he asked.

"He was shot in the side. It's a serious wound because the bullet pierced his colon. Luckily Kerri and Ethan were right on the spot when it happened. It was all a horrible mistake. I think Ethan thought Colton was in danger, and then our idiot brother decided to tackle Danny and got himself into the line of fire."

He nodded, his throat thickening. The situation was enough to shake Micah's faith. He'd arranged the deal with Kerri. He'd brought Colton and Danny together. Why had this happened?

He crossed the room and sat down next to Kerri. She

looked up, tears streaming down her face. "Micah, I just want you to know that this is not your fault."

"No?" He was tempted to rage that if it wasn't his doing then surely it was God's. He had been trying to help.

She shook her head. "I think Danny wanted to hurt himself. Or maybe get Ethan to do the job for him."

"Where's Danny now?" he asked.

"Ethan arrested him on a gun charge. Poor Ethan. He feels horrible about this. I hate to think what might happen if Colton doesn't..." Her voice faded off into a tear-choked silence.

"He'll pull through," Micah said, based on nothing but hope. Sometimes hope was the only dependable thing, though.

She buried her hands in her face, and her shoulders shook. He gently gathered her into his arms and let her sob for a while, all the while making promises that only God and the surgeons could keep. He hoped like hell Colton realized that Kerri was the real thing.

"Come on, girl. You listen to Reverend St. Pierre," Marcie said. "Colton's going to pull through this."

Kerri let Marcie take charge of her. And Micah led everyone in a prayer for Colton. And then he sat down on the hard waiting room chair and studied the ceiling. He could not bear to look at his family.

No one had said a word about his plans to leave. Did that mean Colton hadn't had a chance to tell them about it? Or had Colton kept that secret from them?

It didn't matter, really. No matter what the reason, he was going to abandon them.

Again.

Chapter Twenty-Five

Micah hadn't been in the waiting room for more than twenty minutes before Jude moved across the room to sit down beside him.

"So, is it true?" he asked.

Ah, so Colton *had* spilled the beans. Micah nodded. "I know this is hard to understand, but I have to go."

"You *have* to?" The anger underlying his brother's words flayed Micah's heart. He'd left Jude once before, when his younger brother had been thirteen or fourteen. Right before he'd gotten on the bus to go to college, Micah had foolishly told Jude to take care of Daddy. By that time, Daddy was drinking too much.

There had been a time when Daddy had tried to keep things together, but that fell apart when Mom left. And Micah had handed an impossible job off to Jude all those years ago.

Of course Micah had intended to come home for Thanksgiving. But once he'd gotten away from the daily grind and the drama of home, once he'd made friends and fallen in love for the first time with a lovely girl named Sarah, he'd found every excuse in the book to avoid coming home. He'd spent his holidays at Sarah's parents' place.

But he'd broken up with her senior year, and then he'd left the state, choosing to get his master's degree at the Virginia Theological Seminary in Alexandria. From there, he'd sought appointment as a naval chaplain.

End of story.

He had never come back until a few years ago, when he'd seen Heavenly Rest's call for clergy. And it had seemed almost like the hand of God. Like God had sent him here.

And now he was being called elsewhere. He just didn't understand why God wanted him to abandon his family a second time.

"I'm sorry," he said, bracing his elbows on his knees and staring down at his sneakers.

"Tell me exactly why you *have* to go?" Jude asked.

He wasn't about to gossip about Ashley. He had no one to blame for this untenable situation but himself. And he had to shoulder this decision on his own. "If things work out, I'll be at a church not far away. Close to Orangeburg. I promise I'll come home this time," he said.

Jude said nothing, his silence damning. A moment later, his younger brother got up and crossed the room to sit beside his wife.

Micah raised his gaze, aware that everyone in the family had been listening to his conversation with Jude. So Colton had told the entire family, then. Everyone knew now. And he saw the judgment in their gazes.

He couldn't bear it, so he got up and left the room,

abandoning them again. He headed down the hallway, taking two left turns, which brought him to the doors of the hospital's small nondenominational chapel. He spent a lot of time here, helping families come to terms with grim prognoses. Holding hands. Praying. This part of his job reminded him the most of his years as a chaplain.

Now it was his time to pray.

He stepped into the room's cool, dark interior, folded his hands, and prayed for Colton and for Danny. He also prayed for Jude, hoping his brother could find a way to forgive him.

He prayed for his family, who had so many reasons to be angry with him.

And then he prayed for Daddy, hoping God would send him happiness with Mom. And he prayed for himself, asking God to help him forgive the things that had happened in the past. Asking for a road map that would allow him to let go of that pain, so he could move forward.

And finally, he prayed for Ashley and Jackie. Not because they needed his prayers, but because he hoped God would keep them and protect them. Because he loved them both and had to leave them.

He lost track of time until the sound of the chapel door whooshing open brought him back into the present.

The step-tap of a cane across the floor caught his attention. Aunt Daisy was making her slow way up the aisle.

He jumped up. "What are you doing?" he demanded, taking her elbow. "Did you walk here all by yourself?"

She peered up at him out of her trifocals. "I told everyone I was going to the ladies', and I didn't need help. I'm sure Charlotte is having a heart attack by now. But I knew my way here. And I knew this is where I'd find you." She gestured to the pew. "Let's sit. My legs hurt."

"I'm going to get a wheelchair, and—"

"Hush now. Sit down." It was a command.

He sat.

"I sure hope God has taken the time to slap you upside the head," she said once she'd eased herself down.

He chuckled in spite of himself. "I guess I've been here hoping He would," he said.

"Well, that's half the battle. Look here, Micah, I need to be honest with you, okay?"

He nodded. Maybe if God couldn't show him the way, then Aunt Daisy could. Because, near as he could remember, she'd been the one who'd told him to take the full ride to Clemson and get himself out of town. Of course, Aunt Daisy had probably never anticipated that it would take him almost twenty years to find his way back.

"So," Daisy said, in a slightly breathless voice, "the truth is I don't have many days left. And I'm worried."

"You're worried about dying?" he asked, sliding right into the comfortable role of chaplain. He'd had so many conversations about death and dying with scared sailors and marines, and with elderly and sick members of his congregation.

"No. I'm looking forward to going home. I'm worried about what happens after I go."

"Well, I don't—"

"Hush. I'm talking now." She paused a moment as if gathering her thoughts. "I been holding this family together for a long time. Momma used to help but she's been gone for years now. And I'm proud of the way you boys turned out, even though God knows your momma and daddy didn't do you much good. I'll take a lot of the credit."

"You deserve it."

She nodded, pursing her lips for a moment. "Micah, so do you."

"What?"

She took his hand in hers. "You deserve some credit for the way your brothers turned out. And I wonder... things might have turned out different if you hadn't been there."

"I wasn't there. And you—"

"Hush. I checked up on y'all after your momma left. I expected to have to move right into Charles's house, which would have been a problem because I was looking after Momma. But you know what? You were managing just fine. You got those boys up every morning, you got them dressed, you sent them off to school, you helped them with homework, and you managed to get yourself a full ride to college too. You went to church on your own, Micah."

"Well, I—"

"And all those years ago, when I told you to go off to Clemson," Daisy said, not letting him get a word in edgewise, "it was the smartest thing I ever did. You needed to go. Momma was gone by then, and I had the time to take over with Colton and Jude. I have never been angry about the fact that it took you twenty years to come back. It made sense to me. Because I was the one who let you take care of things. You rose to the occasion."

He stared down at her hand in his. Her skin was dry and wrinkled, her hands knobby from years of making seagrass baskets. The bones were twisted now and frail.

Tears filled his eyes. "I don't want you to go,"

he whispered. "But that's my own selfishness coming through again."

"Yes, probably. I'm ready, Micah. I'm tired and my hands hurt. My whole body hurts. I'm ready for the Lord to call me home. But when I go, I need you here. Not some other place. I need you to promise me that you'll stay in Magnolia Harbor, and you'll watch over this family. Because this is what you've been called to do. It's what you were called to do when you were just a little boy no higher than that."

He blinked. And said nothing. The knot in his throat precluded any words.

She nodded. "You see, you're the one who is ready to hold things together when I'm gone. There ain't no one else, honey. You have to be here."

"But I—"

She squeezed his hand. "And for that, honey, you need to follow your heart, not some wrongheaded idea of righteousness."

"My heart?" he asked.

"Oh, Micah. Any fool could see that you love Ashley Scott and that boy of hers. It's been plain as day for anyone who took the time to look. Have you told her how you feel?"

He barked a laugh. "I asked her to marry me."

"Well, good. I hope she said yes."

He shook his head.

"She didn't? Why not?"

He frowned and stared down at their joined hands as he reviewed the last few weeks. And something astonishing unfolded in his mind. He'd been asking for guidance over and over again. And God had sent it multiple times. He just hadn't been listening.

Finally, God had sent him Aunt Daisy, like an angel from on high, to kick his butt and get all up in his face and push him to see the truth.

"You know, Aunt Daisy, a couple of weeks ago, Mom called me a hero child. And I didn't want to listen to what she said. I didn't get it."

"What's this got to do with Ashley?"

"Everything." He huffed out a breath. "Mom told me I was trying to wipe away the shame that she'd brought on the family with her drug abuse. That all that stuff—taking care of the boys, getting good grades, going to school, was my way of trying to redeem the family."

"Well, that makes sense, but the boys still needed someone to take care of them, Micah. You did that because you loved them."

He nodded. "I know. But the thing is, I never stopped."

"Stopped what? Loving them? I hope not."

"No. Trying to follow every damn rule in the book. I made sure I stayed on the straight and narrow at all times. I don't know if that was Mom's addiction or simply because I'm Black and had to work harder than other people."

"Uh-huh, I know how that goes, son. But you still haven't explained what happened with Ashley."

"I've been letting the rules run my life. In the navy, and here as well. I asked Ashley to marry me, but I told her that we'd have to move away."

"Why on earth did you do that?"

"Because of the rules. Because I'm not allowed to fall in love with her. Because she's a member of my congregation. We can't date, but we could marry. I asked her out of the blue, though, and before she was ready. And then later I messed it up further by kind of suggesting we could solve the problem by leaving Magnolia Harbor."

Daisy snorted. "Ashley *Howland* Scott living somewhere else? Son, that was not a smart move." Daisy's sarcasm was laced with the tiniest bit of humor.

"I know." He swallowed hard. "But here's the thing. I can't have it all, Daisy. If I follow the rules, I lose Ashley. If I don't, I have to leave town. If I stay, I lose my calling."

"Oh, Micah. Look, I understand this rule of the church's. It's a good rule, but maybe it's not a good one for you. Let me ask you, what's more important, the church rules or love?"

He grunted because the question pierced his heart.

"Honey, let me say something. Your momma is right about you. I can see that now. You have spent a lifetime trying to follow the rules in the hope that it would earn you love or respect or whatever. But the truth is we always just loved you because you're you.

"And you know this is how love works. Of all the people in this family, you are the one who knows this best of all. Real love doesn't require anything. God's love is given freely. So, let me ask you again, Micah St. Pierre, what's more important? The church's rules or love?" Daisy squeezed his hand.

He almost laughed because he recognized this advice. He often gave it to others.

And here was the truth: No matter the question, love was the answer.

The heaviness in his chest lifted. "God has always called me to follow love," he said out loud. "Not the rules."

"Yes, He has, honey."

And the words became an answer to his prayers. So many prayers, and yet only one single answer: Love.

* * *

"Mom, give it up. The ghost isn't going to talk to us," Jackie said in a shaky tone that tore at Ashley's insides.

They'd been standing by the old live oak for the last hour, talking at the tree, urging Captain Teal to either go into the light or let them know what he needed before he could go. But the captain had been silent.

Now that the sun had gone down, the warm spring day had turned cold.

"I think maybe we shouldn't have burned the sage," Ashley said. "Burning sage smells bad enough to drive the living away. I'm sure it works the same on ghosts."

"Mom," Jackie said in an ominous tone. Her son was not in the mood for jokes. And she couldn't blame him. He'd had a tough day.

"I'm sorry," she said.

"I don't think the captain cares about the sage. I think he doesn't like to talk to grown-ups," Jackie said.

"So you think Granddad and I should leave?"

He shrugged. "I don't *know*. Maybe we should just give it up. I never had to try so hard to get him to talk to me."

After all these years of denial, suddenly Ashley didn't want to give up. Not on Jackie or his ghost. Suddenly the ghost's true existence seemed essentially important.

"Okay, so maybe we should—"

"Can I help?" The voice came from behind her and raised her temperature by several degrees. A good thing in the suddenly cool evening.

Micah strode across the grass, carrying a flashlight. He was dressed like a man who'd come from the gym.

He wasn't even wearing a sweatshirt, and he didn't look cold, either.

God, he was delicious in that muscle shirt. She resisted the urge to fan herself and waited until he was close enough for her not to have to yell. "We were trying to use your do-it-yourself exorcism kit," she said.

He drew close, his eyes red and puffy as if he'd been weeping. A huge rush of concern flooded her. "Are you okay?" she asked, ready to throw her arms around him and take care of him, or maybe feed him some cake.

He ignored her. "Do-it-yourself what?" he asked.

She held up the chasuble, which she'd been using for the last half hour. The sage had burned itself out so it was useless now. Assuming, of course, that it hadn't driven the ghost away. Oh boy, she wasn't sure what she believed anymore.

"You left a box with some stuff in it yesterday. We decided to see if it might work," she said.

He blinked but said nothing. He might have swayed a little on his feet.

"Have you slept? Recently?" she asked.

"Not much," he muttered. "And, uh, I came over to see if Jackie was okay after what happened this afternoon."

"Oh, you heard about that, huh? I've been wondering how it all played out. Is Danny okay?"

He nodded, his lips tight. "Yes. But I'm afraid he created a crisis this afternoon." He glanced at Jackie and then back at her. "I'll give you the whole story a bit later, but evidently Ethan thought Danny was threatening Colton with the gun. He wasn't. But Ethan did what any policeman would do when someone doesn't put a gun down."

"Was Danny hurt?"

He shook his head. "No. Colton jumped in front of the boy and took the bullet. He was shot in the abdomen. He's been in surgery, but the docs say the prognosis is good for him."

"Oh my God." She glanced at Jackie, whose face paled.

"It's okay, Jackie. You did the right thing," Micah said. "I just wanted to come by to say that you were a good friend to Danny today. I think he was very sad and needed help. And you got him help."

"But Mr. Colton—"

"It's not your fault. A lot of other boys wouldn't have told anyone about Danny. So you did the right thing."

"Where's Danny now?" Jackie asked, concern ripe in his voice.

"Well, he's in jail because he wasn't supposed to have a gun in the park. But I made a few calls. And there are lots of people ready to help him, Jackie. What he did was wrong, but it was also a call for help. And I promise you, Danny is going to get the help he needs. So I don't want you to worry about any of this. Understand?"

Jackie looked down at his sneakers and scuffed the grass.

Micah crossed the distance between them and pulled him into a fatherly hug. The boy clung to him. And Ashley's heart began to shatter.

What was wrong with her? She cast her glance over the lawn to the big historic house she'd turned into a business. She loved her business, but she could bake biscuits anywhere. In fact, maybe it would be better to just follow Micah to that little town with the funny name.

Maybe she was in the wrong here. She watched in growing sorrow as Micah murmured things to Jackie that she could not hear. And it struck her right then. Maybe

Jackie had stopped seeing Captain Teal because he'd found a friend in Micah. Maybe Micah had already sent Jackie's ghost packing a long time ago, and no one had really noticed until right this minute.

"So," she said aloud when Jackie finally squirmed away from Micah, proving that in some deep way her bookish son was still his father's child. "Micah, there's something I need to say to you, you know, about that question you asked me on Saturday. I—"

"No, I need to explain a few things first," he said. "To start with, that wasn't a do-it-yourself ghost busting kit. I had intended to organize a real ceremony of some kind."

"Oh. You mean you were going to officiate?" she asked.

He nodded.

"But I thought—"

"Yeah, technically I'm not supposed to organize any kind of ghost busting without permission from the bishop. But I'm ready to break the rule, for Jackie and Captain Teal. And for the record, the bishop no longer has any say over what I do."

"What? What have you done?"

"I've made a choice I should have made a while ago. I'm choosing to break the rules, Ashley."

"But—"

"And I'm going to try my hardest to let go of the ghosts that haunt me. Someone recently told me that I needed to do that in order to find happiness. And you know what, she was right. While I was at the hospital, I sat down with my mom for a long time, and we talked. It was hard. I don't know that I have fully forgiven her, but it's a step. And I realize that so much of what I've done and how I've behaved has been in pursuit of some messed-up idea of goodness. Good doesn't come from following the rules. It comes from the heart."

She blinked as tears filled her eyes. It was almost like one of his sermons, the ones that always left the congregation thinking hard about what really mattered in life. Only this was a sermon he was delivering for his own benefit.

And maybe for hers.

"But I've been thinking too," Ashley said. "You know my business is important, but it—"

"Ashley Howland, I do not want you to leave Magnolia Harbor. This is your home. Your people have been here as long as my people have been. Heck, your ancestor and mine once lived together right on this spot. I don't think either of us should have to leave this place because of some stupid rule. Or because people might look askance at a white woman and a Black man falling in love. Or because a priest has come to love one of his parishioners.

"A bunch of very evil rules forced Henri into slavery and Rose into a kind of prison made by the mores of her time. They didn't get to love each other three hundred years ago. We don't want to make that mistake again.

"I love you. I've loved you for a long time. And while I got lost for a while, and maybe I'm stupid or romantic, I believe God calls us to follow love. Every time. Even if it means giving up Heavenly Rest. I called the bishop about ten minutes ago and resigned."

"No. Micah, I was trying to tell you that I'll give this up. I'll follow you if—"

"No. I can't leave. My family is here. And they need me. And I belong to this place, the way you do. Neither of us wants to leave. Why are we so ready to go?"

She had no answer for that question. "You resigned?" she asked, her brain struggling to process what he'd done.

He crossed the distance between them, and she felt the warmth of his hands as he grasped her shoulders. "I love you. I want to be with you. I want to share a life with you. And I get that you might not be ready to marry again. So I'm cool with that. Can I take you out to dinner tomorrow night?"

She didn't know whether to laugh or cry. "Are you asking me out on a date?"

"I am, Ashley."

"There will be so much gossip."

He shrugged. "There might be less gossip than you think. So what do you say?"

She threw her arms around his neck. "Yes. I will go out to dinner with you." And then she kissed him for a long time until Dad cleared his throat.

"So, I take it the exorcism is off, then," he said.

Ashley and Micah broke apart, but not before giving each other knowing glances that promised alone time later.

"Well," Ashley said, turning toward Jackie, "what do you—" She stopped speaking mid-sentence because her son was staring up at the old live oak, his hands in his pockets, as something like St. Elmo's fire danced through the tree branches.

"What the hell is that?" Dad asked.

"It's the captain," Jackie whispered. "He showed up a minute ago."

Micah gently moved Ashley behind him, in a protective move that warmed her heart even though she was a competent woman who wasn't really frightened by odd dancing light in the tree. It was kind of beautiful.

But strange and otherworldly. And the chill of the night seemed to grow colder as she studied the lights, while Micah stepped up behind Jackie and put one of his big hands on the boy's shoulders. Another protective gesture.

Maybe it was a good thing they had a priest on hand.

"We should send him into the light," Jackie said. "He came when The Rev started talking about Rose and Henri."

"Of course he did," Micah said in an oddly firm voice. Then he threw his head back and spoke in that voice he always used from the pulpit. "We've learned the lesson," he said. "The circle of Rose and Henri's love has been closed. Now go to your rest and reward. God and the spirits of those you loved have been waiting for you."

The lights swirled for a moment, getting brighter, and then suddenly all went dark.

"He's gone," Jackie said, pausing a moment. "I mean he's gone. All the way."

He turned toward Micah. "You did it. You sent him into the light."

"No. I didn't do that. We did. We all did. By discovering Rose and Henri's love and by honoring it," Micah said.

"Well, one thing's for sure," Dad said. "When Micah talks to a ghost, he projects his authority. They actually listen. Unlike the demon in that coffee machine of yours."

And everyone laughed. And they all hugged. And in that moment, a new family was born under the old oak tree where Rose Howland and Henri St. Pierre had once planted daffodils three hundred years before.

Epilogue

Mom was getting married. Today.

And Rev. Pasidena would be the preacher at the ceremony out on the lawn because Mom and Jackie and Micah didn't go to church at Heavenly Rest anymore. It would have been rude or something if Micah had attended church there since he'd been the preacher at Heavenly Rest once.

The Episcopalians had a new preacher now. Rev. Gorka lived in the house across Lilac Lane with his family, including Abigail.

Abigail was in the seventh grade and sat next to Jackie in history and had the same lunch period. She was super-interested in pirates, and he liked her a lot. But she wasn't here today, which was kind of good because he had to wear this stupid suit and be the "dude of honor," which was BS. There was no such thing as a dude of honor. Jackie knew this because he lived at an inn and had observed a lot of weddings. It was humiliating that he had to stand next to Mom where the bridesmaids usually stood. He was not a bridesmaid.

And heaven help him if anyone at school ever found out he had to pretend to be a bridesmaid. Jayden would give him crap, of course. But Jayden had never punched him again. Probably because of what happened with Danny.

Mom said that Mr. Walsh had a "come to Jesus" moment after Colton got shot. She gave him credit because, instead of blaming Danny for what happened, he admitted that he was partly to blame. He even brought Jayden over to the house one day last year and made the jerk apologize.

Jackie didn't really want to accept the apology, but Micah said it was always best to forgive. And Micah was usually right about stuff like that.

So Jackie didn't have to go to St. Mark's school. And that's how he got to sit next to Abby in history.

Things had turned out okay for Danny, even though he got into big trouble because of the gun. Luckily Colton recovered, so Danny didn't have to feel guilty about that. But he wasn't supposed to have a gun. Since Danny was only seventeen, the judge cut him a break and only made him do some community service instead of sending him to jail. He also had to see a psychologist a couple of times a week, but that was probably a good thing. Jackie had been there and done that. It wasn't so terrible to talk to a psychologist.

Danny was also living at Colton's house, working part-time for him, and going to school too. On Saturdays, as part of his community service, he ran a skateboard safety program at the skate park. Danny was here today with Kerri and Colton, who were married now. Danny's biggest problem was that he was sad because his mom and dad had died. But he was never a bad guy. And Jackie was certain Danny wouldn't say anything about the whole dude-of-honor thing.

Of course, other than being required to wear a tie that was too tight and have a stupid flower on his suit collar, Jackie was down with Mom marrying Micah. Jackie had stopped calling him The Rev, though, because he wasn't a preacher anymore. He had a job at the hospital working as a chaplain. Which was sort of like being a preacher except he didn't preach anymore.

Micah was also going to college to earn a degree in social work. So they did their homework together sometimes.

Mom said that she was proud of Micah. Jackie liked the fact that he was living in the cottage behind Howland House, and Granddad had moved across town to that new apartment for old people. Granddad had a girlfriend. One of Mom's quilting ladies.

Mrs. Jacobs was kind of nice. Granddad seemed a lot happier now.

But anyway, with Micah living in the cottage, Jackie got to spend a lot of time with his brothers, who, after today, were going to be his uncles. He wasn't standing over on the boy's side at the wedding because Micah's brothers were serving as the best men.

Colton was the one who had made up the dude-of-honor thing, and Jackie didn't feel like he could tell his uncle-to-be just how lame that was. After all, Colton hadn't been to as many weddings as Jackie had. So he let it go. He *forgave* him. Sort of.

And also, Colton was helping Jackie turn his platform tree house into the real-deal thing, with walls and a roof.

His other soon-to-be-uncle, Jude, was giving him sailing lessons and had promised that he could crew on *Synchronicity* the summer he turned fourteen. Which was still two years away.

Jackie was also getting a new set of grandparents. Granddaddy St. Pierre had a fishing boat and had taken Jackie out a few times. It was fun. His new granny had joined Mom's quilting group. Mom said she hoped that would help Micah forgive. Jackie wasn't sure what that meant, just that Micah and his mom had their moments.

Sort of like Granddad sometimes said not-very-nice things about Great-Grandmother. Jackie had decided he was pretty lucky when it came to Mom, especially since, once she married Micah, Jackie would inherit a really big family filled with a bunch of St. Pierre second and third cousins who were close to him in age. His only first cousin, Samsara Daisy St. Pierre, Jenna's baby, was only six months old. Sara, as they called her, was boring and stinky. But the second and third cousins were fun.

So things were a lot better than they had been last year.

He was standing by the gate to the backyard with Granddad, waiting on Mom.

"Are you ready for this?" Granddad asked.

"I guess," Jackie said. He was ready for Mom to marry Micah quick so he could take off his tie, but he didn't say that to Granddad. Granddad would probably give him a lecture for just thinking that.

Mom finally came through the gate to the garden dressed up in a dress that wasn't white like most brides. Instead it was kinda pink and not nearly as fancy as the one in the photograph he had on his bedside table of her and Dad getting married.

It was her second time. He understood. And she'd told him that she was never, ever going to stop loving Dad.

That was nice, but Jackie didn't much care. He didn't remember Dad. Only a vague impression of a man in a uniform.

Mom leaned down and gave him a kiss on the cheek. She smelled nice, but it was embarrassing. She must have known he didn't like being kissed in public. So she backed away, her mouth twitching like she might start crying at any moment.

Which would be worse than being kissed in public.

"I'm good, Mom," he said, in the hope of heading off any tears.

Cousin Karen, who was coordinating things, said, "Jackie, it's time."

Right. So he headed down the path, all on his own. Ella Killough, Mrs. Jacobs's granddaughter and the violinist who often played music at Howland House weddings, was doing her thing, playing something slow and fancy. He walked down the path, not too fast and not too slow, and stopped when he got to where Rev. Pasidena, Micah, Colton, and Jude were standing.

Micah winked at him, which was somewhat reassuring since he was standing over here where the bridesmaids were supposed to be and he'd had to come down the aisle, which the guys almost never did in weddings. And now here came Mom, walking with Granddad, her eyes kind of glittery. With tears. He was pretty sure.

But everyone else was smiling and happy. Even Mrs. Bauman, who had been ticked off at Mom for a long while after Micah stopped being a preacher.

But Mrs. Bauman was at the wedding. And Mom said

it was because she was related to Jude's wife. So she kind of had to be there.

Mom got close enough to take Micah's hand. And then it got kind of boring. They did all that "I do" stuff, and they kissed. Everyone clapped like Mom kissing Micah was a really big thing, when the two of them kissed all the time.

And *finally*, he could take off his tie and have some barbecue and cake and go hang with the cousins, who wanted to hear the story about the night Micah sent Captain Teal into the light.

Jackie was happy to tell the story because everyone loved hearing it. But it wasn't nearly as good as the stories Captain Teal had told Jackie about his life on the high seas.

So when he finished telling the story about how the captain went into the light, he immediately launched into another story—about the time Captain Teal stole a whole shipload of gold from some sleeping Spanish soldiers.

His audience, which included Abby Gorka, who had sneaked into the party from across the street, clapped when he'd finished. And then Abby said, "Jackie, you're a born storyteller. I bet one day you write a book about Captain Teal."

And that's when Jackie's face got really hot. Because he had already started writing stories about Captain Teal. He hadn't shown them to anyone. And he wasn't about to tell a soul about them. But maybe now he might. Because Abby really seemed to understand him.

He was really, really glad Micah had moved out of the house next door. Otherwise, he might never have met Abigail Gorka, the minister's daughter.

About the Author

Hope Ramsay is a *USA Today* bestselling author of heartwarming contemporary romances set below the Mason-Dixon Line. Her children are grown, but she has a couple of fur babies who keep her entertained. Pete the cat, named after the cat in the children's books, thinks he's a dog, and Daisy the dog thinks Pete is her best friend except when he decides her wagging tail is a cat toy. Hope lives in the medium-sized town of Fredericksburg, Virginia, and when she's not writing or walking the dog, she spends her time knitting and noodling around on her collection of guitars.

You can learn more at:
HopeRamsay.com
Twitter @HopeRamsay
Facebook.com/HopeRamsayAuthor
Instagram @HopeRamsay

Fall in love with these small-town romances full of tight-knit communities and heartwarming charm!

THE BEACHSIDE BED AND BREAKFAST
by Hope Ramsay

Ashley Howland Scott has no time for romance while grieving for her husband, caring for her son, and running Magnolia Harbor's only bed and breakfast. But slowly, Rev. Micah St. Pierre has become a friend... and maybe something more. Micah cannot date a member of his congregation, so there's no point in sharing his feelings with Ashley, no matter how much he yearns to. But the more time they spend together, the more Micah wonders whether Ashley is his match made in heaven.

THE SUMMER SISTERS
by Sara Richardson

The Buchanan sisters share everything—even ownership of their beloved Juniper Inn. As children, they spent every holiday there, until a feud between their mother, Lillian, and Aunt Sassy kept them away. When the grand reopening of the inn coincides with Sassy's seventieth birthday, Rose, the youngest sister, decides it's time for a family reunion. Only she'll need help from a certain handsome hardware-store owner to pull off the celebration...

Find more great reads on Instagram with @ReadForeverPub

SOMETHING BLUE
by Heather McGovern

Wedding planner Beth Shipley has seen it all: bridezillas, monster-in-laws, and last-minute jitters at the altar. But this wedding is different—and the stakes are much, *much* higher. Not only is her best friend the bride, but bookings at her family's inn have been in free fall. Beth knows she can save her family's business—as long as she doesn't let best man Sawyer Silva's good looks and overprotective, overbearing, older-brother act distract her. Includes a bonus story by Annie Rains!

HOW SWEET IT IS
by Dylan Newton

Event planner Kate Sweet is famous for creating happily-ever-after moments for dream weddings. So how is it that her best friend has roped her into planning a best-selling horror writer's book launch extravaganza in a small town? The second Kate meets the drop-dead-hot Knight of Nightmares, Drake Matthews, her well-ordered life quickly transforms into an absolute nightmare. But neither are prepared for the sweet sting of attraction they feel for each other. Will the queen of romance fall for the king of horror?

Connect with us at
Facebook.com/ReadForeverPub

SUMMER ON BLACKBERRY BEACH
by Belle Calhoune

Navy SEAL Luke Keegan is back in his hometown for the summer, and the rumor mill can't stop whispering about him and teacher Stella Marshall. He never thought he'd propose a fake relationship, but it's the only way to stop the runaway speculation about their love lives. Pretending to date a woman as stunning as Stella is easy. Not falling for her is the hard part, especially with the real attraction buzzing between them. Could their faux summer romance lead to true love?

FALLING FOR YOU
by Barb Curtis

Just when recently evicted yoga instructor Faith Rotolo thinks her luck has run out, she inherits a historic mansion in quaint Sapphire Springs. But her new home needs fixing up and the handsome local contractor, Rob Milan, is spoiling her daydreams with the realities of the project…and his grouchy personality. While they work together, their spirited clashes wind up sparking a powerful attraction. As work nears completion, will she and Rob realize that they deserve a fresh start too?

Discover bonus content and more on read-forever.com

HER AMISH SPRINGTIME MIRACLE
by Winnie Griggs

Amish baker Hannah Eicher has always wanted a *family* of her own, so finding sweet baby Grace in her barn seems like an answer to her prayers. Until *Englischer* paramedic Mike Colder shows up in Hope's Haven, hoping to find his late sister's baby. As Hannah and Mike contemplate what's best for Grace, they spend more and more time together while enjoying the warm community and simple life. Despite their wildly different worlds, will Mike and Hannah find the true meaning of "family"?

THE AMISH FARMER'S PROPOSAL
by Barbara Cameron

When Amish dairy farmer Abe Stoltzfus tumbles from his roof, he's lucky his longtime friend Lavinia Fisher is there to help. He secretly hoped to propose to her, but now, with his injuries, his dairy farm in danger, and his harvest at stake, Abe worries he'll only be a burden. Yet, as he heals with Lavinia's gentle support and unflagging optimism, the two grow even closer. But will she be able to convince him that real love doesn't need perfect timing?